STREETS
OF
GLASS

ALSO BY MICHELLE D. ARGYLE

STREETS
OF
GLASS

MICHELLE D. ARGYLE

www.mdabooks.com

Streets of Glass / First Edition

Summary: "The heir to a drug empire finds her long-lost sister, only to discover she's planning to bring down the family business."

This book is a work of fiction. Any resemblance to actual persons, living or dead, events, or locales, is entirely coincidental.

ISBN: 978-0989970099

Edited by Diane Dalton

Cover Design by Melissa Williams Design

Visit author Michelle D. Argyle at http://michelledargyle.com/

TO MY TREASURED WRITING GROUP

*Without you, this book would still be nothing more
than a mess in my head.*

ONE

Starry entered the fifteen-digit code to her private surveillance room. The door clicked open and she slipped inside, eager to start her day. She loved this room and the power it gave her.

Blowing on her mug of steaming black coffee, she sat down to face several rows of monitors, each one displaying various angles of a different key location of her father's Los Angeles drug syndicate: warehouses, backrooms, parking lots, vehicle interiors, homes.

One particular monitor caught her attention. It covered the home of one of her father's lieutenants, or his Top Eight, as he called them. The closest CCTV feed showed the exterior near a crosswalk on the corner. Every morning there was a student or two waiting to cross the street. Today it was a teenage girl in her school uniform, pristine and perfect.

Starry settled into her chair and watched the girl, wondering what life was like for someone like that. She looked eighteen, Starry's age, but everything about her seemed innocent and unremarkable—normal, as the rest of world might describe her. Starry could hardly remember her own time in school when she'd been a part of that "normal" world. All of that had changed when she'd turned eight and her father had told her what he really did for a living—and then started training her to work beside him. He'd pulled her out of school at that point and given her private tutors for basic education and the other skills she'd need to run the syndicate one day.

"How's the new program coming?" a voice rang out from her speakers. It was her father, Glenn Ramsay, the most influential, formidable drug lord in Los Angeles. That was what all the law enforcement agencies called him, anyway. People made things sound so sensational.

Starry laughed under her breath as she transferred her dad's office video feed to her main monitor. Right now, that "influential, formidable drug lord" was sitting at his desk eating a bowl of cereal. He was down the hall from Starry, but it was easier to get work done without talking in person. She'd see him at lunch, anyway.

"Why are you eating corn flakes?" she asked as he shoveled a spoonful into his mouth and typed something into his laptop with one hand. "Didn't Maria make you breakfast?"

"I was in a hurry. This was faster," he grumbled. "Answer my question. How's the program coming?"

"I'll iron out the last of the bugs today."

He took another bite of cereal. "Keep the cost low. I know it's something we need, but Luis keeps showing me numbers and they're not ideal."

She set down her mug a little too hard, splashing coffee onto her desk. "Didn't he show you my reports?" she asked, wiping up the spill with her thumb. "I've run the numbers myself. This program will save you two billion a year. It costs a lot now, but it will pay for itself in three months, sooner if we roll it out to the East coast too."

Her dad smiled up at the camera on his ceiling and she smiled back, even though he couldn't see her. "What would I do without you?" he asked.

Starry picked up her coffee again. "You'd die of a broken heart."

There was a long pause and Starry watched her dad shuffle some papers on his desk. A few slipped off the edge, fluttering to the floor. He swore and leaned down to grab them. "You're right. I probably would."

Starry cringed. She hadn't meant to fluster him, but any time she ever mentioned something that might make him think about how lonely he'd be without her, like how lonely he'd been when he'd lost her mother so long ago, he got clumsy. She couldn't blame him. She was his only blood family, and he hers. She didn't like to think about how her life would be without him, either. It was lonely enough with just the two of them.

"Come on, Dad," she said cheerfully, eager to steer him back to a smile. "You know I'm not going anywhere. Why would I?"

He flashed her a brief, genuine smile. "Let's get back to work, honey. I'll see you in a few hours."

"Sounds good." She pushed aside her coffee. Enough stalling. She had too much work to do.

Switching off the office feed, she began her review of the previous evening's activities, a few hours slipping by before an alert blinking on her screen stopped her cold.

Suspicious communication found.

She clicked the alert and it took her to a string of emails, texts, and audio recordings. Monitoring her father's Top Eight was a full-time job, and letting the software she'd designed herself do some of the labor eased her workload. It still had bugs, but today it was working fine. The suspicious communication it had flagged belonged to two of the Top Eight, Andrews and Chavez.

Damn. Why those two?

She listened to a recorded conversation and read through a group of recent emails and texts. Piece by piece, she put it all together and then slammed a hand on her desk, nearly tipping over her cold, unfinished coffee.

"You bastards," she hissed at her computer. "You think secretly working with another syndicate is a good idea? He gives you everything and this is how you repay him?"

Only one of her dad's lieutenants had ever betrayed him, and the punishment hadn't been pretty. Starry had watched her father torture him. He'd made sure the man stayed conscious as he cut off his toes one by one, then his fingers, his tongue, and then slit his throat. It was the first time Starry had ever watched him kill someone. She had been eleven, maybe twelve.

Now, listening to Andrews and Chavez talk about their plans in a vague, roundabout way they probably thought she'd never pick up on, her blood boiled. They'd been in her father's syndicate for twenty years now, longer than she'd been alive. They knew she monitored them. They knew leaving her father meant he'd hunt them down and kill them and everyone they cared about. Why would they be so careless? Her father paid them well and nothing in their lives had seemed abnormal lately. If anything, the syndicate was getting more powerful and more rewarding. Her father was unstoppable.

13

She pushed the intercom to her father's office. "Dad, we need to talk. Are you there?"

No answer.

She switched the video feed to his office. The room was empty. She pushed her chair out from her desk and rushed into the hall. She looked at her watch. 12:20. He was probably swimming laps in the pool at the other end of the house. She would check his bedroom first on the way. Rounding the corner, she stopped at a set of heavy double doors. One of them was cracked open, as if her father had been in a hurry to get inside and forgotten to close it all the way. He was probably changing into his swim clothes.

Starry raised her hand to knock, but stopped when her father's voice carried through the crack.

"I need to know where she'll be in the next year," he said gruffly. "I don't want her anywhere near Starry. Opposite sides of the country doesn't feel far enough away anymore."

Who didn't he want near her? There was a long pause and Starry leaned closer to the crack, intrigued. She'd never had a reason to eavesdrop on her father's phone conversations before, but hearing her name piqued her curiosity.

"That's a promise I'll keep if you stick to your end of the deal," her father said coolly. "I've never stuck my nose in your business, and I never will unless there's a reason to. I've trusted you for years now, but this is information I need, Sam. I'm asking nicely. Don't piss me off."

Who the hell was Sam? Starry racked her brain and came up with nothing. Inching closer, she caught sight of her father standing next to his bed. His back was to her, shirtless. He had a swimmer's build, strong and broad-shouldered, and the muscles under his skin rippled as he rubbed the nape of his neck near his graying hair. For a fifty-year-old man, he was in excellent shape. He had to be to stay at the top of his game.

"That sounds better," her father snapped into his phone. "Keep me updated. What? No, that's fine." He tapped his finger against the back of his neck for a minute and then tensed. "I will never send you pictures. You already have Emma. You don't need a picture of Starry. They're sisters. They're bound to look alike."

Starry's blood ran cold.

Sisters?

When had that happened? How was that . . . she couldn't even . . .

Holding her breath, she watched her father say goodbye to "Sam" and end the call. When he walked over to his closet and reached for his swim bag, Starry backed away from the door and took off down the hallway. She didn't know what to do. She wanted to face him, but at the same time she had to get away and process what had just happened. How could her father keep something so important from her?

She rushed through the house and slipped out the back door to the pool. The sun hit her in the face and she shaded her eyes as she sat down on a white plastic lounge chair. It smelled like coconut lotion from the last time she'd sunbathed. That had been last week, when she'd thought she was an only child and would have laughed at the idea of her father keeping secrets from her.

The back door opened and closed. She kept her eyes on the pool as her father walked down the porch steps and dropped his bag next to her chair.

"Taking a break?" he asked as he leaned down to kiss her cheek.

She shrank away from him and scrambled off the chair, her hands balling into fists at her side.

He stared at her, confused. "Is something wrong?"

She folded her arms. "I have a sister? When were you going to tell me?"

His eyes hardened with a flash of fear that was gone so fast Starry almost missed it. "You don't have a sister," he said nonchalantly, reaching down to zip open his bag. He pulled out a pair of swim goggles.

Oh, no way was he going to pull a lie like that. "Bullshit! I heard you on the phone in your room! Since when do you lie to me? We've always told each other everything."

She didn't know what hurt more: the fact that he was lying so blatantly to her, or the fact that he'd hidden her sister from her. He knew how alone she'd always felt. She'd never known her mother and it wasn't like friends came easy, especially when most of her time was spent training to take over the syndicate one day. Besides, the syndicate was too dangerous for casual relationships. People were either in or out, loyal or disloyal. There was no in between.

But a sister. A sister would always be around no matter what. A sister was blood. Family. How could her father steal that from her?

His face annoyingly calm, he walked up to her and pulled her into a gentle embrace. She stood stiffly, unsure if she wanted him anywhere near her.

"I'm sorry," he whispered against her dark curly hair. "I'm sorry. That was stupid of me to deny what you heard. You do have a sister. Her name is Emma. She was mine and your mother's, but you can't ever meet her. It's impossible."

Her mind raced as her anger slowly subsided. Her world was tipping onto its head. Nothing made sense anymore.

"Tell me everything," she ordered.

"I can't. It breaks my heart, but I can't. The way things are . . . the promises I've made . . . it's too complicated. You two can never meet. I saw her once as a baby and that was it. I had to give her up and so do you." His arms tightened around her. Almost too tight. "Promise me you'll forget about this."

"What?" She ripped away from his embrace, her heart hammering. The sun felt so hot she was breaking into a sweat. "Are you crazy? That's all you're going to tell me? And you *haven't* given her up. You were getting information about her from that Sam guy! Whoever the hell he is."

A dark expression settled across her father's face. It was the same look he gave people before he killed them. It made Starry take a step back.

"Drop it," he ordered. "I don't want to hear you mention her ever again. You know she exists and that has to be enough, do you understand? It's over."

Trembling, she glared at him, her anger and confusion boiling so hot she felt like she might erupt into flames. "This is insane." She couldn't decide if she wanted to hit her father or fall to her knees and beg him to change his mind. "I can't forget about my sister on demand."

He put a hand to his forehead. "This is just like anything else you've had issues with, Starry. You'll move on from it. You're strong. That's what I love most about you."

Ugh. Seriously? He was going to play the love card? She loved him too, but that didn't mean she had to like what he was doing.

She leaned up into his face. "It might be too difficult for me to keep friends because of the syndicate, but you can't take a sister away from me. That's going too far. I'll dig until I find her. You can't stop me."

A slap cut across her cheek. She stumbled backward.

He had never hit her before.

Never even come close.

Touching her cheek with trembling fingers, she shook her head in an effort to bring her focus back. Her legs bumped into the chair behind her and she teetered. Her cheek was hot, prickling and stinging like a thousand tiny stabs, each one sliding slivers into her heart, cracking it wide open with anguish.

"I *will* stop you," her father snarled. "*Do not* try to find her."

He was blurry through her tears now. She imagined hitting him back, breaking his nose, his jaw. She was strong enough to take him on, but she knew it wouldn't last long.

He was stronger.

"I need to get out of here," she huffed, and spun around to leave.

She stopped when her dad's hand landed softly on her shoulder. "We'll talk about this later when you've calmed down."

She hated how calm he was, as if none of this was a big deal. She stared ahead, clenching her jaw as she shrugged his hand off and marched away from the pool. She had to get as far away from him as she could or she was going to lose it. He was right about one thing: she had to calm down.

As she grabbed her purse from her bedroom, she remembered Andrews and Chavez's betrayal. A sick smile lifted her lips. Those two were a bomb waiting to explode. Maybe she'd let that go off in her father's face without any warning at all. She could keep secrets of her own. It would serve him right, even if it did get a bunch of his men killed. He would yell at her later about it, for sure, but she didn't care at the moment.

She got in her car just as her phone buzzed in her pocket. She pulled it out, and was surprised to see the call wasn't from her father. It was Rhys Marshall. She'd been installing a new surveillance system for him the past few weeks . . . among other things. The last time she'd seen him they had ended up doing a lot more than wiring mics and cameras.

Her heart raced at the memory of how quickly they had connected with each other—and how quickly she'd rushed home and showered that night so her father wouldn't catch on that she'd had sex with someone he worked with.

She'd been with a handful of men over the past few years, but her father had always known about them and approved of them. Rhys was different, probably the main difference being that he was older than her—eight years older—but when she was with him the age gap never felt quite as big as it sounded. Despite the fact that he managed one of her father's clubs and used it to launder money for the syndicate, he was the cleanest and nicest man she'd ever met.

Backing out of the garage, she put her phone on speaker and maneuvered her way down the long, curving driveway and out onto the street. "Hi, Rhys," she said, trying to make her voice as upbeat and casual as possible.

"So good to hear you," he answered in the deep hello-baby voice he'd been using to greet her lately. She imagined him on the other end, his dark messy hair, his sharp suit and tie, his chalky blue eyes.

"What's up?" she asked, grinning. "Don't you usually sleep until five or six? It's one o'clock in the afternoon."

"I've got meetings with people on normal day schedules. And last night I discovered camera three is shot. Do you have time today to come look at it?"

"Hell, yes. I'm on my way right now. So is it really your camera or is this an excuse to see me?"

He laughed. "Can I say both?"

"Absolutely." She was relieved to feel no awkwardness with him over the phone. Maybe this really could go somewhere serious. "I'll be there soon."

"I'll be waiting."

She ended the call and let out a velvety sigh. Whenever she was with Rhys, he made her feel slushy and warm and soft all at the same time. It was like nothing else mattered but him. The last time she'd been with him, he seemed to feel the same way. The horrible thing was that if her father found out what was going on between her and Rhys, no matter how small it was, he would probably kill Rhys for messing around with his daughter behind his back, and that would suck.

Her father had never liked her dating older men, so she hadn't pushed it past the one time she and Rhys had been together, but now . . . now . . .

Now everything was wide open. When her father had slapped her, he'd killed every rule in the book.

She looked in her rearview mirror, her house sliding out of view as she rounded a corner. A part of her never wanted to go back.

Maybe she wouldn't.

TWO

"You're not the Chinese food delivery guy," Rhys said as soon as he opened the door to his apartment above the club. "Guess I'll have to keep waiting." He shrugged and started to close the door.

Laughing, Starry shoved her weight against the door to keep it from closing. She didn't know how Rhys could make her laugh and smile when she was so pissed off at her father, but that was part of why she liked him so much. He made all the crap in her life go away.

"I'm better than Chinese food," she whispered through the crack where Rhys was smiling at her. "Let me in and I'll prove it to you."

The resistance against the door let up and Starry stumbled through the doorway, right into Rhys' arms. He held on to her so tightly she was sure he didn't intend to let her go anytime soon. That didn't bother her in the slightest.

"You can start proving your worth now," he said teasingly as he pushed the door with his foot. It clicked shut and Starry stared at it for a moment. She was safe. There was no way her father would find her here.

Turning to Rhys, she smiled and took a deep breath of soap and cologne. He was always so clean and put together, and she loved that. She leaned close enough to him so her nose almost touched his. It surprised her how comfortable she felt in his arms.

"Joking aside," she breathed against his lips, "I'm here to hide from my father." She said it carefully, hoping the mention of her father wouldn't scare Rhys off.

His teasing smile fell into a straight line. "I was afraid something might be wrong when I talked to you on the phone." His arms tightened protectively around her. "You sounded upset. Are you okay?"

She shrugged. "I'm fine, but he can be such a bastard sometimes." The anger she'd felt on her drive over to Rhys' place returned like a slow-burning fire in her gut. She put a hand to her cheek, as if touching it might wipe away the memory of her father's slap. It only made it worse.

Rhys' eyes fastened on the hand on her cheek. "He hit you?"

She nodded. "He'd probably say I drove him to it, but I know better. He doesn't respect me the way I want him to and it pisses me off. I don't know how to fix it."

Rhys loosened his hold on her as the muscles in his jaw clenched. "I could beat him up for you, but I doubt that's what you want right now."

Laughing weakly, she stepped away. "You know me well. And you know he'd kill you, so yeah, don't even try." She looked away as the anger in her gut grew stronger. "I want to see how he manages without me, that's all. Nobody can do what I do for the syndicate. He can't keep lying to me or I'll leave forever."

Rhys cocked his head and raked a hand through his dark, still-damp hair. Most people would probably say Rhys was rather plain, but his attitude more than made up for any of that. He was alluring and he knew it. He wore confidence like an expensive designer suit because the club he ran depended entirely on the strength he projected. "What did he lie to you about?" he asked.

Heaving a sigh, Starry walked into the living room. Rhys' apartment was definitely his own space, decorated in charcoal grays and blacks with the occasional white piece of furniture breaking it all up. She sat on the white leather sofa and looked up at Rhys still in the entryway.

"I have a sister he's kept a secret from me my entire life. Her name's Emma and she lives somewhere across the country. That's all I know."

Rhys' eyes went wide. "Wow, that's quite the secret. What can I do?" His expression filled with concern. "Besides hiding you here, of course."

Starry settled into the sofa and folded her arms. "I don't know." It was true she wanted to stay away from her father long enough to show him how angry she was, but she also wanted to find Emma. "I can't properly hack anything without the right equipment. I was so angry when I left, I didn't grab any."

Rhys nodded. "We can take care of that. Tell me what you need and where I can get it."

Starry looked up at him, surprised. She hadn't expected him to offer anything. "Rhys, you don't have to—"

"I'm as stubborn as you are. You need help, so I'm going to help. Got it?"

She rolled her eyes, but couldn't stop a smile from lifting her lips. A knock on the door made her jump. She snapped her eyes to the entryway, her heart beating in her throat at the possibility of her father finding her so soon. He couldn't have sent someone to follow her. She'd left too fast and she'd parked in a public garage half a mile away in case he used the car's GPS tracker to find it. Maybe she was underestimating her father. If he found out Rhys was hiding her, he'd kill him in two seconds flat.

"Calm down, Star," Rhys laughed as he walked to the door. "It's the Chinese food, not your father."

"Am I that obvious?" She put a hand to her forehead. It wasn't like her to feel so jumpy and on edge.

Rhys paid for the delivery then closed the door and turned around with a big brown sack in his arms. The smell of Chinese food made Starry's stomach growl. She hadn't realized how long it had been since breakfast.

"Don't you usually eat cereal before work?" she asked as she got up and followed Rhys into the kitchen.

"I thought you might want lunch. And if I got lucky and you stayed the night, we'd both be hungry when I got off work." He set the bag on the table. "This is better than cereal, anyway." He started pulling out little white boxes with bright red Chinese symbols stamped on the sides.

Starry picked up one of the boxes. "How did you know I love this place?"

"You do?"

She nodded. "They have the most amazing garlic shrimp and their baozi is to die for. How did you know?"

Rhys sat down and ripped open a package of chop sticks. "I *didn't* know," he laughed. "This is the best Chinese takeout in town. I figured anyone worth knowing would love this stuff. You're obviously worth knowing."

Chuckling, Starry sat down across from him and opened the box in her hands to find three of the steamed, pork-filled buns she loved more than any other food on the planet. The sweet scent of Chinese barbecue and dense bread wafted up to her nose. Her mouth watered. "You got the char siu bao. Please tell me you ordered garlic shrimp too."

Rhys grabbed a box and opened it up. "Of course I did. I'm not insane." He plucked a shrimp from the box with his chopsticks and leaned across the table so he could put the food close to Starry's lips. "See?"

Starry slid the shrimp off the chopsticks with her teeth, chewing slowly as Rhys sat back in his chair. He looked amused as he watched her. She couldn't blame him. Finding out they both loved the same food made her happy, even though it was a shallow thing to cling to.

"I think this makes me want you more than I've ever wanted you," she said as she picked up a pork bun from the box in front of her. She kept her eyes on Rhys as she took a big bite of the bun, the sticky-sweet sauce coating her tongue.

Rhys put a shrimp in his mouth and looked sadly at his watch. "Unfortunately, I have a meeting downstairs I'm already late for. We're interviewing a new assistant manager."

Starry nodded with disappointment. She didn't know much about the club, but she did know it took most of Rhys' time and energy. It wasn't easy to work for someone like her father.

"Help yourself to anything you want," Rhys said after he ate a few more shrimp and then stood up from the table. "I'll be back around two or three tonight, hopefully earlier if things are running smoothly."

She rolled her eyes. "I'll probably be asleep. I don't know how you've completely turned your sleep schedule around. I'm not a vampire like you."

He walked around the table to her chair. "Stay here long enough and you'll turn into one," he teased. "All the other girls do."

Starry set down her pork bun and stood up to face Rhys nose-to-nose. "I'm not one of your strippers. If that's how you think of me, I'm out of here. I don't care how many dancers you've slept with, I'm not—"

His kiss cut her words short and she fought against him for a second before giving in. She'd forgotten how well he kissed. He tasted like garlic. The smell of him surrounded her as he pulled her close and kissed her like he couldn't get enough. His fingers inched up her neck and tangled in her hair. She moaned, not wanting him to leave.

Pulling away, he looked her in the eyes and placed a hand gently on her cheek, right over the spot where her father had slapped her. It still felt hot and sore.

"I've never slept with any of the strippers," he said solemnly. "It's not only bad business, but I'm not that kind of man. And just so you know, I could never think of you that way." He lowered his hand from her face and kissed her cheek. "I'll be back as soon as I can."

29

"I'll be here."

When he was gone, Starry sat down and tore open a package of chopsticks. She grabbed the box of garlic shrimp and shoved several bites into her mouth, wondering how long she could stand being with someone who made her feel so sentimental.

THREE

Emma slid a mound of scrambled eggs onto a plate and carried it to her father at the kitchen table. "I didn't salt them," she said, setting the plate in front of him. "I used some tarragon instead."

Dressed in his usual suit and tie, her father lowered his newspaper and raised an eyebrow at the eggs. His light brown hair was combed and he was freshly shaved. He looked sharp except for a grease stain on the left cuff of his white shirt. Emma cringed. It was probably from last night's dinner.

"Eggs without salt?" he laughed uneasily as he set his newspaper aside. "Are you crazy?" His smile fell as he studied her frowning face. "You're serious."

Emma pushed her dark blond hair off her shoulders and folded her arms. "Your blood pressure's too high. The doctor said if you don't cut out more sodium it'll get even higher and you'll have to go on meds. Don't you care?"

He studied her, his frown finally lifting into a weak smile.

Feeling a little guilty, Emma walked around the table to give him a hug. She wasn't the kind of daughter to order her dad around, but when something affected his health she didn't mess around. Nobody else was around to watch out for him, and he knew it.

"Love you, Dad," she said as she hugged his broad shoulders and pecked his cheek. She hadn't inherited his swimmer's build, but she was almost as tall as he was. He often jokingly told her she wasn't allowed to get taller than him or he'd lose all of his self-confidence.

She walked back to the stove to put some butter in the hot pan for her own eggs. She was in charge of three things at home: meals, laundry, and keeping up with school. Her dad kept the apartment clean, fixed stuff, managed bills, and went to work every day to support them. It had worked that way since Emma had learned to cook and operate a washer and dryer, but she had totally slacked on the laundry the past few Saturdays and it was beginning to show. She looked down at the rumpled shirt she had now worn four times in a row without washing. Good thing tomorrow was laundry day.

"We meeting for lunch today?" her dad asked as she finished cooking her eggs and put them on a plate.

Nodding, she sat down at the table. She had a long lunch at school on Fridays, so it was a good excuse to get together with her dad. "You want tacos or the Italian place? Either one probably has too much sodium, but I guess it's okay once a week if we watch all your other meals." She gave him an encouraging smile.

"Let's do Italian then. I've been craving their pizza."

"Sounds good."

Her father's phone beeped and he pulled it out of his suit pocket, his smile fading as he read whatever message had come through.

Emma's stomach sank. He was a CPA for a major New York tax firm, and they were nearing the end of tax season. That meant her father was so stressed out that every work call and message nearly sent him over the edge.

"What's the matter?" Emma asked. It was difficult to stand by and watch her father fall apart every time he got a text.

His shoulders slumped as he looked up from his phone. "It's nothing you can help with, honey. They've been talking about a new wave of layoffs after the season's over, that's all, and sometimes I'm afraid I'll be in it."

Emma leaned all her weight against the table as worry gnawed at her gut. Her father couldn't lose his job. They were barely scraping by as it was and she was going to college in the fall. Or, at least, that was the plan. Not that she was sure she'd go. A part of her wanted to attend one of the local universities that had already accepted her. That way she could live at home. Most of the schools her dad wanted her to attend were expensive and far away. She'd miss him like crazy. He'd never been very good at taking care of himself. Knowing him, he'd eat TV dinners and takeout every night and give himself a heart attack.

And what if he lost his job? He'd need her even more.

He looked up from his phone and put on a forced smile. "Enough of this depressing talk," he said cheerfully. "Let's focus on the good things, okay?" He slipped his phone back into his pocket. "Have you had any other acceptance letters roll in?"

"No, but I'm not sure I want to go even if I do get accepted to one of the bigger universities. It costs so much money."

He reached across the table and squeezed her hand. "Money's not an issue. I'm sure they'll offer you a scholarship. Even if they don't, there are grants and loans and ways to make it work."

"But it's more than that," she muttered. Her shoulders felt heavy. "I'm not like everyone else at school. They all want to move out and get away from their parents. I'm weird, I guess." She stared down at her unfinished breakfast. "I'm scared to leave you, and I'm scared to move away, and I'm scared I'll never be happy anywhere else."

She looked up when her dad squeezed her hand again. His eyes were soft and understanding, and she realized that made everything worse. He was her family—her *whole* family. Her mother had died in a car accident when Emma was only a few weeks old. Emma had never met any extended family because they were either dead or shunned to the point of nonexistence. Her dad had mentioned a brother once or twice, but apparently they never spoke and never would. So her father was all she had and she couldn't imagine leaving him willingly.

"This is some deep stuff," he said, rubbing his thumb across her palm. "How about we talk about it a little more over pizza while we sit in the nice spring weather? It's supposed to be close to seventy degrees today."

Emma smiled. "Deal."

"Great, I've got to get going." He stood up from his chair and headed into the living room where he'd left his briefcase and suit jacket. "You have anything fun going on at school today?" he asked as he slipped on the jacket. "Anything planned with friends?"

"Not really." She had a few friends at school, but she'd never been close to any of them. Her dad always told her it was because she was too focused on her grades, like he had been when he was in school, but she wasn't sure that was it at all. It was more like she never felt connected to anyone.

Her dad frowned at her answer, but didn't say anything before his phone started ringing. He pulled it from his pocket and answered with a hasty hello. Emma tuned him out as she got up from the table and took the dirty dishes to the sink. Her dad would clean them when he got home from work.

"That's not what we agreed to!" her dad's voice rose above its normal pitch. "Tell them they'll have to look at the contract again. It clearly states in the last section . . ."

Emma turned to look at him as he kept raging into the phone. She hated it when he got this upset. Whenever she thought about him at work, she imagined him yelling at people all day long just like he was doing now. It scared her.

He continued yelling into the phone as Emma went to her room to grab her backpack and shoes. He was still yelling when she sat down on the sofa to put them on. Finally, he ended the argument and gave Emma a sympathetic look as he walked past her into his bedroom. He emerged with a package the size of a large shoebox under his arm. Emma smiled. At least there was something good for him to look forward to.

"What are you selling today?" she asked as he set the box next to his briefcase on the sofa and buttoned up his suit coat.

He smiled proudly. "Antique decorative eggs from China. They're made out of petrified wood. A good find, I'd say. I should get a lot for them."

"Well, good. Maybe you should take me to a movie tonight."

"Maybe I should." He picked up his briefcase just as his phone rang again. His smile fell immediately. "I swear," he muttered as he pulled his phone out of his pocket again. "Maybe it'll be a good thing if they lay me off."

Emma rolled her eyes as he answered the phone and opened the door to leave the apartment. He waved goodbye and Emma watched the door close behind him. Maybe he did need a new job. Sometimes she dreamed he'd make enough money buying and selling antiques, but so far they didn't seem to bring in more than a few hundred dollars a month. Certainly not enough to live on, and he'd been doing it for as long as she could remember.

Standing up, Emma swung her backpack onto her shoulders and started toward the door, her eyes landing on the box her father had left on the sofa. She groaned to herself. It wasn't the first time he'd forgotten to take a package with him. He usually stopped by one of the antiques stores on his way home from work.

Emma stared at the box, a niggling thought at the back of her mind. She'd never sold antiques for him before, but how hard could it be? There was an antiques store a block from her school, one she was sure her father had sold to before. Plus, it opened early. Selling the eggs for him would get one more thing off his plate. He'd be that much less stressed.

Making up her mind, she reached down and picked up the package. It was heavy, but not unmanageable. If she couldn't sell it she'd leave it in her locker until lunch and give it to her dad then. He'd thank her for being so thoughtful.

Antsy Antiques was not what Emma expected. As she stepped inside off the busy New York sidewalk, she was surprised by how quiet it was. Passing wicker chairs, spindly lamps, and glass knickknacks lining ornate shelves, she reached the back counter and came face-to-face with a tall, angry-looking woman writing something down on a pad of paper. She reminded Emma of a crow, her hair like shiny black feathers smoothed around her narrow face, her chest puffed out as if she owned the entire world and not just some hole-in-the-wall antiques shop in Brooklyn. Her name tag read *Paula*.

Emma felt creeped out all of a sudden. Maybe it was Paula's inky eyes that bored holes into Emma's forehead. Or maybe it was the faint smell of marijuana in the air, mixed with dust and spicy cologne. None of these things were particularly alarming, but it was such a different feeling from the city bustle outside, Emma felt strange rules applied here. And she had no idea what they were.

She lifted the box onto the counter. "I'm Sam Coleridge's daughter," she explained coolly as Paula looked up from her pad of paper. "You buy from him, right?"

Paula studied Emma's face. "Yes, I buy from Sam all the time." She leaned forward to look down at the shipping label on the box. Her eyebrows immediately drew into a knot and she was silent for a moment before looking back up at Emma. "Does he have you delivering the goods now?" She pursed her peeling lips.

"Um, not really. It's tax season. He's crazy-busy this time of year so I thought I'd do him a favor."

"I see." Paula opened the box and reached inside to pull out one of the antique eggs. Inspecting its brown, swirling exterior, she hefted it from one hand to another. It was quite beautiful. By the size of the box, there had to be at least twenty eggs inside.

A wicked smile ghosted Paula's lips as she set the egg back into the box and peered at the shipping label again. "Well, Miss Coleridge. This has been quite enlightening." She opened a drawer and pulled out a pad of pre-printed invoices. Filling out the blanks with thick, black ink, she ripped off the top paper and handed it to Emma. "Tell your father he'll receive his payment in his account later today. I still need to appraise these properly, so if I decide they're worth more than the base price listed on the invoice I'll deposit the difference by tomorrow."

Emma looked down at the invoice, her heart slamming into her throat. "They're worth six thousand dollars?" she asked, her voice hoarse with surprise. "Are you sure?"

Paula's eyes narrowed to glittering slits. The look was so menacing it made Emma take a step backward. "My sellers never argue with payment. Tell your father if he has a problem with it he can come in here himself."

"Y–yes, of course." Emma turned on her heel and left the store. When she was back out on the sidewalk she took a long, deep breath and looked down at the invoice again. Either her father was keeping it a secret how much he profited off his antiques, or those Chinese eggs were worth way more than he'd thought.

Emma sat down in her seat and raised an eyebrow at her father's mini pizza. "Goat cheese and raw jalapeños?" she asked. They were eating al fresco at the Italian place, just a few feet away from the long, snaking line at the outdoor pick-up window. "But you hate jalapeños. You won't make it through half that."

Flourishing a hand, her father lifted a slice and bit off the end. "This is my punishment for this morning." Already, his face was turning bright red from the heat of the peppers. "I don't have ten dollars to put in the Swear Jar."

Confused, Emma leaned back in her chair and took a sip from her Coke. She couldn't remember her father swearing this morning, but she was so used to tuning out his yelling that she must have filtered out all the swearing too. She watched little beads of sweat form on her father's forehead.

"Fine," she chuckled. "If you eat that entire pizza, I'll waive your Swear Jar fee."

Her father swallowed and gulped down a few swigs of water. "Thank you," he gasped, and took another bite of pizza. "I like the taste, but the heat kills me. Just remember this when it's your turn to pay up. You'll have to eat anchovies on your pizza."

Emma pulled a disgusted face. She didn't hate fish, but she got queasy at the thought of eating little shriveled up fishes, heads and all. "Agreed. I'll be sure to save up my cash."

41

"Or just don't swear. You can manage that, right?"

Emma rolled her eyes. The Swear Jar was more of a fun game than it was about actually swearing. "I rarely slip, Dad, but sure, I'll try my hardest."

Her father's smile faded as he took another bite of his pizza. He had already removed his suit coat and rolled up his shirt sleeves. It was almost seventy degrees outside, but Emma was certain the bright sunshine beating down on their heads had nothing to do with her father's discomfort. He couldn't stand anything even remotely spicy, so eating jalapeños seemed an extreme alternative to dropping a ten dollar bill in the Swear Jar, especially considering the six thousand dollars he'd made off the eggs this morning.

"So, Dad," Emma said after polishing off a few slices of her own pizza. She leaned over to pull out Paula's invoice from her backpack. "I, uh, wanted to do you a favor this morning, but I'm a little confused now."

Finishing up his second piece of pizza, her dad wiped his brow with one hand and leaned forward. "Sure, honey, what is it?"

"You left the box of eggs in the apartment. I decided to take them to Antsy Antiques for you on my way to school." She set the invoice carefully in the middle of the table between their two pizzas. Her dad's eyes landed on the paper and his chewing slowed until it stopped altogether. He looked up at Emma, his eyes widening.

"Dad?" she said when it was obvious he wasn't going to say anything. "I'm confused about how much she's paying you for those eggs. I know it's not my business, but . . . I mean, do you make that much on all of your antiques? Or did you pay a lot for the eggs in the first place? If you're making a huge profit, that's awesome, but I . . ."

Her voice faltered and died in her throat as her dad picked up the invoice and stared at it so hard it looked like his eyes might burn holes through the paper. He started chewing again, but it was slow and methodical. His eyes filled with pain and then something like fear. "I wish you hadn't done this," he said in a low, trembling voice.

Oh, crap. Emma swallowed a lump in her throat and shifted uncomfortably on her chair. She'd done something wrong. Terribly wrong. The amount he was receiving wasn't a good thing after all. Maybe she should have pushed for more money if they were worth more. "I'm sorry, Dad," she whispered. "I thought I was helping you out. Paula said she'd pay you more if they're worth more than that."

He lifted his eyes to her, the fear in them switching to concern. "Oh, Em, it's not the money." He folded the invoice in half and set it down by his pizza. "Of course you meant well. I'm not upset with you. My

43

antiques hobby is something I never intended for you to get involved with, that's all. Those eggs cost a lot, so my profit isn't the entire six thousand dollars, but it's still quite a bit. It's just . . . I wish you hadn't delivered them to Paula. She's not the person I . . ." His voice faded as he glanced nervously at the invoice and reached up to loosen his tie. His forehead was still beaded with sweat and it seemed to be getting worse. He'd only eaten two pieces of pizza so far.

Emma watched him carefully, her insides tying themselves into a hundred different knots. She felt guilty and frightened and confused. Her father had never acted so nervous around her before, but she had also never butted in on his hobby before. Had he promised those eggs to a different dealer? Was that why he was so upset?

"What can I do?" she asked. "I want to fix whatever I messed up."

He looked so pained Emma thought he might start crying. "There's nothing you can do, honey. I'll fix it, don't worry."

"But do you really make that much on all of your antiques?"

He looked over at the passing traffic and took a deep breath. Emma waited for him to say something, but he stayed quiet. He couldn't possibly expect her to take silence as an answer.

"Dad," she urged. "What are you doing with—"

"Please stop asking." He kept his eyes on the traffic.

Emma snapped her mouth shut and lowered her eyes to the pizza on the table. Everything was fine a minute ago. Now it was a mess, one that she'd made. The tension rolling off her father felt a million times worse than when he yelled at clients and coworkers on the phone. This was a quiet sort of anger. It almost felt dangerous.

"I've gotta go now," he said, turning back to Emma. He scooted his chair away from the table. "I'm sorry, honey." He grabbed his suit coat from the back of his chair, put it on, and then walked around the table to Emma's chair. "Promise me something," he said.

"Anything, Dad." She pushed her chair away from the table and stood up to face him, her heart aching. She had upset him and there was no way to take it back.

"Promise me you'll always stick to what you know is right." He pulled her into a tight hug. "Please, Emma."

She squeezed him and tried not to think about the strangeness of his request. "I'll always do what's right. You know me better than anyone, Dad. You raised me that way."

"Yes, I did." He loosened his hold and reached across the table to grab the invoice. He folded it into a small square and put it in his suit coat pocket. "Don't worry about anything," he said, leaning forward to kiss her on the cheek. "I'll see you tonight, okay? Make me a good low-sodium dinner?"

Emma relaxed a little and laughed. "You got it, Dad."

They said goodbye and he walked away, disappearing around the corner as Emma sat back down. She stared at his unfinished pizza, her heart aching. He'd eaten all those raw jalapeños just for her. She had to message him or she'd go nuts. She pulled out her phone.

EMMA: *Sorry for what I did. I hope you can fix it. Tell you what . . . you can curse as much as you want in front of me and I won't make you put a cent in the Swear Jar. Deal?*

DAD: *I love you, Emma. It's a deal.*

FOUR

Emma felt sick for the rest of the school day. When her last class finally ended, she walked the few blocks home as fast as she could, berating herself the whole way. She changed her clothes and started making dinner, but she couldn't get her dad's words out of her head: *I wish you hadn't done this . . .*

She wished she hadn't, either, but she also wished she could stop scolding herself. It wasn't like she'd meant to upset him. The best thing to do was get back into a comfortable routine. She was halfway through dicing an onion when the door buzzer sounded. She walked to the entryway and pushed the intercom button. "Yeah?"

"UPS delivery," a familiar male voice chirped. "For Sam."

"Come up." Emma pushed the buzzer to unlock the lobby doors. It was so routine to get packages that she'd almost forgotten her father would be getting a box of antiques today—possibly worth thousands of dollars.

A few minutes later someone knocked on the door. It was Erik, the usual UPS man who delivered to the building. He handed over an electronic tablet for Emma to sign. She scribbled her name on the tablet and handed it back.

"It's a heavy one today," Erik said as he bent down to pick up the box he'd lugged up with him. It was big enough to hold an entire set of pots and pans and felt just as heavy when Emma took it from him. She said goodbye and shut the door with her foot before carrying the box to the kitchen table. A part of her wanted to open it, but she turned away before the temptation got too strong. She had to finish dinner.

EMMA: *Hey, Dad. I've had dinner ready for two hours. Where are you?*

No response.

EMMA: *It's been three hours now, in case you've lost track of time. Do you want me to bring your dinner to the office? I'll bet you're swamped, huh?*

No response.

EMMA: *Please answer your phone, Dad. I'm bringing you something to eat.*

No response.

Even though it was close to 8:30 at night, two receptionists still sat at the front desk of her father's CPA firm. Emma walked across the marble-floored lobby toward the receptionist she knew dealt with her father's office wing.

"I'm surprised to see you, Emma!" Carol said as she leaned forward on her elbows, her red lipstick a pretty shock of color on her face. "How is Sam feeling? We were so sad to hear he caught that flu bug going around."

Emma almost dropped the bag of food she'd brought with her. "What?"

Carol's expression turned sympathetic. "It's an awful bug. The entire third floor has been wiped out by it. I've heard hot lemon tea helps, so be sure to give him some of that. Keep him hydrated." She tapped a few keys on her keyboard and squinted at her monitor. "So what did you need, dear? Did he send you over here for a file or two? Still trying to work while he's sick?"

Dumbfounded, Emma tried to move her feet, but they felt like cement blocks holding her down. Her mind zipped through a thousand things she could say to cover her father's deception. What if this affected the company's decision about laying him off?

"I knew he wasn't feeling well," she said quickly. "But he tries so hard, you know? It must have been really bad for him to leave. Do you know when he went home?"

Carol looked up from her screen. "What? Oh, a few minutes after he came back from lunch. He looked horrible."

Emma leaned forward, gripping the edge of the tall counter with her free hand. "Did you talk to him? Did he say where he was going?"

Carol eyed Emma's white knuckles. "I assumed he went home. Why?"

Emma tried to swallow the lump in her throat, but it wouldn't go down. Maybe her father had gone to the doctor, but that seemed unlikely. Even if he had, why hadn't he answered her texts and calls? His phone could have died, but she knew he'd find some way to contact her if he could. It wasn't like him to leave her hanging like this.

"Oh, it's nothing," she said and peeled her fingers off the edge of the counter. "If it's that bad he should've gone to the doctor, that's all." She waved a hand toward the direction of the elevator. "I'll go get that file he wants."

Carol nodded, unfazed. "Okay, dear."

Emma turned and made her way to the elevators, her finger trembling as she pushed the button to go up to the eighth floor. She'd been to her dad's office countless times to visit him during lunch or meet him for dinner, but never when he wasn't there.

Once she was inside the office, she closed the door behind her and stared at the empty desk chair. A part of her had hoped she'd find her dad up here despite what Carol had said. Sure enough, the office was empty.

Emma set the bag of food on top of the desk and sank into the leather chair. *Where is he?* She'd be deluding herself if she didn't assume his absence had something to do with the antiques. Maybe he was in the middle of fixing whatever it was that had to be fixed. That was it. He'd be home soon. It was fine.

Looking down at a desk calendar penciled with appointments and doodles, Emma ran her finger over one of the doodles. A blinking light on the desk phone caught her attention. New messages. Before she could stop herself, she pushed the button. There were three voicemails from clients, all work related, and then a message recorded two hours ago. It was a familiar voice, the words clipped and angry:

"Sam, it's Paula. I know you told me never to call you at work, but you won't answer your cell. Consider this our last contact. You're out. I've told him everything."

The line went dead and the voicemail beeped to indicate there were no more messages.

Emma leaned forward, panic constricting her throat as she rubbed her arms. They were covered in goose bumps. He was *out*? That sounded like something more serious than a simple, "I don't want to buy antiques from you anymore."

The suspicion that her father had done something bad wormed its way into her mind. She tried to bat it away, but it wouldn't leave. Standing up from the desk, she left the office and passed a door with a name tag she recognized: *Alex Sheffield, CPA.*

Alex was one of her father's friends. It must have been three or four years ago when Emma had first met him. A few months after that, her father had given her his phone number and told her if there was ever an emergency, Alex was the one she should call. He'd been very adamant about it and made sure she put the number in her phone.

Now, as she passed Alex's office, her feet slowed to a stop. Maybe he would know where her father was. She looked through the little side window by the door, but the office was dark and empty. She couldn't quite bring herself to call him yet. If anything, she should call the local hospitals first to see if her father had checked in anywhere.

Leaving the building as fast as she could, she made a few calls on her way home, but no hospitals had any record of a Sam Coleridge, or any unidentified men with his description being admitted in the past six hours. While that was comforting, it was also unsettling because now she had no idea where to look.

She stepped into her apartment, disappointed to find it empty. Her heart pounded as she stared at the box on the kitchen table. She took her phone out of her pocket and looked down at the texts she had sent her father. She typed another one and then tried to call him, but there was still no answer. It was 9:30 now. He had never, ever gone this long without telling her where he was.

Finally, she walked into the kitchen, set down the bag of food, and picked up a pair of scissors. She walked to the box of antiques, her curiosity growing as she cut the tape and pulled open the flaps. Inside was a massive amount of bubble wrap and wadded-up brown paper. She dug through it all and pulled out four oval packages the size of footballs. Unwrapping one, she found a large ceramic owl. She turned it over in her hands. It was painted in shades of turquoise and sea green. Its big yellow eyes stared blankly at her.

A beep from her phone made her jump a full inch in the air. The owl slipped and fell to the floor, cracking around the neck. She swore out loud. So much for not needing to put money in the Swear Jar.

Pulling her phone out of her pocket, she read the incoming message. Her heart sank. It was nothing but a text from one of her teachers' automated systems reminding her of a specific assignment due on Monday.

She tossed her phone onto the table and knelt down to inspect the broken owl. Knowing her luck lately, it had to be worth thousands of dollars—*before* it was broken, anyway.

Or maybe it wasn't worth much at all.

Maybe she'd never know.

Her father had to tell her more about what was going on. They'd never kept secrets from each other. Why would he do it now?

Her phone beeped again and she stood up to look at the message. It was from the same teacher clarifying something about the assignment. Would he stop already about the assignments? Her father was missing. He wasn't answering his calls. He was possibly lying to her. She didn't care about school!

She looked down at the owl, shocked to see the crack had grown. The owl was broken beyond repair. Even if it ever had been worth a lot of money, she'd ruined it now. She'd upset her father and she'd ruined everything.

Anger rippled through her, and for a split second she understood exactly why her father lost his temper over the phone all the time. It was impossible *not* to be furious with herself right now. There was only one way to get rid of that anger. Letting out a guttural yell, she threw the owl as hard as she could at the wall. It shattered, releasing a heavy plastic package that fell to the floor with a thud.

Emma froze. Her breaths came hard and sharp until finally she moved forward and picked up the package. It was so tightly sealed the little packets inside bulged against the thick plastic. There were at least a hundred of them, each one half the size of a business card and filled with small crystal-like chunks.

Emma's head pounded as one word filled her mind: *drugs.*

What else could it possibly be? She'd seen enough drugs passed around at school to at least know what they looked like. Meth, cocaine, heroin. This particular package looked like meth. She wracked her brain, but couldn't come up with anything else it could be. That meant Paula was buying drugs. That meant Emma's father was a . . .

No, he couldn't be. There was no way. She thought about Paula's creepy message on the voicemail: *You're out. I've told him everything.* Who had Paula told? Was she talking about other drug dealers? Would they hurt her father?

Her breath catching in her throat, Emma dropped the package onto the table and put her hands on either side of her head. Her father had kept this part of his life a secret from her. It made sense why he wouldn't want her to know, but it made *no* sense why he would do it in the first place.

Or maybe . . .

She lowered her hands. Maybe he didn't know all of the antiques he sold were filled with drugs. Or maybe this was the first package that had ever contained drugs and it was simply a fluke she'd discovered them.

Yes, that was it. It had to be. She looked at the curio cabinet in the living room where her father kept several valuable antiques: a few Hummel statues, some 19th century vases, some Navajo woven baskets. She was certain none of those had drugs inside of them. The Hummel statues were hollow and had a hole in the bottom. The vases were empty and so were the baskets.

Turning back to the box of owls, Emma thought back on how Paula had acted in the antiques store. Considering that, it seemed more plausible that drugs were involved with those Chinese eggs and that her father knew exactly what he was doing.

Emma turned away from the table and sat down on the sofa in the living room. She put her head in her hands and tried to keep her breaths measured. She had to stay calm or she was going to fall apart. She could wait for her father to come home. He would answer all of her questions then.

But what if he never came home? Should she call the police? But if she called the police and showed them the drugs, that might get her father thrown in jail when he did come back. What would she do without him? She stood up from the sofa, her entire body breaking out in a sweat. There were no answers to her problem, and even worse, she had nobody she could go to, nobody she trusted with something like this.

Then she remembered seeing Alex's name plate on his office door. Rushing to the table, she grabbed her phone and pulled up Alex's information. She hit the call button.

"Hello?" a scratchy voice answered on the other end.

Emma took a deep, nervous breath. "Alex? Hi, this is Emma . . . Sam's daughter . . . you know?"

"Oh, Emma . . ." He cleared his throat. "What's going on? You okay?"

She walked down the hallway, stopping when she got to a portrait hanging on the wall. Her mother's smile beamed at her, framed by two sparkling brown eyes and a mass of tight dark curls Emma had not inherited.

"Is my dad with you?" Emma asked as she moved into her room and sat on her bed. "Or have you heard from him?"

There was a long, dead pause. "No, he's not with me, and I haven't heard from him since before lunch. What's wrong?"

Emma's throat closed up, but she forced herself to keep talking. "He's . . . he's missing. He left work after lunch and never went back. He told them he had the flu, but he never came home. I can't get a hold of him."

There was another long pause.

"Are you there?" Emma asked.

"Yes, I'm here. Has anything been out of the ordinary lately? Besides him going missing?"

Emma looked up at the ceiling. Things were way out of the ordinary. "Yes. I delivered one of his boxes of antiques this morning and he got upset about it. They paid him a lot of money for it too. And then he got another package today and I looked inside it and I found . . . I found . . ."

She couldn't bring herself to say it. She didn't trust this man enough to tell him about the drugs. She barely knew him. Still, her dad trusted him. He worked with him. They were friends.

"It's okay, Emma," Alex said gently when Emma's silence filled the line. "I know you don't know me very well, but I've promised your father to help you in an emergency. I care about you as much as I care about him, okay?"

Emma relaxed enough to keep talking. "I found drugs inside one of the antiques." Tears immediately filled her eyes. It was the first time she'd cried over any of this. "At least, I think they're drugs. A lot of them. I don't know what else they could be."

"Right. Listen, Emma, it's very important we meet. Is there any way I can come to your place tonight, or you to mine?"

A shudder ran down Emma's spine. Alex was divorced, all his kids grown up and gone. She'd been to his house over in Bay Ridge with her father. It was small and very quiet because he lived alone.

"I-I don't know," she stuttered. "Could we meet tomorrow morning instead? My dad might still show up. It's only been a few hours, right?"

Alex was so quiet she started to think he'd hung up. "Are you sure? I think your dad would appreciate me keeping you safe. There are things I need to tell you."

The eagerness in his voice made Emma's jaw clench. "Why can't you tell me now?"

"It's too complicated to explain over the phone. Have you called the local hospitals?"

"Yes, he's not at any of them."

"Hmm, you should visit the police station in the morning and file a missing persons report. Maybe don't tell them about the drugs yet, though, okay? Not until you know more about what's going on."

"Okay." Her voice was trembling now. Hearing Alex's suggestions made everything seem that much more real, but maybe he was being overly cautious. Her father had probably given Alex the impression she was helpless and he should do everything possible to take care of her if she ever called him. She could handle things on her own, especially for one night while she waited for her father to show up.

"Call me in the morning?" Alex asked. "Even if Sam shows up?"

"Sure."

"Oh, and Emma?"

"Yes?"

"Promise me you won't go searching for him out on the streets. That could be dangerous, especially this late at night."

"Yeah, that makes sense. I'll talk with you tomorrow."

Her hands shook as she ended the call and got off her bed, weary but wide awake at the same time. She had to do something to distract herself.

She shuffled into her father's room and flipped on the light. Blinking in the brightness, she thought about all the times she'd washed her dad's bed sheets, all the times she'd curled up with him to watch a movie or read a book, all the times he'd kissed her forehead and told her how precious she was in his life. She remembered the grease stain on his shirt and headed for his dirty clothes hamper. Like her, he had very few clean clothes left to wear. The least she could do was separate the clothes to get ready for the laundry. He'd want clean clothes when he got back.

Because he *was* coming back.

She busied herself with the clothes and then started going through his drawers to see if he'd put away dirty stuff to wear again since she had taken so long to do the laundry. She had never gone through his drawers before. When she reached his sock drawer, her hands froze.

Near the back was a gold key. She held it up to the light, turning it around and around. Why would he hide a key in his sock drawer? There was nothing in the apartment that locked with a little gold key. There was the front door and the windows, but she and her dad kept those keys on their key chains.

She looked around the room. She checked under the bed. Nothing. In the bottom of his closet. Nothing. The top shelf of his closet. Bingo. There was a box near the back behind a bunch of file crates. She slid it off the shelf. It was the size of a large shoebox and there was a lock built into it. Her fingers trembling, she slid the key into the lock and turned. It fit perfectly and the box opened. She breathed a sigh of relief. It wasn't drugs, at least. There was nothing in it but a little notebook and photographs. She lifted the first photo and frowned. It was a baby picture, the kind taken at the hospital when the baby is still in the nursery. It was her baby picture. It looked just like the one she had in her baby book in her bedroom. Same faded pink blanket and everything.

Or was it?

Her heart pounding, she jumped off the bed and ran into her room to retrieve the book. When she was back on the bed, she flipped to the first page and compared the two pictures. The babies were clearly separate individuals. The hospital tags on their wrists had different numbers and dates. Emma had caramel brown hair. The other baby had dark hair.

Emma scrunched her forehead in confusion. Why would her father keep a picture of a random baby in a locked box?

She set down the picture and lifted out the other pictures in the box. There were two: one of Emma's mother holding the baby in the hospital and one of that same baby about a year old, her hair a mass of dark brown curls on top of her head. She was grinning at the camera, a plastic giraffe halfway in her mouth.

Emma's throat closed up. Was this her sister?

She looked at the background, trying to piece together where the picture had been taken, but nothing looked familiar. It was furniture she'd never seen before, carpet she'd never felt, toys she'd never played with.

The baby must have died.

Emma squeezed her eyes shut. Her father had obviously kept this from her because he hadn't wanted her to feel the sense of loss coursing through her right now. Not that she had ever known her sister, but now that she knew *about* her, something inside of her felt empty.

She lowered the picture and looked at the one with her mother again. She was about the same age as she was in the picture hanging in the hallway, so beautiful, thin, and elegant.

Lucy.

Emma knew that was her mother's name, but it sounded strange. It had always sounded strange because she had never known the woman. And she had never known this other baby, either, whoever she was.

Emma turned back to the box and lifted out a little leather notebook. When she flipped through it, every page was filled with pretty cursive writing. She read eagerly.

May 20th, 1997

Starry is a punk, just like she was in my tummy. She cries if I leave the room, so I have to carry her everywhere, which seems like a lot, even if this apartment is small. I haven't done laundry in a week,

but Sam is helping as much as he can, bless his heart.
He loves us both so much.

Emma ran her finger over Starry's name. If Lucy had given birth to Starry, then Starry really was her sister. Based on the date of Starry's hospital photo, she would have been almost nineteen if she were still alive. Emma had just turned eighteen in March. They were less than a year apart.

Emma's heart ached as she imagined what it would have been like if Starry had lived with her. They would have shared so many things, maybe fought a little, but would probably always be best friends.

Emma read on, flipping through a few short entries about how difficult it was for Lucy to care for Starry, financial stresses, how much she loved Sam, how happy she was, but busy too. Then Emma reached an entry dated six weeks after the first entry. One paragraph stood out:

Here I thought nursing a baby was good birth control. I was wrong. I'm pregnant again! What have Sam and I done? It's crazy! We've had to hire a nanny to help out with Starry so I can keep managing the rehab clinic. Sometimes I wonder if it's even worth it. Money is so tight and being pregnant again so soon, I'm too tired to do much with Starry by the time I get home. I'm not sure how long I can keep it all up.

Emma's heart sank at the thought of being an added burden to her parents. She'd had no idea her mother had worked at a rehab clinic. Working after having a baby and then getting pregnant again seemed like too much for anyone. She kept reading, but nothing else stood out until she reached an entry on the last page, dated in January:

Sometimes I think back on high school and wonder what my life would be like if Sam hadn't exposed Glenn's steroid habit and shown his true colors. Would I still be with Glenn if that hadn't happened? Over the years, he has shown Sam and me that he is rotten to the core. He will never change.

Emma kept looking at the name Glenn, her thoughts jumbled as she tried to remember if her father had ever mentioned someone by that name. Her mother made it sound like Glenn had been a part of their lives even after high school. Emma supposed it wasn't too strange that her father had never mentioned him, but at the same time, it made her think about how little he talked about his past. All she knew for certain beyond a few stories he'd told her was that his parents had died in a car wreck when he was a teenager and that he'd gone to college for computer science and then a trade school for his CPA training.

And right now Emma couldn't ask him about anything. If she tried to search for her sister, what would she find? An old obituary? News articles? Had she died in the same accident as their mother? Starry was a unique name. It couldn't be too difficult to find her.

Emma grabbed her phone and took a few pictures of the most important journal entries before getting on her computer to search for Starry Coleridge. But as far as she could find, Starry had never existed.

FIVE

Starry rolled over in bed as Rhys' alarm blared through the room. She pushed his shoulder and he grunted. He should have been up hours ago, but she'd talked him into taking half the night off so he could get more sleep.

"Wake up," she yawned. "Unless you'd rather stay here with me."

Rhys turned off the alarm and rolled over to her. "As nice as that sounds, it's probably already a mess down there without me. What time is it?"

"Eleven. You'll only have to go down there for three or four hours, right?"

"Yeah."

Starry melted against him and thought about how good it felt to be connected to someone. She'd never felt this way before. "Maybe you should take the whole night off. The club won't fall apart without you for one night." She nuzzled his earlobe. "Please? All we ever get is tiny chunks of time and it's usually when I'm half asleep."

Rhys gave her a longing look and climbed on top of her. "We've got a few minutes."

He felt so good, his warm lips on her bare shoulders, his fingers tangling in her hair. She wrapped her legs around him. No matter how many times she had him, she always wanted more.

"A few minutes, huh?" she whispered into his ear. Her stomach growled a second later and she stifled a laugh. "Um, maybe I should eat something first? My body apparently wants something other than you."

Chuckling, Rhys reached across the bed and grabbed a half-empty bag of Doritos. "Will these do?"

Sitting up, Starry snatched the bag. "I love these. I know they're terrible for me, but I don't care." She ate a few chips before Rhys took the bag away and grabbed her hand, inspecting it with a look of concern.

"Dirty," he scoffed and rubbed his lips across her fingers covered in nacho cheese powder. "Very dirty." He sucked her index finger clean and licked his lips. "Just how I like it."

Starry slapped his shoulder. "You're a dork."

"A sexy dork, you must admit." He smirked and tugged on her panties. "Now, back to those few minutes."

Half an hour later, Starry rolled onto her back, hot, satisfied, and sweaty. "That was a few great minutes," she gasped.

"Good to know you're so pleased." Rhys wrapped her in his arms again. He smelled like fresh laundry and Doritos as she breathed him in. She'd washed the bed sheets that afternoon and she'd straightened up the apartment too. She was becoming a damn maid, but a part of her deep, deep down didn't mind.

Sliding her hand up Rhys' side, she felt a long scar between two of his upper ribs. He'd never told her how he'd gotten it and she'd never asked, but she could only imagine it had something to do with his reckless past. She hoped in time he'd tell her everything.

"I have to go shower now," he said, looking regretfully into her eyes. "I want more time with you too, but I have too much going on. We've got three new girls coming in the next half hour. Ginger's going to have her hands full even with my help, and I've got to finish training Mark."

"Who's Mark?"

He rolled onto his back and groaned. "My new assistant. I'm not sure I'm going to keep him." He put a hand on his forehead as he started in on Mark, quickly outlining a few huge problems he could foresee.

Starry watched his mouth as he spoke, noting the way he pursed his lips when he was irritated with someone. When he finished, she tenderly brushed a finger up his shoulder.

"So you ordered my equipment?" she asked. The only reason she'd avoided doing it herself was because her father could be watching her phone as well as the company she'd told Rhys to order from. It was the only place she trusted.

Rhys nodded. "I split the order between several different names and addresses, like you said. It'll be delivered here and to a post office box we use for the business. Nobody should be able to trace the order back to you." He grabbed his cell phone from the end table and pulled up a few screens, finally stopping on one. "Here you go."

Starry took the phone and looked over the orders. "I'm impressed. So I can pick up the ones at the post office?"

"I'll need to pick them up, but I can get up early on Monday and get them for you."

Starry frowned. "That's a long wait."

Rhys' eyebrows knotted with concern as he rolled onto his side to look at her. "I know you want to find Emma, but please don't dig too deep on this. I don't want you pissing off your father any more than you already have. I couldn't take it if he hurt you."

What the hell? Starry narrowed her eyes. "Don't you want me to find her?"

He kissed her on the cheek. "Of course I do. I've gotta go get ready."

She watched him walk into the bathroom. Once the shower was going, she got out of bed and pulled on some clothes before picking up Rhys' phone and entering the access code. She'd memorized it the first time she'd seen him punch it in. Not that she'd planned on ever using his phone, but she knew she could never be too careful with anyone.

She quickly dialed the shipping company's number. Something wasn't sitting right. Why had Rhys told her not to dig too deep? It was a red flag waving madly in her face. She kept her eyes on the closed bathroom door as she was put through to several different people.

"What do you mean none of those names are in your system?" she snapped after the person on the other end explained they had no record of any of Rhys' orders.

"There are no orders under those names, ma'am," the man answered. "Do you have the order numbers?"

She looked at the numbers on the phone and then recited them to the man.

A full minute passed.

"Nope, nothing under those numbers. And you said the payment already went through? Do you have a record of that?"

Starry gritted her teeth. She had no idea how Rhys had paid for the equipment. She'd assumed he'd used one of his personal credit cards.

"I don't have that information right now," she said.

There was a heavy sigh. "Then I have no other way to track the orders. Would you like to place the orders again? I'll give you a discount. If the other ones go through, we'll refund you later."

Starry stared at the bathroom door again, every inch of her wanting to throw something at it and scream at Rhys that he was a dirty liar.

But why had he lied?

Or maybe he hadn't lied and the company had screwed up. Or Rhys had covered his tracks in a way she wasn't considering. Or maybe her father or one of his security people had somehow managed to erase her orders. That didn't make sense, though. If they knew about her orders, her father would know where she was, and if he knew where she was, she wouldn't still be here.

The truth was she didn't know Rhys well enough to implicitly trust him. She hated that feeling. There was nobody she could trust right now. Not even her father.

"Ma'am?" the man on the phone said.

"Tell me," she said, "is there any way you can find out about other inquiries regarding those names?"

"I can look into it. I'll put you on hold for a moment."

"Fine."

A minute later the man came back on the line. "No other inquiries have been made. I'm sorry, ma'am."

"It's not your fault." She ended the call and stared down at Rhys' phone. It felt wrong to snoop into his business, but she couldn't shake the feeling that something was wrong. A second later she was looking through Rhys' text messages and phone call history and then opening up his email and scrolling through that, as well. Nothing looked amiss. There were phone calls from her father to Rhys, but none of them were very long. It certainly wasn't strange for her father to talk to Rhys once in a while. He was his boss, after all.

She put Rhys' phone back on the end table and started pacing the room. Rhys had tossed his clothes on the floor earlier. She stepped over them, irritated. She had done his laundry. She had cleaned his apartment. She'd had sex with him less than twenty minutes ago. And what did she get in return? A bunch of lies.

She squeezed her hands into fists. If Rhys really was lying to her, she'd kill him before her father even got a chance.

SIX

Emma sat up in bed, sleep clinging to her eyes. She had been up most of the night, tossing and turning as she waited for her dad to come home. She must have finally fallen asleep. Scrambling out of bed, she looked around the apartment. It was empty.

Her phone beeped with a text message:

ALEX SHEFFIELD: *Hi, Emma, I've tried calling you several times but you haven't answered. Did your father come home? If not, can we meet? It's really important I talk to you soon.*

Emma stared at the message. She wanted to meet with Alex, but she didn't feel comfortable with letting him into her apartment. She looked over at her overflowing clothes hamper and typed a response.

EMMA: *No Dad yet. Let's meet in the laundromat around the corner from my place. Do you know where that is?*

ALEX: *Sure do. See you around 1:00?*

EMMA: *Sounds good.*

Heading into the kitchen, Emma quickly snapped a few photos of the antique owls and the box they'd arrived in, just in case Alex might want to see them. Then she got all the laundry together and headed out the door half an hour later. Her arms were aching from the weight of the three laundry bags by the time she got to the laundromat. The sign above the door read: All Washed Up. This was the most depressing place on the whole block, but it was still less depressing than her empty apartment right now.

Hoisting her bag of laundry onto one hip, she opened the door and held her breath. She'd always believed a laundromat should smell clean. Dirty clothes go in, fresh ones come out, but this place always smelled like urine and wet dog mixed together with the faint stench of newspaper ink. The rows of linked plastic chairs on both sides of the room were a rainbow of faded reds, yellows, and blues, some of them cracked.

Emma made her way to the only empty machine along the wall of washers. Eyes followed her, flicking up from phones or books. She started a load and sat down. A second later she realized she needed to go to the bathroom and stood up just as the laundromat door dinged. An Asian guy with a scruffy face and messy black hair zipped straight toward the restroom. Right as he rounded the corner, he looked over his shoulder and locked eyes with Emma. It was an intense look, as if he was trying to figure something out. Before Emma could do or say anything in response, he turned away and disappeared into the restroom.

Emma cringed. Just her luck, there was only one restroom. Jiggling her legs to relieve the tension in her bladder, she waited. And waited. Twenty minutes later, she marched over to the restroom door. The guy had looked around her age, at least, so she didn't feel too intimidated confronting him. Or maybe she should avoid that and go next door to the café. She was pretty sure they had a restroom, but she'd heard stories of people stealing unattended clothes, whether they were finished washing or not. She didn't want to risk it.

She knocked lightly on the door.

"Someone's in here!" a voice called out. "Wait your turn."

Emma scowled. Someone had carved crude sayings into the door and she bit her tongue in an effort to keep similar words from coming out of her mouth. "You've been in there for twenty minutes," she said loudly.

The door opened and Emma's eyes widened. Had Scruffy Guy slipped out when she wasn't looking? This couldn't be the same guy. But it was. He'd taken off his jacket and rolled his T-shirt sleeves up to his shoulders. His face was clean-shaven, his hair dripping wet, and he smelled like soap and mint.

"Oh," Emma said softly. Scruffy Guy was no longer scruffy. He was kind of hot. Not that it mattered.

"I'm almost finished," he said calmly, as if what he was doing was completely normal. "Sorry."

The door closed and Emma wondered if maybe it would be worth it to go next door and risk her clothes being stolen. This guy was seriously weird.

Thirty seconds later he came out with a bag slung over his shoulder. His hair was styled away from his face. "It's all yours." He swept an arm at the filthy restroom.

Emma charged past him. "Thanks. Sorry if I rushed you."

He gave her an apologetic smile. "I'm sorry I took so long." He looked like he might want to say something else, but the door closed between them and Emma turned to look at the restroom. It was disgusting. There was a hypodermic needle on the floor next to the toilet. *Gross.* Had Scruffy Guy been shooting up in here? He hadn't seemed high or anything.

She used the toilet without touching the seat and then stood at the sink to wash her hands, stopping when she spotted a sleek, black cell phone near the faucet handle. It had to be Scruffy Guy's. No way would something that nice last long in a place like this without being stolen.

She quickly finished washing her hands, snatched up the phone, and opened the door. When she rounded the corner, she couldn't see Scruffy Guy anywhere. Her heart sank. She felt guilty for rushing him out of the bathroom.

She made her way back to her seat and cradled the phone in her hands before pushing the button to wake it up. It opened to a passcode screen. Maybe he would come back in looking for it.

It buzzed and she looked down at the lock screen showing a text.

DAD: *Give me a call. I want to know how things are going.*

Emma stared helplessly at the message, her fingers itching to respond. This guy's dad wanted to talk to him and there was nothing she could do. Shaking her head, she tucked the phone into her bag and looked up to see someone emptying a washer next to hers. When they were finished, she hurried to fill it up with a load of darks. By then it was just past 1:00. She pulled out her phone to text Alex.

EMMA: *You on your way?*

He called a moment later. "Hi," he said, sounding a little flustered. There was bustling in the background. "I'm sorry. I was just about to call you. I got tied up in Manhattan with a client. I'm on the subway home and then I'll drive over. Should be an hour, possibly longer if traffic is bad, is that okay?"

She stood up to sort through the rest of her laundry. "Sure. There's parking not too far from here."

"Oh, that's good, thanks. So, Emma . . ."

She waited for him to go on as she pulled a white sock from a pile of her dad's khakis. "Yeah?"

"I know it's difficult for you to trust me. I haven't handled any of this as well I should have, and I'm sorry. The truth is, I'm scared to tell you what your father never wanted you to know, but there's no way around it now. He's still missing, so I have to suspect the worst, and that's a frightening scenario."

Emma dropped the sock in her hand. "Okay," was all she could manage to get out. She hadn't even tried thinking about worst-case scenarios yet.

"I don't think you should go back to your apartment," Alex continued. "I don't think it's safe. You should stay at the laundromat until I get there. Once we've talked you can decide what you're comfortable doing, whether you want me to help you or if you want to take another course of action. I'll support you either way. Your father asked me to take care of you if anything ever happened to him, but it's your call once I've told you what you need to know. I'm here if you need me, okay?"

Leaning against the dryer in front of her, Emma tightened her grip on the phone. *Not safe in her apartment?* She didn't want to think about what that could possibly mean.

"Thanks," she said. "I'll wait for you to get here and then we can talk."

"I'll be there as fast as I can. Have you filed a missing persons report yet?"

She winced. "No, not yet." She'd been putting it off, simply because filing the report meant she'd have to fully accept the danger her father might be in. Whether she filed a report or not, it was obvious now that she was going to have to accept it.

"We can do that once we've talked," Alex said. "I'll keep my phone on if you need to call me. Hang in there, okay?"

"Thank you." She said goodbye and tucked her phone in the pocket next to Scruffy Guy's. She couldn't go back home, and that made her anxious, like the ground had rushed away from her and left her suspended in the air with nothing to hold on to except Alex.

⚬⚬⚬

Emma opened her eyes and realized she was sitting crooked on a set of hard chairs, her bag clutched tightly in her lap, her head leaning against the wall. There was a nasty smell in the air. Oh, yes, the laundromat.

She leaned forward with a little gasp and looked around. Her sleepless night had obviously caught up with her. The last thing she remembered was shoving her first two clean loads into the only available dryers and starting two more loads in the washers. She must have sat down and drifted off after that.

Rubbing her eyes, she saw that the laundromat was empty now except for her and two other people: an old man with a cane who was kind of a regular fixture there, and Scruffy Guy. He was arguing with the old man.

Emma's eyes widened. He'd come back! She pulled her bag all the way onto her lap and reached into the pocket to grab his phone.

"Look, dude, all I'm asking is if you've seen it somewhere," Scruffy Guy addressed the old man. "I'm not accusing you of anything."

The old man lifted his cane. He moved as if it was painful, but he seemed to stand just fine without the cane as he waved it at Scruffy Guy a few feet away. "Get out of here," he snapped, like the laundromat was his personal domain. "Kids like you never respect your elders and I'm sick of it. Get out!"

It was then that Scruffy Guy turned to see her. Relief washed over his face and he moved toward her, ignoring the waving cane as it followed him. The old man's glare melted into fear. He lowered his cane and shuffled toward a dryer where it looked like he'd been pulling out some clothes.

Scruffy Guy came right up to her. "Hey, can I borrow your phone? I think this grandpa stole mine. He's been acting fishy since I came in here."

Emma smiled. "I have it. I found it in the bathroom."

He straightened and cast a guilty look at the old man. "Oh . . ."

Emma's fingers wrapped around a phone. It was hers. She pulled it out, sure the other one was in her bag somewhere. That was where she had put it. She frantically searched the rest of her bag and then leaned down to look around the floor. It must have fallen out when she'd fallen asleep.

It was nowhere.

"Crap," she said as Scruffy Guy turned back to her. "It's gone. I fell asleep and it must have fallen out." She gave Scruffy Guy a helpless look and they both turned to the old man, who was hurrying toward the door as fast as he could. "Quick, call your number," Emma said, unlocking her screen before tossing the phone to Scruffy Guy. He dialed a number and a muffled ringtone sounded from the old man's vicinity.

Scruffy Guy rushed up to him before he could get out the door, lowering Emma's phone from his ear so he could end the call. The ringtone stopped and the old man leaned on his cane as he gave Emma a death glare over his shoulder. "*She* stole it!" he yelled, and turned back to Scruffy Guy. "It fell out of her bag. I was going to turn it in to the cops, I swear."

"What?" Emma cried out.

Scruffy Guy rolled his eyes and held out his hand. "Hand it over, dude."

The man pulled the phone from his pocket and shoved it into Scruffy Guy's hands. "Maybe you shouldn't leave it lying around." He hefted his laundry bag and pushed his way out the door.

When he was gone, Scruffy Guy turned to Emma and returned her phone. "Thanks a million. What can I do to thank you?"

Emma furrowed her brow. "You don't need to thank me. Wouldn't most people do what I did?"

His rich brown eyes widened. "Um, no. I think most people who come in here would have stolen it." He raised an eyebrow. "Can I ask your name?"

"Emma. Yours?"

He smiled warmly. "Jack."

"You don't have to do anything to thank me, Jack," she said, glancing out the window where the old man was now crossing the street. "Seriously, it's no big deal."

Then she realized the sun was a lot lower than before. She looked down at her phone, her mind instantly switching gears as she snapped back to reality. It was almost 4:00. She'd been asleep for hours!

She leaned forward in her chair, her heart pounding. Where was Alex? Had he arrived while she was sleeping? No. He had been so concerned about meeting her he would have woken her up. She dialed his number and waited for him to answer, but it went straight to voicemail. She texted him.

EMMA : *Is everything okay? I fell asleep. Did you come by the laundromat yet?*

She waited a minute, but there was no response. What could possibly have happened? He'd told her not to go back to her apartment. It wasn't safe. He was going to meet her. He was going to help her, and now he was going to ignore her?

Jack leaned forward. "Hey, are you all right?"

She slumped in her chair, her head swimming. "I don't know. Someone was supposed to meet me here, but he hasn't shown up." She looked around frantically and then stood up with her bag. "I'll go see if he's outside."

She rushed out of the laundromat, looking up and down the street for a car with someone waiting in the driver's seat. Flashbacks of trying to reach her father slammed into her. She would stay calm. Maybe he had run into bad traffic and his phone had died. Even so, it was two hours after the time he had said he would be here. Something was wrong.

Walking up the sidewalk toward her apartment, she glanced at every car parked along the curb. They were all empty. She looked at every person on the sidewalk. Nobody looked like Alex. She stopped when she reached her apartment building, her body breaking into a sweat as she stared at the glass lobby doors. Nobody was in there that she could see. She reached out to punch in the code to let herself in and then hesitated, her finger hovering over the buttons.

It's not safe in your apartment.

Was Alex crazy? She had to accept the fact that there was a lot she didn't know. She couldn't assume he didn't know what he was talking about. She backed away from the door and turned around. When she got back to the laundromat, Jack was still there. He was standing right by the door, a worried look on his face as he opened it for her.

"Hey," he said, his eyebrows knotted. "You left your laundry here. I thought I'd watch it for you."

She gave him a curious look, surprised at his thoughtfulness. "My dad's friend was supposed to meet me here and he was going to tell me—"

She zipped her lips closed. Way too much information. She didn't even know why she was spouting it out in the first place. He hadn't asked for an explanation.

"Never mind," she said and headed for her clothes. "Thanks for watching my stuff."

Jack followed her. "Maybe I can get you a coffee or a pastry or something while you wait for your friend? It'll be my way to repay you for helping me out."

"Oh." She hadn't eaten anything all day, but she was so anxious she was sure she'd be able to run on adrenaline alone for the next few hours. Still, coffee sounded good. "I guess so, sure. Milk, no sugar."

He smiled and pocketed his phone. "Great. I'll go next door."

She watched him leave and then turned to her laundry. The loads in the dryer were finished, but there were still two more to dry. She was lucky nobody had taken anything while she was sleeping.

She emptied the dryers and loaded them up again before sitting down to try to call Alex one more time. Still no answer. What was she supposed to do? She blinked back tears until Jack returned, a steaming coffee in one hand and a paper sack in another. He handed her the coffee and set the paper bag on top of a dryer.

She stared up at him, the coffee cup warm in her cold, trembling hands. "This was really nice of you, thanks."

He laughed. "It's coffee, not a big deal."

She looked down at the steam wafting from the hole in the lid. "No, it's not that. It's . . . I feel so . . ."

Alone.

But she couldn't say it. She *was* alone. Completely alone, and Jack was the only person around she could connect to. She wasn't close enough with any of her friends at school to tell them about her dad's apparent drug dealing and disappearance. Maybe it was because of how much additional responsibility she'd had to take on, but kids at school always seemed so immature. Emma had always been closer to her father than anyone else. The good thing now was that Jack seemed to want to connect with her. At this point, she'd take anything she could get.

"So," she said, eager to change the subject to anything other than her own discomfort. "You want to tell me why you were cleaning up in the restroom? I'm curious. You don't look homeless or anything."

Shrugging, Jack looked away. "I've been helping my dad out at work early in the mornings and sometimes I'd rather sleep than shower. On busy days, I don't have time to fight traffic all the way home and back before my shift starts at the drugstore down the street. Dad's company is pretty snobby, so I think they'd freak if they saw some teenager shaving in their restrooms, and the one at the drugstore doesn't have a mirror. This one's convenient and nobody asks questions." He gave her a little smirk. "Until now, anyway."

She hid a smile and looked away. "Right, well, uh, maybe just one more question? I promise it has nothing to do with the restroom."

Jack sipped at his coffee. "Sure."

"If you have a job and you've also been helping your dad at work, I'm guessing you're not in school?"

He nodded. "Yeah, I graduated last year." He snatched the bag off the dryer and reached in to pull out a stuffed croissant. "I got two of these. Want one?"

She took another sip of coffee and shook her head. "Not right now, thank you. I'll finish my coffee first."

"No problem." He bit into his own croissant as Emma looked down at her phone, her thoughts spinning around Alex and what she was going to do. She couldn't stay in this laundromat forever, and she didn't feel like she could go back home. She had to go to his house to see if he was there. He had said he was going there to get his car. Maybe one of the neighbors could tell her if they had seen him leave or come home.

"Hey," Jack said, nearly finished with his croissant now. "Did I say something wrong?"

She let out a nervous laugh, realizing how long she'd been zoned out. "No, it's not you."

"Well, is there anything I can do to help, then?"

She shrugged. "Not unless you can help me find my dad's friend."

Jack's worried expression switched to anticipation. "I could try."

She hadn't expected him to actually offer, but maybe he could help. He'd made it sound like he had a car. It was a twenty-minute drive to Bay Ridge in decent traffic, probably agonizingly longer by bus, especially when she didn't have the address and had no idea which route to take. She didn't have enough money to pay for a cab. She'd spent most of her cash on the laundry, and her father hadn't transferred her allowance into her account in over two weeks.

Could she find Alex's house if she had to? She'd been there a few times for Christmas dinner, once right after she'd received her license and her dad had made her drive. She was pretty sure she could find the place again if she had to. It was too bad her father had sold their car since then.

"You mentioned fighting traffic to get back home. Does that mean you have a car?" she asked Jack.

He nodded. "Yeah, it's my dad's. We share it."

"Could you possibly give me a ride over to Bay Ridge? You'd be 'fighting traffic,' though, so I understand if you don't want—"

"Not a problem," he interrupted. "I'd be happy to."

She raised an eyebrow. "Really?"

He laughed. "Of course. It's not a lot to ask. Bay Ridge isn't far. Not as bad a drive as getting back home. We live in Manhattan."

Emma wondered why he worked at a drugstore here in Brooklyn if he lived all the way over in Manhattan, but decided not to ask. Maybe it was because his dad worked here and it was easier to carpool together. It didn't matter. What mattered was her current problem of getting to Alex. She glanced at the dryer.

Jack smiled. "Looks like that'll be done in a half hour. Wanna leave then?"

She stood up from her chair. "Will you be able to get back in time for work?"

"Won't be a problem. I'll go get the car. It's a few blocks down."

She thanked him and sat down to wait for her laundry to dry. Maybe it was reckless to get a ride with a complete stranger, but it would be dark in a few hours and if she took the bus she would probably have to walk alone for several blocks to Alex's house. Jack could take her right there. He didn't feel dangerous to her, but she double checked to make sure her pepper spray was easily accessible.

SEVEN

Emma hauled her laundry outside as soon as Jack pulled up to the curb in a shiny white Lexus sedan. It looked brand new.

"Let me help you," Jack said as he got out and walked over to the passenger side. He opened up the back door and started tossing her laundry bags onto the tan leather seat.

"Thanks," Emma said, throwing in the last one herself and then moving to open the front door.

Jack grabbed the handle before she got to it. "Allow me, madam," he said in a British accent, and opened the door wide for her to get in.

She stifled a laugh. This guy was crazy weird, but at least he was making her smile. Nothing else was going to at this point. She settled into the front seat as Jack shut the door, making sure her backpack was easily accessible on her lap in case she needed to grab her phone or pepper spray in a hurry.

The car was clean and smelled like Jack's soap and new leather.

Jack got back into the driver's seat and smiled warmly as he pulled away from the curb. "So, you got an exact address?" he asked, turning down the radio.

"No, but I can guide you there as we get closer. Just head toward Bay Ridge for now." Emma buckled her seatbelt and rested her hands on top of her bag. She had brought the paper bag with the croissant too. It crinkled under her fingers. "I shouldn't be nervous to get a ride with you, but I am," she said, giving Jack an anxious smile.

"No need to be nervous." He switched off the radio. "I'm a nice guy. Promise."

Emma forced a laugh. "Isn't that what they all say?"

"I guess you'll have to wait and find out."

He was joking, but a part of Emma seized up inside. She tightened her hands on her bag and then relaxed them.

Jack cleared his throat. "I was kidding."

"I know."

His voice turned serious. "I'll let you out any time you want."

"Thanks."

The rest of the trip was mostly silent. Emma ate her croissant and called Alex's number several more times, but it kept going to voicemail. When they got to the right street she pointed to a home with white wood siding. It was the only white house on the block. She remembered the two spindly pine trees in front of the large bay window. "That one," she said.

"All right." Jack pulled into the driveway. The house had a separate garage in the back, so Emma couldn't tell if Alex's car was here or not. She got out of the car and shut the door. Jack followed suit.

They walked to the front door. It didn't look like anyone was home since all the windows were dark. Emma turned to Jack. "I can find a bus to get back home. You don't have to stay." The last thing she wanted to do was make him feel obligated to stay with her and make him late for work. But he didn't seem to mind as he pushed his hands into the pockets of his jeans and shook his head.

"I kind of don't want to leave you here alone. It's getting dark and this guy might not be home."

He definitely seemed sincere. Emma was suddenly glad he wasn't leaving her. He was the first person she felt had really, honestly helped her. A soft smile lit up her face. "Thanks," she said, ringing the doorbell. There was no answer.

Jack sat on the lowest porch step and stretched out his legs. "Doesn't look like he's home. Maybe try knocking?"

Emma opened the screen door and knocked, but there was still no answer. What were the chances of Alex disappearing within a day of her dad? Right when he was going to give her information he couldn't say over the phone? It seemed too big of a coincidence to be anything but suspicious.

Jack looked up at her. "Is there another place you want to check?"

She glanced up and down the block. A few lights were on inside the houses. "He said he was going to drive out to meet me, so maybe we should check the garage and see if his car is still here. If it's gone, we should ask the neighbors if they've seen anything."

"Good idea."

She walked down the steps and Jack followed her around the corner of the house. There was a security lamp above the back porch. Its bluish light shone brightly across the garage door, revealing strips of peeling white paint. The door was closed.

Jack walked around to the side, running his hand along the edge until he stopped at a narrow window close to the roof. It was too high for him to peer in.

"Hmmm," he said, jumping up to get a peek. It was still too high. "Let's try the door." He walked back around to the front of the garage and reached down to pull up on the handle. The door snapped open so fast it made them both jump back. "Pulled a little too hard," Jack laughed. "I expected it to be locked."

Emma didn't laugh. Muggy air rolled out from the garage as she swept her eyes across boxes and lawn equipment and Alex's dark blue Mazda. It looked like somebody was sitting in the driver's seat, perfectly still.

"That doesn't look good," Jack said, stepping into the garage.

Emma looked at him, dumbfounded. He was a lot braver than she was. He walked to the driver's side of the car and motioned for her to follow. Forcing her feet forward, she inched her way to the car.

"Is that him?" Jack asked.

A little cry left Emma's throat as her eyes landed on Alex slouched against the door, his head touching the window. His eyes were wide open, staring into nothingness, his lips colorless. Dark red blood was smeared across the glass near his head.

Choking back a scream, Emma steadied herself against the car and looked away. She had to suck down three huge breaths before she could speak. "Yeah, that's him," she whispered.

"You should call the police. It's obvious somebody murdered this dude."

"Wh-what?"

Jack pointed to a spot on the back of Alex's head that Emma had completely overlooked in the shadows. The skull was caved in, hair matted over a slick spot of blood and some other substance she didn't want to think about. Were those his *brains*?

No. No way. No. She covered her mouth, bile rising up her throat as she took a step back.

Jack shuffled closer to the car and let out a low whistle. "Somebody messed him up bad before they killed him. Look at his arms."

How could he be so calm about this? Emma leaned forward, trying to keep her eyes away from Alex's brains. Jack was correct. Alex's arms were crisscrossed with over a dozen fresh, savagely deep cuts, each one coagulated with blood.

"Why would someone do that to him?" Emma stuttered. Her skin started crawling with what felt like a million tiny roaches. "We should go. I don't think we're safe here. We shouldn't be here."

Jack took her by the shoulders and she focused on a little freckle by his nose to keep herself steady. "Why would somebody kill this guy?" he asked.

Tears stung her eyes. "I don't know, but if he's dead, my dad . . . my dad . . ."

Was her dad dead like Alex?

Panic hit her in the chest. It felt thick and wet, like a wave of sludgy water washing over her, filling up her mouth and lungs. She ripped out of Jack's hold and stumbled backward, bumping into a shelf full of gardening tools. A terra-cotta pot fell to the floor and shattered into shards, just like everything inside of her. She couldn't get any air. She ran out of the garage. She had to get away from everything. Now.

"Emma!" Jack yelled, but she kept running. She reached the side of the house and tripped over her own feet. The ground came up to meet her, but Jack caught her by the waist and lifted her upright.

"It's okay," he said calmly, turning her around to face him. "Let's get in the car and call the police. I should probably leave before they get here, but I'll stay as long as I can."

Oh yeah, he had to get to work. She pulled away from him and shook her head. Getting into the car didn't sound like a good idea. Neither did sticking around here. Nothing sounded good.

Jack kept his concerned eyes on hers. "What do you want to do?"

"I don't know." She put a hand to her clammy forehead, willing herself to think straight, but everything stayed jumbled and frantic. She took another step away from Jack. Why was he so calm about all of this?

He stayed rooted to the spot. "I think the first thing you should do is call the police," he said. "One thing at a time, okay?"

She shook her head. "I don't think I can call them. I don't think I can tell them about Alex and . . ." She touched her head and then her arms and felt like she might fall over. She had to get away from here.

Jack looked at the ground, his voice shaky as he said, "I'll call."

Emma scrunched her forehead, confused why he seemed nervous to call the police when seeing Alex's dead body hadn't bothered him in the slightest. He pulled out his phone.

"Yeah," he said after a moment, "my friend and I found a guy dead in his car. It looks like he was murdered." He paused while the operator spoke. "In Bay Ridge." He walked around the corner to look at the front of the house, rattling off the address before answering a few more questions. He ended the call and pocketed his phone, returning to Emma. "She said they'll be here soon and we should stay put if we don't feel like we're in danger. I'll stay with you."

Emma stared at him, open-mouthed. "Don't you need to get to work?"

He shoved his hands in his pockets and looked up at the sky and then back at the garage. "It'll be okay. I can't leave you here like this."

"Thanks, but can I ask why you seemed so nervous to talk to the police? Alex's dead body didn't even phase you."

He sighed. "It's my dad. He does some illegal stuff and I don't want to get anywhere near the police." He glanced back at the garage. "That guy was definitely murdered. If we're sucked into the investigation, who knows what the police might dig up. Anyway, yeah, I don't want to be a part of any investigations, that's all. I'm putting off school to help my dad get out of the hole he's dug, not to get him arrested and thrown in jail."

Emma felt herself collapsing inside. She wanted to ask Jack what his father was doing that was illegal, but swallowed the question. What he was doing for his dad made her think of her own loyalties to her father and how much she loved him no matter what he did. Then again, deep down she didn't believe he could have done anything wrong. She did not doubt he was a good man. She wondered if that was how Jack felt about his father, completely torn and confused.

"It's okay if you need to leave," she said. "Seriously, I don't want to get you or your dad in trouble."

"It's fine. I'd feel worse if something happened to you because I left you here alone."

"But you don't even know me."

A crooked smile lit up his face. "I told you I'm a nice guy. You still don't believe me?"

She didn't know if she should smile or keep her guard up. "I don't know what to believe anymore. My dad is missing. Alex was the only person I knew who was willing to help me find him, or at least give me information on whatever my dad was up to. Now I might never know and nothing I've found makes sense. If someone killed Alex, they might be after my dad too." She held back the tears trying to break through. "If they are, he could already be dead."

Jack looked at her blankly. She didn't dare mention the drugs now.

"I'm sorry," she said. "I didn't mean to dump all of that on you."

"You're right." He moved closer. "I don't know you, but you're not alone, okay? The police are coming. They'll help you. I'll make sure they help you."

She nodded as she looked into his eyes. If he had wanted to hurt her, he would have done it long before now. She had to trust that he wanted to help her. But she had trusted Alex too, and look where that had gotten him.

The police arrived a few minutes later. They separated Emma and Jack to ask them questions. Seeing the ambulance and paramedics and officers made everything even more real to Emma than it had been before. Terrifyingly real. She turned hysterical, tears running down her face as several different officers tried to calm her down. She didn't want to be such a problem, but it was as if something had broken inside and she couldn't fix it.

A woman who introduced herself as Officer Chen finally managed to calm her down with a combination of kindness and unlimited patience. She handed her off to Detective Daniel Harris, who assured her he would be the last person she would have to talk to tonight because this was now his case and he'd be helping her with her father's disappearance, as well.

She answered his questions as best she could, trying not to leave out any details. She even told him about the drugs in the owls. Tears filled her eyes, and then she couldn't continue.

"I'm sorry," she sobbed as her tears broke free again. "I feel weird. I can't do this. I can't. Am I putting my dad in more danger now? I don't want him to get in trouble. I don't want—"

"Let's sit down." Harris led her to a bench in Alex's backyard. A tree above them cast skeleton shadows across the tiny lawn in the light of a security lamp attached to the house. The bench was at the opposite end of the yard from the garage, but Emma still felt it was too close to where Alex had died. They hadn't even taken the body away yet. People kept milling in and out of the garage, all of them with latex gloves, some with cameras, and some with notebooks and plastic bags.

When they were sitting down, Harris leaned so close to Emma's face that she was forced to look at him. "Listen to me, Emma. You are going to be okay. You're not in trouble, and neither is your dad. Do you need to speak to Officer Chen again?"

Emma shook her head, swiping furiously at her tears. She glanced at Jack. He looked calm and collected as he talked to an officer, the complete opposite of how she felt. Why couldn't she pull it together like that?

"I'm fine," she muttered, turning back to Harris. His eyes were an unruffled sort of blue, like the sky right before sunrise. Emma concentrated on them as hard as she could in an effort to keep herself from bawling like a baby again.

"We're going to try to find your father," Harris said gently, "but we need all the information you can give us, especially if you think his disappearance is connected to Alex's death. I'm not sure it is, but it's somewhere to start."

"I've already told you everything."

Harris had an uncanny ability of keeping his eyes open without blinking. He held Emma's gaze like a trainer soothing a frightened animal. "I'm sure you've told me everything you possibly can right now, but you're in shock and you're probably forgetting details." He pulled a cardholder from his back pocket. "Here's my number. You call me any time of the day or night, even if it feels silly. If you remember something, you call me. If you get scared, call me. Officer Chen told me you said there's nobody you can stay with?"

She shook her head, her heart sinking at how pathetic it was that she really had nobody she could go to in a time like this. It hit her all of a sudden how maybe that was more strange than pathetic. Harris certainly seemed to think so judging by the look on his face. "Alex was the only one," she said, knowing Harris wouldn't ask her about Jack. They had already established she and Jack had only just met.

"You don't have any friends from school who could have you over for a few days?"

She shook her head. "I'm not that close to anyone."

Harris reached out and took hold of her right hand, uncurling her fingers so he could place the card in her palm. "I know Alex told you it wasn't safe at your apartment, but we'll check it out tonight and put some patrol cars around the block to keep an eye out for you, okay? We'll take those drugs you told me about and see if those give us any more clues. Tomorrow afternoon, after you've had some sleep, I'll come pick you up and take you to the station to answer a few more questions. Until then, we'll make sure you're safe, okay?"

Of course they would make sure she was safe. She was a link in Alex's homicide, so she doubted they'd let her out of their sight. Harris seemed to truly care about her well-being, though, which put her a little more at ease. "Okay."

"Do you have a cell phone you can put my number into?" he asked. "I'd feel better if it were somewhere you can't lose it."

"Right here." She pulled out her phone.

"Okay, good. Send me a text so I have your number too."

Once she'd input the numbers, Harris stood and held out his hand for her. "Let's get you home and make sure the place is safe."

She nodded and followed him out of the backyard, glancing at Jack, who was still being questioned by an officer. He gave her a hopeful, attentive look as she passed him. Although she still didn't know how to feel about him, she hoped this wasn't the last time she ever saw him. She gave him a grateful smile. It collapsed a moment later when she and Harris passed by the garage where two men wearing latex gloves zipped up a body bag laid on a stretcher.

"Looks like meth to me," Detective Harris said as he leaned over to inspect the package Emma had placed on the table next to the shards of the broken owl. She hadn't touched any of the owls or the box since yesterday.

"Yes, it's meth," an officer named Detective Suárez confirmed. He snapped on a set of latex gloves and lifted the package from the table. "We've been seeing drug packages disguised as antiques for years, but they're tricky to track down."

Emma's heart sank as she faced Detective Suárez. "My dad's been selling antiques for a long time. Do you think all of them were drugs?"

Detective Suárez gave her a sad smile as he dropped the meth into an evidence bag and handed it to another officer, who took it away. "I can't answer that for you right now. I'm in the narcotics division, so I'll be asking you some questions later when Harris gives me the go-ahead. We'll talk more about it then, okay?"

Emma nodded and turned to Detective Harris. "I promise my dad's never done drugs before. This is the first time I've ever . . ."

Harris held up a hand. "Let's discuss all of that tomorrow when I take you down to the station. I'd like you to rest before we do another interview. You're still in shock."

Emma nodded as he led her into the living room and motioned for her to sit down. He was right about her needing rest. She felt strained, like she'd been wrung dry and laid out in the sun. She was parched and hungry and exhausted, not to mention weirded out at seeing police officers milling around her home.

Detective Harris sat down next to her on the sofa. "We're almost done here," he explained as she watched an officer pull her father's favorite chair away from the wall. "I'm stationing a patrol car on the street. They'll keep an eye on the building for as long as we need, okay?"

Emma nodded. "That sounds good. When will you come get me tomorrow?"

"As soon as you're feeling up to it. I'll call you by noon if I don't hear from you earlier."

"Okay." Emma looked into Harris' eyes and forced herself to smile. "Thank you for helping me."

He patted her hand. "That's what I'm here for."

EIGHT

Groggy from another night of tossing and turning, Emma stood in her kitchen and stared at the dirty dishes in the sink. It was her dad's job to wash them, so she hadn't touched the sink in years. The thought made her feel hollow. She and her dad had become so dependent on each other it now felt like her left arm was missing.

Knowing she should eat something, she turned to the fridge and pulled out a loaf of bread. She put a slice in the toaster just as her phone buzzed with a new text message.

UNKNOWN NUMBER: *Hey Emma, I'm sad I didn't get to say goodbye to you last night. I hope they got*

you home okay. If you need anything, let me know. —
Jack

Emma read the message over and over, her heart beating faster each time. She wanted to answer him, but didn't know what to say. Could she trust him and turn whatever they had into some sort of friendship? Did she *want* to? She looked up and realized her toast had popped up, mostly burned.

Rushing forward, she pulled it out and tossed it into the garbage can. Stupid toaster. It was useless if she didn't stand right over it and pop things up manually. She looked at her phone and typed a reply to Jack.

EMMA: *Thanks for your concern, and thanks for helping me last night. It meant a lot to have someone there with me.*

She didn't know what else to type. Jack seemed so nice, but at the same time there was so much she didn't know about him. After everything that had happened, she wasn't sure she should trust anyone outside of the police. Even if she did trust him, she didn't want to drag him into more danger. Her phone beeped again.

UNKNOWN NUMBER: *Anytime. So, you might think I'm crazy, but do you want to hang out today?*

I'm kind of keeping your laundry hostage until you agree.

A laugh burst out of Emma's throat. She didn't know why. Maybe it was how casual Jack sounded after they'd found a dead body together, or maybe it was because he was the only ray of light left in her mess of a life. Either way, his question made her feel blissfully happy for a whole minute. She'd forgotten all about leaving her laundry in his car. She typed five different replies before finally sending the last one.

EMMA: *Yes, I want my laundry back! The police are going to come and get me for more questions later, but maybe we should meet in the café next to the laundromat for a bit?*

There. It was done. A second later her phone rang, making her jump in surprise. It was Jack's number.

"Hello?" she answered.

"Texting is stupid," he laughed.

Emma was surprised how good it felt to hear his voice. "Yeah, it kind of is." She went back to the fridge for another piece of bread. "So, uh, why do you want to hang out? I thought for sure all my drama would have scared you off."

"What drama? I have no idea what you're talking about."

Emma grinned. "When do you want to meet?"

"Right now, if you can. I'm starving."

Looking down at the piece of bread in her hand, Emma cringed. "I am too. Those croissants were pretty good."

"Yeah, I'm going to order three of them. And a large coffee. I have to go into the station to answer more questions too."

Emma put her bread back in the bag. "I'll head down in a bit."

"Awesome, see ya."

"See ya." Emma lowered her phone and looked at the dirty dishes in the sink again. She didn't feel any better about her father still missing, but at least she didn't feel like she was going to fall apart now.

"Did you get the ham and cheese?" Jack asked as soon as Emma came over to the table with her coffee and a croissant breakfast sandwich.

"Yep, it's all they had left." She settled into her chair across the table. "But it's what I wanted, anyway."

"Oh, good." Jack bit into his croissant and sent some flaky crumbs scattering across the table. He was wearing a leather jacket and his shirt was rumpled.

Even disheveled, he was attractive. Emma wanted to trust him so badly, but how far could that go?

"Hey, Emma?"

Emma blinked and realized she had zoned out. She was doing that a lot lately. "Sorry." She took a sip from her coffee cup. "I'm worried about my dad, that's all."

"It's going to be okay. The police are trying to find him. They know what they're doing."

She nodded. "Is Detective Harris the one questioning you too?"

"Yeah, maybe we should go in together."

"Sure." Emma's shoulders slumped as she thought about all of the questions they would ask. "I keep worrying I'll forget to tell them something important. Like, on Friday I found this old journal of my mom's. I had a sister I never knew about, so why didn't my dad tell me about that? I mean, that can't have anything to do with why he's missing, can it?"

She was mostly talking to herself, but Jack gave her a worried look. "Is your mom gone?" he asked softly.

She nodded. "Yeah, she died when I was only a few weeks old. Someone hit her with their car when she was crossing the road. There was ice."

A half smile flitted across Jack's face. "Guess we were both raised by our dads. My mom died in her sleep when I was six. Brain aneurysm. I was the one who found her."

Emma's mouth dropped open. "What a terrible memory to have. I'm sorry."

"Thanks. Mostly, I'm sad she had to die that way, and so young. It seemed random, but apparently it happens a lot."

"Doesn't make it any easier for you," Emma sighed. "Or anyone, I'm sure."

"Yeah, my dad took it super hard."

Emma took a small bite of her croissant even though her stomach felt unsettled. Jack had told her last night that his dad was involved in something illegal. She was crazy curious about what that might be, especially when she thought about her father's antique owls filled with drugs.

"I can tell you're close to your dad," she said as Jack finished his croissant. "I hope you didn't have to tell the police anything last night that might get him in trouble. And I hope you weren't fired from your job or anything."

He looked away. "Nah, my job is . . . fine. As far as my dad goes, I had to tell a few white lies to the cops, but nothing that will affect their investigation."

"Will today be any worse?"

He shrugged. "I hope not. There's not much more I'll be able to tell them."

"Can I ask you what illegal stuff your dad does? I promise I won't tell the police."

Jack's eyes widened and Emma cringed. She'd gone too far. How could she ask him something so personal when they hardly knew each other?

"I'm only wondering," she said quickly before Jack could respond, "because I found out my dad might be involved with drugs. So, yeah, you're dad's not the only one doing illegal things."

Jack's eyebrows knotted in confusion. He seemed to be thinking hard about something before he finally nodded. "Right," he said as he sat back in his chair. He folded his arms and looked out the window. "Well, that's what my dad's involved with too. I've never seen him use any drugs, but I know he sells them."

Emma's breath caught in her throat. What were the odds of her father and Jack's father both dealing drugs? "That seems like a weird coincidence," she said.

Jack turned away from the window. "Your dad deals too?"

"I don't know. He's been buying and selling small antiques for as long as I can remember. I accidentally broke one the other day and a bunch of meth fell out."

She pulled out her phone and opened it to the picture she'd taken of the owls and the meth. She handed it over to Jack. He stared down at it in surprise and then swiped to the next one in her phone. It was a snapshot of the shipping label on the box. "All the way from Los Angeles, huh?"

She leaned forward and grabbed her phone. "Yeah." She looked closely at the picture Jack had pulled up. "They always come from LA. He has good suppliers out there."

He snorted. "Yeah, a lot of drugs come through California straight out of South America. Do these packages always come from the same address?"

She shrugged and shook her head, trying to remember if the addresses were always the same. "My dad had to get good money for drugs like that, right?"

Jack's eyes widened. "Are you kidding? Just one of those owls is worth thousands of dollars on the street. Well, not the owl—the drugs—but you know what I mean."

"Right." She put a hand to her forehead and thought about the six thousand dollars Paula had paid her dad for the Chinese eggs. The owls were larger and able to hold a lot more drugs, so they were probably worth ten times as much.

Jack looked confused. "If your dad was selling drugs like this every single week, he had to be raking it in. And I mean *hardcore* raking it in. I don't think my dad's ever sold that much shit. Does your dad have a regular job too?"

Emma nodded. "He's a CPA here in Brooklyn. I don't know why we didn't have more money if he was doing this. We're not destitute or anything, but we're definitely not rich. He's always been so careful about spending money."

Maybe he had been sending the money somewhere. Or saving it for something, like to pay for her college tuition. Her heart sank as guilt swept through her. Had he been doing all of this for her? That seemed so extreme it was crazy. Why risk so much if she could get scholarships and grants like he had said?

"Hey," Jack said, "if it helps you feel any better, it's hard for me to accept anything about my dad too. He's ruining my life, but I'm still not leaving him."

Emma picked at her croissant. She had only eaten half of it even though she knew she should eat the entire thing. She was going to make herself sick if she didn't eat a normal meal soon. "You said you were putting off school to help him, right?"

"Yeah, I'm supposed to be a freshman at Cal State right now."

Emma forced herself to take another bite of the croissant and swallowed it with a sip of coffee. "What do you want to study?" she asked, feeling a little easier now that the conversation was moving into more normal territory. It was nice to look at Jack and think of him as a regular guy with aspirations instead of someone who had discovered a dead body with her last night.

He leaned forward, excitement in his eyes. "Forensic science. I know this sounds weird, but my mom's death is what started it all. Ever since then, I've been interested in ways people die, and that led to forensics. I got to do some stuff with it my senior year, like watching an autopsy and visiting the lab. It was awesome."

Emma let out a sigh of relief. "So *that's* why seeing Alex's dead body didn't bother you."

He turned slightly pink. "You must have thought I was a freaking psycho."

"Actually, I had this crazy idea you were somehow part of the murder or my dad's disappearance or something. I mean, what kind of a person sees a dead body like that and doesn't freak out?"

He groaned. "I'm sorry for making you worry. Blood and guts don't bother me at all." He looked down at the table. "Maybe I am a psycho."

"That might be going a little far."

"Are you sure? I'm keeping my dad's drug dealing from the police, and you thought I might have something to do with a murder. You should be running away from me as fast as you can."

She flashed him a teasing smile. "Maybe I just want my laundry back."

He nudged her laundry bags closer to the wall with his foot. "Does that mean I'll need to keep these hostage if I want to see you again?"

She took another bite of croissant and chewed slowly, making a show of thinking hard about his question. The conversation was once again entering uncomfortable territory, this time because she had never been very good at flirting. She sucked at it, in fact, but for the first time since meeting Jack, she didn't feel nervous.

"Hmm, keeping laundry hostage too," she said, raising a hand as if to tick off the offending marks he'd put against himself. "Maybe I *should* run away."

He leaned forward, his grin falling as her phone rang on the table. She grabbed it and looked at the number. It was Detective Harris.

"Hello," she answered.

"Hi, Emma, it's Detective Harris. Are you all right? The officer outside your building said you left your apartment half an hour ago."

She ran a finger around the rim of her coffee cup. "I'm having some coffee half a block down with Jack. Sorry if I worried you."

"No, no, it's fine. I was just checking. Do you and Jack want to come to the station and answer some more questions? It's only a few blocks from where you are."

"Let me ask him." She lowered the phone and asked Jack if he wanted to go in. He nodded, and Emma put her phone back to her ear and told Harris they'd be there soon.

"Great, see you in a bit."

"Well," Jack said as Emma ended the call, "there goes the rest of our quiet afternoon." He jerked his head toward the café menu above the registers. "Do you want to grab something to take with you?"

Smiling, Emma shouldered her bag and stood up from her chair. "That sounds good, but I'm making you carry my laundry up to my apartment before we head to the station."

Jack raised an eyebrow. "You trust me enough to let me into your apartment?"

She looked him up and down, smiling at the awkward way he was trying to hold her three bags of laundry with one arm. "I didn't say I'd let you *inside* the apartment . . ."

Jack laughed. "Okay, okay, I get it. One step at a time, right?"

"Right."

NINE

Starry stared down at her phone, her fingers itching to text Rhys a reminder to look into her computer supplies. Not that he seemed worried about it. She had charged into the bathroom after calling the company and accused him of deceiving her, but he'd only shrugged and said something must have gone wrong and he'd call customer service. It was Sunday now, and he still hadn't called. Starry wasn't desperate enough to go digging into his personal files to figure it out herself, but all the same, she couldn't get his words out of her head: *Please don't dig too deep on this.*

Why wouldn't he want her to find Emma? It had to be more than him wanting to protect her. That seemed too simple. And why the hell couldn't she work up the courage to demand an explanation? Maybe it was because she was too afraid of the answer. But that was ridiculous. She wasn't afraid of anything he might say.

She started typing a message to him on her phone, then stopped. It would be best if she went down there in person. She looked at her clothes and groaned. There was no way she could go into the club dressed in Rhys' boxer shorts and a T-shirt. Her other clothes were in the washer, but they weren't dressy enough anyway.

She thought for a second and then dialed Ginger's number. Ginger was the strip club's house mom, who handled everything from making sure the dancers paid their club fees to handing out granola bars and listening to all their latest relationship dramas. She had helped Starry install the cameras in the dressing room and the two had hit it off right away. She was the closest thing to a friend Starry had.

"I've got thirty seconds, sweetheart," Ginger said as soon as she picked up. "Go."

Starry quickly explained that she needed some clothes to get into the club and Ginger assured her she'd bring them up in ten minutes. Ending the call, Starry turned to the refrigerator and pulled it open. She had eaten dinner with Rhys before he'd gone down to work, but that had been hours ago and she was starving. The nightclub schedule was seriously screwing her up.

She rolled her eyes as she looked into the fridge. How did Rhys stay so fit and healthy when all he kept in his fridge was eggs, half a loaf of bread, and fake cheese? It was the kind her dad used to give her when she was a kid—individually wrapped orange squares. Rubbery. Hardly edible. She opened one and bit off a corner, melting as memories rushed back.

"I miss you, Dad," she sighed. "Why do you have to be such a bastard?"

As she fried up two eggs and set them on a piece of bread, she thought of all the times her father had taken her to the shooting range when she was a kid, all the times he'd personally sat in on her karate lessons, taekwondo, and boxing, and then eagerly cheered her on at the tournaments. It was a regular thing for him to sit down with her to show her where the syndicate currently ranked in the drug world. He'd taught her about drug politics, his relationships with senators and governors, drug trade routes, finances. He'd given her a good childhood, even with no mother around.

Despite her lingering anger over Emma, she missed being around him. She missed golfing with him on Saturday mornings, the way he'd mess up a shot so she could get ahead of him. He would never do that for anyone else. She missed eating lunch with him every day, ranting about their work problems together.

Now her lunches were nonexistent. They were snacks she ate at midnight. Alone.

She stared down at the fried eggs on the bread and gently set a piece of rubbery cheese over them. Disgusting. She picked it up to take a bite and was saved by a knock on the door. She put the sandwich down and rushed to the door. Maybe there would be food down in the club.

Ginger smiled as the door opened. She was a thirty-year-old natural platinum blonde who wore nothing but pantsuits. Somehow, she managed to make them look sexy.

"Here you go," Ginger said as she handed over a neatly folded outfit, some underwear, and a pair of six-inch black stilettos. She looked Starry up and down and raised an eyebrow. "It's certainly better than what you're wearing."

"Right?" Starry sighed. "Thanks, Ginger." She turned to go change, but Ginger grabbed her arm.

"Wait one sec. What's all of this about? Did you two decide to get more serious?" There was excitement in her voice.

Starry had been keeping her in the loop about Rhys since there was nobody else she could talk to about him. Ginger was the perfect confidant thanks to her job. She took relationship secrets more seriously than anyone Starry knew.

Starry leaned against the wall. "Yeah, we're together now, but it hasn't been very long, and I think he might be keeping something from me."

Ginger folded her arms and leveled her gaze at Starry. "What could he be keeping from you?"

"It's a long story."

Ginger put a perfectly manicured hand on Starry's shoulder. It was something Starry had seen her do with the dancers downstairs. "I've got a few minutes," she said.

Starry shifted away from her hand and started pacing the entryway. "I think he's lying to me about something."

"Oh? Can you tell me what it is?"

Starry gave her a wary look. All Ginger knew about her father was that he was a wealthy businessman who owned countless clubs and other businesses. She had no idea what he really did. "It's complicated," she sighed. "In a nutshell, there's something I need to find and he's trying to keep me from finding it by lying to me."

"Why?"

Starry gritted her teeth. "He thinks I'm in danger, but there's got to be more to it than that." She motioned for Ginger to follow her down the hall to Rhys' bedroom. "I'm gonna change and go ask him what the hell is going on. I can't be with anyone who's lying to me."

"I don't blame you," Ginger said as she leaned against the open doorway. "But I've known Rhys for a long time and he wouldn't lie without a damn good reason."

"Well, then I'll find out what that reason is. No matter what it takes." She stood by Rhys' bed and stripped down naked before pulling on the underwear Ginger had given her. "Can I keep these? I'm really tired of washing my only clothes over and over."

Ginger laughed. "Sure, but why don't you bring more clothes from home?"

Starry slipped on the black leather skirt and sequined halter top. "I'm safer staying here for right now, but that's another long story. I'll tell it to you when some of it's resolved."

"You don't have to tell me anything, honey," Ginger said as Starry went over to her purse on Rhys' dresser and pulled out some makeup. "I'm pretty good at reading between the lines."

Starry snorted. "And what are you reading right now?"

Ginger shrugged. "You say it has to be more than Rhys wanting to protect you. What if that's all it really is? Maybe he cares about you that much."

Starry froze with her lipstick halfway to her bottom lip. "Maybe," she muttered.

"Then you shouldn't go barreling down there in a fiery blaze."

Ginger had a point. Starry looked down at her bright red lipstick and cringed. Did Rhys care about her so much that he'd try to protect her from any danger at all, no matter how unlikely? He had to know her father would never really hurt her *that* much. But nobody should have to lie to the people they cared about. The truth was always better.

Besides, Starry didn't need protecting. She was the one protecting Rhys by not telling her father about him. Hiding here at his place was nothing more than her trying to gain the upper hand over her father.

She lowered the tube of lipstick as her stomach twisted. She was gaining the upper hand over her father at Rhys' expense. If she wasn't careful, he could die and it would be her fault. She cared more about Rhys than she wanted to admit, and it made her weak. Her father had always warned her about this kind of weakness, but she couldn't help it. At the same time, she couldn't ignore catching Rhys in a lie. She deserved the truth.

"I won't barrel down there in a fiery blaze," she concluded out loud as she finished applying her lipstick. "I'll ask him what's going on. Calmly. Nicely." She applied some mascara and then slipped on the black stilettos.

Ginger smirked from the doorway. "Well, at least you're calmer than when I got here. I thought you might storm down there and rip the poor man's head off."

Starry walked past Ginger in a breeze of black sequins and leather. "Oh, I could still rip his head off," she growled.

But she hoped she wouldn't have to.

TEN

Emma's phone beeped. Gasping, she grabbed it and sat up in bed, but her vision was so blurry she couldn't see the message. She blinked until the words came into focus.

JACK: *Hey, are you up?*

Her brain finally clicked out of sleep mode. She looked at her clock. Almost 1:00. The last thing she remembered was brushing her teeth in the bathroom, desperate for a good night's sleep after her emotionally draining afternoon at the police station.

She read Jack's message again. She hadn't seen him since they'd gotten to the police station. They'd been led to separate interview rooms, and Jack was nowhere to be seen when she came out.

EMMA : *How was the station?*

Her phone rang a second later and she answered it immediately. "Jack?"

"Hi, I'm so sorry I didn't text you when I was finished at the station. They kept me there forever."

Rubbing her eyes with her free hand, she stifled a yawn. "That's okay. How long were you there?"

"Until three."

Emma's eyes widened. "Seriously?" she gasped. "I thought I was there a long time, but I left at one."

"Yeah, they found out about my dad, that's why."

"I'm so sorry. What happened?"

"They kept saying there was a connection between my dad and your dad, but they wouldn't tell me anything outside of the fact that they've apparently known each other for years. Harris convinced me to wait there until they brought in my dad."

Confusion slammed into Emma like a freight train. Her dad knew Jack's dad? For *years*? "What else do you know about this?" she asked. "The police must have told you more."

"Nope, nobody will tell me anything. The police took my dad in a room and questioned him for two hours. When they let him go he was so pissed off he wouldn't even look at me, so I went home and dug around in some of his paperwork to see if I could figure anything out, but that didn't get me anywhere. He still won't answer any of my questions. He keeps saying he won't talk to me until he can talk to you."

Emma looked over at her window where moonlight spilled thinly through the glass. "What do you want me to do? Should I talk to him over the phone?"

"He says it needs to be in person. He wants to meet with you right now, if you can. I'm sorry. I know it's late. I woke you up, didn't I?"

Emma appreciated how concerned he was, but if meeting with his dad got her any closer to finding her father, she didn't care what time of night she had to do it. "How will this work?" she asked. "Where does he want to meet? No offense, but I don't want him here in my apartment."

"No, I understand. He doesn't want to be seen around your place, anyway. There's an all-night Italian takeout restaurant one block north of your apartment. We go there for dinner all the time when he has to work late. Would that be okay? There's always a lot of people around."

A lump formed in Emma's throat as nostalgia washed over her. "Bella's Fast Italian?" she choked out.

"Yeah, you know it?"

She blinked back a few stinging tears. "My dad and I eat there all the time."

"Oh."

"No, it's fine." She got out of bed and walked over to her window. A police car was parked on the street.

"Okay, as long as you're sure. I'm right around the corner. Can you meet me down here in a few minutes?"

She frowned at the police car, wondering if she'd be able to sneak past without the officer noticing her. No doubt he'd tell Harris she was leaving her apartment in the middle of the night. "Sure, but the officer down there might—"

"He's asleep. If you hurry, he won't see you."

"So much for security," Emma mumbled. She didn't like the idea of sneaking past the policeman to go and meet with a drug dealer friend of her dad's. But she didn't see how she could refuse. How else was she supposed to find out what was going on? She needed to know.

Pulling on a pair of jeans and a sweatshirt, she grabbed her phone and pepper spray and headed downstairs. Once she was in the lobby, she peeked out the door and saw that Jack was right about the policeman. He was resting his head against the seat, his eyes closed.

Emma pushed open the doors and hurried down the street. When she rounded the corner, Jack stepped away from a brick wall. "You ready?" he asked.

She nodded and took a deep breath as she glanced over her shoulder. She'd grown up in the city, but there was something about being on the streets in the middle of the night that put her on edge.

"Let's go, then." Jack stepped close enough to take her hand. It happened so fast Emma was surprised when she looked down to see her own fingers curling around his.

She looked up at him.

"Is this okay?" he asked, his lips curving into a nervous smile.

She nodded. It felt natural to hold his hand, like she'd been stupid not to have held it earlier.

They reached Bella's Fast Italian Takeout a few minutes later. The traffic was heavier here and a lot more people were milling around. Jack let go of her hand as they approached the line of grungy-looking customers snaking out the restaurant door. The inside was nothing more than a small room with an ordering counter.

"My dad wants me to order some food," Jack said as Emma shoved her hands into her pockets.

Emma nodded and started searching for a man who looked even remotely like Jack. She didn't see any. "Where is he?" she asked.

"He's on his way." She turned back to Jack and realized he was still dressed in the same clothes as that morning. He looked as rumpled as the rest of the people hanging around.

"There's something I have to tell you," Jack said as they moved forward in the line.

Emma rocked on her feet as she shivered. It was colder out here than she'd thought it would be. "Okay."

Jack stared at the ground. "Haven't you wondered what I was really doing in the laundromat yesterday?"

"I guess I haven't thought much about it since then. We had a whole conversation about it. You said—"

"I lied," Jack interrupted, his eyes intense as he searched Emma's face. "I don't have a job at the drugstore. I needed to clean up, but I could have done that anywhere. I chose the laundromat restroom because you were there. I'm sorry I lied to you." He looked down at the ground, guilt spreading across his face. "I was tailing you."

Emma took a step backward, nearly bumping into the person behind her. "T-tailing me?" she whispered, hardly able to get the words out. "*Why?*"

There was nobody she could trust. Not one person. Maybe the police, but right here, right now, she was not safe.

Jack shoved his hands into his pockets. "My dad asked me to watch you and make sure you were okay. I was supposed to tell him if anything seemed wrong. He wouldn't tell me why."

Emma took another step back. The person behind her backed up too and gave her a dirty look. She looked over her shoulder, searching once again for Jack's mysterious father. She didn't want to meet him now. She needed to get home. Fast.

"I gotta go," she mumbled, and turned to leave the line.

Jack grabbed her arm and let her go a second later. She wanted to run, but stopped herself when she caught the desperate pleading in Jack's eyes. "Hear me out," he said softly. "Please, just give me a few minutes to explain."

Emma inched away from him. "You *lied* to me. After everything I've been through. You lied. How long have you been tailing me? What have you seen?" Her mind raced through all the scenarios of someone watching her. Had he been looking into her apartment windows from a telescope across the street? Why would his dad ask him to do something so creepy?

The more questions she came up with, the more hysterical she felt, until she finally realized she was all the way out of the ordering line and people were looking at her like she was nuts.

Jack left the line and walked calmly to her. "Dad asked me on Friday. I've only tailed you to the laundromat and kept an eye on your building's front doors to see when you came and went. That's it. All my dad said was to make sure you were safe."

She shook her head. "It still doesn't make sense," she said loud and shrill enough to get more weird looks from most everybody in the line. "Why would your dad care about my safety? Did my dad ask him to do this?"

Jack locked eyes with her. "I honestly don't know. It's not the first time my dad's asked me to tail someone for him. Usually it's just to find out if some guy he's working with is where he's supposed to be. I know it sounds crazy I'd do things like that for him, but he's my dad, and none of it's been dangerous so far." He looked down at his feet. "You're the first girl he's ever asked me to tail. He seems genuinely concerned for you."

Emma folded her arms, hysteria giving way to anger. She could run away and tell the cops Jack and his father were drug-dealing stalkers, or she could stay and maybe get some answers about who her father really was and why he'd been living a lie for who knew how long. She looked around the brightly-lit sidewalk full of restaurant patrons and decided to stay. "I'll ask him about it, then," she said boldly, giving Jack a dirty look. "If he ever decides to get here."

Jack looked at the distance between them. "I've screwed everything up, haven't I? I'm so sorry, Emma. If you decide not to ever see me again after this, I'll understand."

"Yeah, well, consider this our last meeting," she snapped. "You're lucky I'm not going straight to that cop outside my apartment building. And I'm telling

Detective Harris about this too, next time I talk to him."

Jack nodded sadly. "I understand." He pointed limply to the end of the line. "I'm, uh, gonna go stand back in line."

"I'll be over there." She went and sat down at the only free table, fingering the pepper spray in her pocket.

———

Jack came to the table with three Styrofoam boxes. "I got you something in case you're hungry," he said cautiously as he set one of the boxes in front of Emma. "It's the four-cheese garlic spaghetti. Have you had that one?"

Emma glared at him, irritated by his thoughtfulness. Maybe she should be making an effort to understand his side of the story, but right now it was all she could do to keep herself from leaving. It was going to take her awhile to cool off. "It's one o'clock in the morning," she snapped.

"And I'll bet you haven't eaten anything since our croissants this morning."

He had her there. She snatched the Styrofoam box, catching a whiff of its contents. Her stomach growled.

"Is your dad ever coming?" she asked, looking around the sidewalk. "And is it always this busy at night?"

Jack glanced at the line as he sat down across from Emma. "They do half-off from midnight to four. Gets them more business, I guess." He took a box and opened it up. The rich aroma of garlic and parmesan wafted into the air. "My dad should be here in a minute." He handed a fork to Emma.

She opened her box to see a mess of buttery noodles, gooey cheese, and caramelized garlic cloves. She took a bite. It was better than anything else she'd eaten here, and that was saying something. She glanced at Jack. "Thanks for this," she muttered as Jack shoveled noodles into his mouth. "I'll pay you back."

He stared down at the table. "Don't worry about it. I don't think there's anything I could do at this point to make up for what I've done to you."

Her chewing slowed. He looked absolutely crushed. Not that it should matter. She wanted him to feel bad for what he'd done. Anybody in their right mind should.

"I wish we'd met under different circumstances," he said softly, still staring at the table. "I don't even know how to begin to tell you how horrible I feel."

Emma took a deep breath. Maybe all of this wasn't completely his fault. Wait, how could she think that? He'd lied to her from the moment they met. *That* was his fault. She didn't want to be friends with a liar. She couldn't.

But he looked so sad. And sorry. And broken.

Something tugged at her heartstrings. Maybe he deserved a second chance. He'd come clean, after all.

She gave him a weak smile and kept eating her pasta. She was halfway through when she noticed Jack was already finished. She set down her fork. "Tell me more about your dad," she said, hoping to pass the time with conversation while they waited for Jack's father. "Something good."

He pushed away his Styrofoam box as a mixture of pride and frustration filled his eyes. "My dad's very intense." He rested his chin in his hand and started tracing a pattern on the table. "But it's good that he's intense because when he says he'll do something, you know he means it. He's loyal and he works hard. He's a hacker for Helios Industries."

Emma's eyebrows rose high. "That's a huge company. But what do you mean, a hacker? That's a good thing?"

Jack nodded and pushed his plastic fork back and forth on the table. "Yeah, you know, a white hat hacker? The ones who protect against other hackers. He helps keep their servers from getting hacked."

Emma had heard of something like that before. "That's kind of cool."

"Yeah, he—here he comes."

136

Emma turned around, her heart pounding. There was a man walking toward them on the sidewalk. He was Asian, slender and small like Jack, but tougher around the edges. A lot tougher. He had a buzzed head and was dressed in a nice pair of slacks and a button-down shirt. His black leather jacket looked worn but clean.

"Hey, Dad," Jack said as he came up to the table. "Emma, this is my dad, Craig."

Craig nodded a curt hello to his son and then turned to Emma with a curious, expectant look. "Hello, Emma. How are you doing?"

She forced a nod. "I'm fine, thanks."

"Good." He walked past her and sat down in the chair next to Jack. He grabbed the untouched Styrofoam box and the fork Jack had set on top and started shoveling noodles into his mouth with the same gusto Jack had.

Jack threw Emma a *see-what-I-mean?* look and cleared his throat. "So, Dad, how do you know Emma's dad? Do you know where he is?"

Craig looked up at Emma, his expression irritated. "I don't know where he is. I also don't know why everyone I've contacted to try to find him is dead. I was hoping you could give me some insight, Emma. When was the last time you saw him?"

A shudder went down Emma's spine at the mention of more dead people. Craig looked angry, as if he blamed her. She tightened her jaw. "I last saw him yesterday afternoon at that table over there." She pointed to the table where she and her father had sat. "He was upset when I told him I'd delivered a package for him earlier. He left and I haven't seen him since."

"What kind of package? One like the police confiscated from you?"

She twisted her hands together. "I guess they told you about that when they questioned you?"

He nodded.

"Yeah, it was like that one. It was antique Chinese eggs, but now I'm pretty sure there were drugs inside. I delivered it to someone named Paula in an antiques shop a few blocks from here."

Craig closed his eyes. "That's how this happened," he muttered.

"What is going on?" Emma demanded. "Who is Paula?"

Craig let out a soft grunt. "None of your concern. All you need to know is your father is probably dead now. I hope he isn't, but death would be better than your uncle getting to him."

Emma scrunched her forehead in confusion. Why would her uncle be trying to get to her dad? She tried to remember his name, but realized her dad talked so rarely about him that she'd forgotten it altogether. In fact, she wasn't even sure he'd ever told her his name. "Which uncle?" she asked as casually as she could.

Craig gave her a mystified look. "How much has Sam told you about Glenn?" he asked icily. His eyes were suddenly cold, as if a light had gone out of them.

Emma's mouth dropped open. "*Glenn* is my uncle?" She wracked her brain to put together what little pieces of information she had. Her mother had written in her journal that she'd left someone named Glenn because he was using steroids and that he was rotten to the core. And she'd ended up with Sam, Glenn's *brother*. That had probably been a terrible situation for everyone. No wonder her father had never talked about it.

The iciness in Craig's eyes melted away as he leaned across the table. "Sam never told me much about you, except that I needed to protect you if things went wrong. To do that, I need you to stay out of the way. Don't look for him. Don't go poking around, okay? It's too dangerous." He glanced at Jack. "I expect you to make sure she stays out of the way."

Jack slapped a hand down on the table. "That's why you wanted me to keep an eye on her? So I could keep her out of your way while you do whatever shady shit you're into?"

Craig sighed. "You've never stuck your nose in my business and you're not going to start now. Do you have a problem with that?"

Jack folded his arms, his expression livid. "I'm tired of doing everything your way. Emma needs answers. You have to give them to her."

Emma nodded. "I can't promise to stand by and not do anything. He's my father. I love him. I have to find—"

Craig's face clouded with anger. He stood from his chair and leaned across the table, grabbing Emma's wrist so hard that she let out a little cry. She stood up halfway, trying to break free from Craig's grip, but she wasn't strong enough. Her pepper spray slipped from her sweatshirt pocket and clattered under the table. She threw a desperate glance at Jack.

"Let her go, Dad," Jack growled as he leaned over and grabbed his dad's arm, but Craig gave him a warning look so harsh that Jack backed off.

"I'm not going to hurt her," Craig said calmly. He turned back to Emma. "I can't tell you more about your father because he never gave me permission to tell you anything. You *must* stay out of this. You're already in danger, but if you stay out of the way there's a chance everything can still run according to plan. We'll all be a lot safer that way."

Emma spotted a shimmer of fear in his eyes. That gave her the courage to strain against his fierce hold. "You *are* hurting me," she hissed, her fingers turning numb. "Let me go."

Jack inched closer to his father, his eyes swirling with anger. "She's right, Dad. Let her go."

Craig nodded and released his hold. Emma backed away from the table, rubbing her sore wrist. The well-lit block seemed darker all of a sudden. When she turned to Jack, he gave her an apologetic look, as if trying to tell her this was not how he'd planned things.

"I'm sorry," Craig said as he sat back down. "I didn't mean to hurt you."

Emma stared hard at him. She had no idea how to get what she wanted out of him. There was a hardness to him that scared her. Maybe it was the fierce lines in his forehead when he got angry, or how strong his grip had been. It wasn't something she sensed in Jack at all.

For the first time, she felt like she might be able to forgive Jack. Eventually.

"I guess this was a wasted trip," she said to Jack. "I'm going home."

He nodded, his expression full of concern and embarrassment as he stood up. "I think that's a good idea. I'll walk you there." He threw a dark glare at his father as they walked away. Emma didn't look back.

ELEVEN

When they were a block away from her apartment building, Emma breathed a sigh of relief.

Jack gave her a pained look. "I hope you don't think I planned any of that. I told you my dad was . . . well, that's just how he is. I'm so sorry. I'm sorry for everything."

"I know you are," she answered. She didn't know what else to say.

"I'm especially sorry he grabbed you like that," Jack said. "My dad's a tough guy, but I've never known him to actually hurt anyone except in self-defense. He scared me tonight. I need you to understand I won't ever hurt you or threaten you like he did."

"I want to believe you won't," she whispered. "But it's going to be really hard to trust you again."

"I get that, yeah. I'm not a bad person. All of this got way out of hand. I didn't mean it to . . . I didn't—"

Emma watched him, torn by the sudden urge to comfort him. She folded her arms, waiting as he stuttered around something else he was trying to say.

"I want you to know my dad's not a bad guy," he finally managed. "I wish I could get him out of whatever he's involved in. But I don't know how. I'm afraid he's gonna get in so deep, he'll end up in prison. I have to stick around and help him as much as I can."

Emma shot him a glare. "What do you mean, 'help him'? Do you mean tail people like you tailed me?"

He shook his head quickly. "No, that's not what I meant. I meant keep him in line, like I did tonight when he grabbed you. I feel like sometimes I'm the only thing grounding him to reality. If I leave, he might really go overboard."

Emma scratched her head. "So that's why you're sticking around? What about you? What about your dreams?"

Jack's pace slowed and Emma slowed with him. "I know it doesn't make sense," he sighed. "But I love him. I have to try to see him through this. I need to know he'll be okay without me. Losing my mom hurt him so much. It hurt me too, and we kinda need each other in a lot of ways."

Emma's heart sank. Those were a lot of the same reasons she wanted to stay with her dad. Despite her father telling her he wanted her to go to college far away, she feared he would fall apart without her.

"Even before all of this went down," Jack said, "I didn't really want to leave for college. We've always been there for each other. When my mom died, we had to stick together. He says he's fine with me leaving, but I don't think he would be."

"I understand," Emma said. "When you've taken care of each other for so long, it's impossible to leave without hurting the other person. I don't want to hurt anyone."

"I don't either."

The crazy thing was that Emma believed him. They were at her apartment building now. She glanced across the street to see the officer still asleep in his car.

"They should sack that guy," she said as she reached for the keys in her back pocket. The keys were there, but her phone wasn't. "Crap," she said, and turned around, not sure what she should do.

"What's wrong?" Jack asked.

"My phone. It was in my back pocket. It must have fallen out at Bella's. These stupid jeans have loose pockets. Stuff's always falling out when I sit down." She felt her sweatshirt pocket and realized she'd forgotten to get her pepper spray from under the table, as well. She took a step back down the sidewalk, but Jack stopped her.

His eyes looked tired but determined. "I'll go back and get it. You go on up and I'll buzz you when I'm here."

She raised her eyebrows. "Are you sure?"

He shrugged. "Of course."

"Well, thanks. You know, Jack, you really are a nice guy—even if you did tail me and lie to me about it."

He laughed. "I'll keep proving I'm nice, too. If you give me the chance."

She shuffled by him to get to the door. "I'll have to think about it, but yeah . . . maybe."

"Emma, wait . . ."

She stopped in her tracks, her body still close to Jack's. He looked at her tenderly, inching closer and closer. It felt like a force was pushing him to her and she wanted to give in and fall into it. How could she when so many things were so wrong right now?

"Yes?" she choked out. Her mouth was dry.

Jack's fingers brushed across her arm and she suddenly wished she didn't have long sleeves. Then his fingers lowered to her hand and touched her fingertips.

"I know this is really fast," he said. "And I know you hate me right now. You have every right to hate me. But I really do wish we'd met under different circumstances. I know we would've been good friends." He glanced away. "Maybe even more."

She looked into his eyes, relieved at the honesty she saw in them. "As long as you promise to never stalk me like that again, even if it's for your father. It's hard for me to trust anyone right now."

He nodded. "I understand, and yes, I promise."

She tried to keep looking into his eyes, but it was difficult. Finally, she turned away. "I don't know if I can believe you, Jack. I hate this. With my dad missing, I feel so alone. I need someone. I can't do this by myself."

Jack leaned closer, making her look up at him again. His eyes were pleading. "Have I hurt you at all since you met me?"

She shook her head. "Well, you lied to me."

"I didn't really know you, then. I thought it was just a favor for my dad. You get that, right?"

"Yeah."

His fingertips brushed against hers again and she held her breath. A part of her knew it was crazy to get closer to him, but the rest of her didn't care. She felt safe. She slid her hand into Jack's and squeezed. "I'll try to trust you."

A soft smile lifted his lips. "I won't let you down. You don't have to be alone, Emma. I'm here, okay?"

"Okay."

He leaned forward, hesitant, before quickly pressing his lips against hers. Emma didn't stop him. Instead, she leaned into him and closed her eyes. She brushed her fingertips along the inside of his hand and he did the same to her. Everything about him was warm and inviting.

He slowly pulled away, his eyes fastened to hers. "I– I'll go now," he whispered. "Go up to your place and I'll ring your buzzer when I'm back. I'll hurry."

She nodded and watched him walk away, her heart pounding as she entered her code into the keypad and went inside. Her thoughts were a jumbled mess, tangling with the emotions pumping out of her heart. She didn't know why she had returned Jack's kiss, but it had felt like the right thing to do. And she didn't regret it.

Swiping a hand across her face, she took a deep breath and concentrated on the buttons in the elevator. She had to focus. The buttons blurred for a moment as her thoughts shifted to her uncle, her mother's journal entries, her father's drug packages.

The kiss.

She shook her head and focused on the buttons again, pressing the one for her floor. There were more important things than Jack.

She had to get answers about her father. Soon.

Stepping off the elevator, she unlocked the apartment door, and immediately fastened the locks behind her when she was inside. She glanced down at a pair of her father's shoes in the entryway, and what Craig had told her came rushing back: *You're already in danger.*

But how imminent was that danger? Emma looked up, her breaths coming faster. She fell against the door as she thought about the frightened look on her father's face when she had given him the invoice. What had been weighing on him right then? Why hadn't he told her about it—about *any* of his secrets? After what Craig had said about her being in danger, and Alex saying the same thing, she wondered if her father had only been trying to protect her from something. Or some*one*.

The buzzer went off right beside her and she jerked in surprise. She hit the button and leaned close to the speaker, her entire body shaking with a rush of adrenaline. "Yes?"

"Hey, is everything all right up there?" It was Jack.

She let out a sigh of relief. "You scared me, but yes, everything's fine here. Why?"

"Let me up. Right now."

Her body was still shaking. "Did you already get my ph—"

"Now, Emma! That cop isn't sleeping. He's *dead*, and I don't think you're safe."

"Dead?" she gasped. "How? I don't—"

"Please, just let me up."

She jammed her thumb against the button to buzz him in. Her fingers turned to ice as she glanced away from the door and saw that the sofa was slightly crooked, something that would have driven both her and her father crazy. Had she simply not noticed it earlier? Then she spotted a broken dish on the kitchen floor by the sink.

Her entire body went numb

Someone had been here . . . and she wasn't entirely sure they were gone.

Jack was right. She wasn't safe.

Spinning around, she fumbled with the door and practically fell out into the hallway as soon as she got it open. She yanked it closed behind her. Not that closing it would stop anyone from coming out to get her. Why weren't her feet working properly? She ran toward the elevator then changed her mind. That felt unsafe. Unreliable.

Breathing hard, she ran for the stairwell, stopping short when a man dressed in dark jeans and a dirty denim jacket cleared the top step.

Emma turned and ran back down the hallway, but the button for the elevator stayed dark when she pressed it.

The man approached her casually, making no sound as he moved. Something glinted in his hand, too thin and small to be a knife. Emma touched her sweatshirt pocket and cursed herself for forgetting her pepper spray. Her body broke into a sweat as panic gripped her and squeezed until she couldn't breathe.

"We've got you trapped," the man laughed. "You can't go in your apartment. You can't go downstairs. No way out, Emma."

He knew her name.

Emma sucked in a breath and choked out, "Who are you? How did you get in? The lobby doors are locked."

He kept advancing. "We've been waiting for you since you left. We figured you'd be back soon."

She stumbled backward, her breath stopping in her lungs. She froze completely as the man came closer, his face swirling into an indistinct blob through her teary eyes. He'd said "we," meaning he wasn't alone. She had no chance at all until Jack arrived. *If* he arrived.

No. She could fight on her own. Her father had always taught her to never give up, and she wasn't going to start now. She had to pull it together.

Gathering her resolve, she assessed her options. She couldn't get past the man, but she could make noise. Turning, she pounded on her neighbor's door and called out for help. There were only four units on each floor and she realized her chances of waking someone up at this time of night were slim. The man who lived in the apartment next to hers was seventy-five years old and wore a hearing aid he always took out at night. The woman at the end of the hall worked graveyard shifts as a nurse, and the other apartment was currently empty.

Had this man known she'd be practically helpless up here? When she looked into his eyes, she guessed he had made sure of it.

"I don't know why you want me," she said as she kept pounding on the old man's door, "but I promise it won't solve anything. I had nothing to do with my father's drugs, or whatever he was doing."

The man smirked. He had sharp blue eyes and light wavy hair. She didn't like how smoothly he moved. She especially didn't like whatever he was holding in his hand. It was mostly hidden, but she could see a needle poking out from between his fingers.

Her mouth went dry and she spun around. Where was Jack? She stopped pounding on the door and ran to the nurse's apartment. She banged on the door even though it was unlikely anyone was home.

"Nobody's going to hear you." He was only a few feet away now. He reached out to grab her, but as he drew closer Emma's panic spurred her to action. She slammed her knee into his groin as hard as she could. A loud *oof!* left his mouth. Emma pushed him off balance and ran for the stairwell. She didn't look back to see if he'd fallen to the floor or not.

"Emma!" Jack was charging up the stairs toward her. "Are you okay?"

"No! Run! Go!"

Jack's eyes widened, but he did as she said and she raced after him down the stairs. Something crashed into her from behind and she hit the wall at the landing, her shoulder smacking against the brick.

When she righted herself and turned around, she saw the man in the denim jacket fighting Jack.

Jack was . . . *good.*

He ducked a blow and then landed a hard punch on the man's nose. Grabbing the man's shoulders, he slammed him into the wall right next to Emma. She jumped down the next few steps past the landing to get out of the way.

Jack gave her a sharp look. "Get out of here!"

"I think there's someone else with him. I can't leave you here alone!"

"I'll be okay," he gasped. "I called the police. Go!"

He turned to land another blow just as the man recovered. The man shook his head, not as fazed this time. His eyes were on fire. Blood dripped from his nose. He'd ditched the needle or whatever he'd been holding. He lunged at Jack, but Jack was too fast. He dodged and elbowed the man's chest just as Emma turned to go.

She stopped as another man appeared at the top of the stairs, looking confused. He was a lot bigger than the denim jacket guy.

Emma blinked. "Look out!"

Jack looked up to see the second man heading straight for him from above. With that extra momentum, Jack had no chance. The burly man kicked him in the ribs and Jack cried out in pain as he smashed into the wall, his eyes squeezed shut.

Emma instinctively moved toward him, but then the bigger man was almost on top of her and she spun around and jumped the four steps to the next landing, her knees wobbling on impact. She felt strong and weak at the same time. Her eyes stung. Jack was going to die. They were going to kill him. How many more people did she have to lose? How much more of this could she possibly take?

Footsteps pounded behind her as she raced down the next flight of stairs, but she didn't dare look back. Her breath wheezed in her throat. She let out a high-pitched scream for help, hoping someone would hear her and open their door. It would take too long for the police to get there. She had to make it to the street. There would be more space to run and places to hide until the police arrived.

She was on the third floor now. So close. Just a few more. The footsteps sounded louder. Something hard slammed into her shoulder and she flew sideways into the wall, her ribs colliding with the metal railing.

"It's over, bitch," a voice hissed in her ear. Heat wrapped around her. Arms, strong and vice-like, lifted her up from her knees.

She screamed again, this time so loudly it seemed to shake the walls. A hand clapped over her mouth. It smelled like bike grease. She tried to bite it, but the man held his palm tightly against her mouth. A moment later she felt a prick in her neck.

The needle.

She fought against the man, kicking her legs and twisting her body to break his hold on her, but nothing worked. Her legs felt heavy, like she was pushing through sand. Finally, she went limp as her thoughts turned fuzzy and her body dissolved into clouds. The hand lifted from her mouth and she gasped for a fresh lungful of air. Maybe if she breathed harder, faster, she'd wake up.

She moved her attention to her attacker. His blue eyes were pretty, like a calm lake on a warm day.

"That's right," he laughed as her body began to float in that lake. "Go to sleep. When you wake up you're going to wish you were dead. Glenn will make sure of that."

She was a fish. She was a swan. She was a feather in a sea of blue. And she never wanted it to end.

TWELVE

"He came out of his office and headed over to the VIP rooms a few minutes ago," one of the club's bouncers told Starry when she demanded to know where she could find Rhys. When she had first come down to find him, he'd been in a meeting. She'd waited and waited and finally decided to go to the late-night Mexican taco shop next door to get something to eat. Now her stomach was full and she felt ready to face Rhys and his lies.

The bouncer scratched his shiny bald head and looked Starry up and down. "Are you the girlfriend?"

Starry narrowed her eyes. "Why is he talking about me to his employees? What has he told you?"

The bouncer didn't reply. He looked her up and down one more time and nodded approvingly. It was almost enough to make Starry hurl a fist into his fat, ugly nose, but she held back. They were standing near one of the entrances leading out to the main floor and the last thing she wanted to do was draw attention to herself.

Taking a step away from the bouncer, she forced down her anger. "Which VIP room?"

The bouncer jerked his head toward the main floor. "One of the rooms down that hallway. I don't know which one."

Starry pushed past him and marched into the club. She had never been on the main floor during business hours. It was packed with people. Most of them were at the bar or seated on black leather couches surrounding small raised platforms with dancing poles. Most of the platforms were occupied by a stripper dancing to the heavy music pounding through the speakers. The whole place smelled like sweat and cologne and energy.

So this was where Rhys hung out every night. Starry knew he worked hard, but how could he complain so much about working in such an environment? It was all pleasure and play.

Reaching the hallway to the VIP rooms, Starry stopped in front of the first door. To the right of the door handle was a glowing red panel.

"Can I help you with something?" a man asked as he approached Starry from the other end of the hallway. He was even larger than the other bouncer.

Starry turned to him, surprised how intimidated she felt by the man's sheer muscle mass. Most of her father's bodyguards were huge, but not this huge. Even in her six-inch heels the man towered over her. She glared up at him. "Which room is Rhys in?"

The bouncer folded his meaty arms. "Who's asking?"

She grabbed the collar of his black button-up shirt. "Someone who has the power to make sure you never work another club in this city," she growled, yanking him forward. He barely moved half an inch.

He took a deep breath through his nose before pushing her hand off his collar. "This way," he said.

She followed him to a door down the hall, standing a few feet away as he pressed the center of another glowing red panel. The door opened a minute later and Rhys appeared. He looked at the bouncer, his expression irritated.

"What is it? I told you not to interrupt us."

The bouncer slid his eyes to Starry, and Rhys' expression switched to confusion. She marched up to the door and leaned into his face. "We have to talk. Now."

"I'm busy," he whispered. "Can it wait a few minutes?"

It was then that Starry realized Rhys wasn't wearing his suit coat. She looked past him into the room. A twenty-something blonde sat half-dressed on a plush red sofa in the middle of the room. A chandelier hung

from the ceiling above her, the lights dimmed. Rhys'
jacket was slung across the back of the sofa.

The anger Starry had been trying so hard to keep
under control burst free.

"You lying, cheating son of a bitch," she hissed, and
kicked the door open farther with her heel. She shoved
Rhys' chest hard enough to make him stumble
backward. "Busy, huh?" The door shut behind her.

Rhys stood up straight and glanced at the woman.
She was only wearing a bra and panties. Her clothes
were strewn across the dark carpet. But something was
off. There were trails of tears and mascara running
down her cheeks.

"Starry, this is Mia," Rhys said. "The guest she was
entertaining noticed her problem and came to tell me
about it."

Mia broke into uncontrolled sobbing and Starry
knotted her brow, confused until she looked at Mia a
little closer. There were large, purple bruises on her
ribcage and all down her legs. All of them were fresh.

"Oh," Starry said, and took a step backward in
surprise. For a second all she could think about was her
father's hand striking her cheek. It was the only time
anyone had ever hit her abusively. She couldn't
imagine what this woman had been through.

"Who did that to her?" she whispered to Rhys. Mia
was crying so hard Starry doubted she could hear
anything being said about her.

Rhys walked up to Starry and frowned before touching her hand down at her side. "Her husband," he answered, and looked tenderly into Starry's eyes. "I'm sorry you thought I was in here cheating on you. Is that why you came storming down here? What's the matter?"

Starry looked down at his fingers brushing across her knuckles. She hated how quickly he made her feel soft and compliant. It couldn't last. Her anger returning, she pushed his hand off hers and straightened her shoulders. "The computer equipment. I'm tired of you giving me the runaround. Tell me right now what's really going on. You don't want me to find Emma, but why? It's got to be more than wanting to protect me."

Surprise flashed across Rhys' face. "Oh," he said, and took a step back. He didn't look flustered, but something about the way he moved suggested nervousness. "Yes, we should talk, you're right." He glanced at the wailing Mia and back to Starry. "Give me a minute?" He nodded to a set of armchairs at the other end of the room.

Starry folded her arms and walked across the room to sit down.

Rhys turned to Mia, who was gathering up her clothes and pulling them on. Her crying had finally slowed. "Take the rest of tonight and tomorrow off," he said.

She looked up, surprised as she zipped up her skirt. "What do you mean? I c-can't take any time off. I need the money."

Rhys folded his arms. "I'm going to have Ginger book you a hotel room until we can deal with your husband. Don't worry, it'll be paid for. And I'll waive your house fees and tip outs for tonight to help make up for tomorrow."

Starry raised her eyebrows. None of her father's strip clubs allowed dancers to work without paying tip outs, and she doubted the club would pay for the woman's hotel room, either. Rhys was probably going to pay for everything out of his own pocket.

When Mia didn't respond, Rhys stepped forward and lifted her chin with two fingers until she was looking him in the face. He lowered his hand. "You have nothing to be ashamed of. You're important here, okay? You matter and we'll take care of you. Nobody will hurt you again, especially your husband. If the police don't make sure of it, I will."

Mia's eyes filled with fresh tears, but this time they were tears of gratitude. She pushed back a mess of curls from her forehead. "Thank you. I've never worked for a manager like you before. I don't know what to say. I don't know how—"

"You don't have to thank me. It's the least I can do."

Mia nodded, her chin trembling as she finished getting dressed and dried her tears. Rhys saw her out the door and then turned to Starry as the door closed behind him.

She looked up at him, stunned. Seeing him deal with Mia had somehow quashed all of her ire. It was maddening and left her wobbling between the anger she knew she should be feeling and a newfound admiration and respect for what he did every night at work. He didn't just manage a club. He took care of people. He protected them.

"Does that sort of thing happen a lot?" she asked as she stood up to face him.

"Not really. I'm surprised she managed to hide it from Ginger, though." He waved his hand. "Anyway, enough about work. What's this about Emma? You don't believe I want to protect you?"

Starry tensed. "It seems fishy to me, that's all. Did you actually order that equipment?"

Rhys glanced down and took a few deep breaths. "No, I didn't. I created those invoices myself."

So that's how it was. Starry's anger flared. "You lied to me, then. You know how much I hate being lied to, Rhys."

He looked up, his expression completely sincere. "I shouldn't have lied to you, you're right, but you're so angry with your father right now. I thought if you had a few days to cool off you might change your mind. I'm afraid of what your father might do if you find her. He could hurt you, Starry. That's all this is."

"My father is more likely to hurt you than me." And that's when it clicked. "Unless that's what this is about," she said, taking a step back. "You're afraid he'll hurt *you*."

But she regretted saying it almost immediately because she knew deep down it wasn't true. Rhys was not a coward. Ginger was right. It was all about protecting her. He had protected Mia too, and probably dozens of others. Maybe that was just the kind of person he was. That made her care for him even more. Infuriating bastard!

He laughed. Loudly. "Oh, Starry. That's not what this is about." He took her shoulders and pulled her close. "I care more about you than myself. If you can't see that by now, I don't know what I'm supposed to do."

Weak-kneed. Slushy. Dizzy.

That's what Rhys did to her. He made her absolutely insane.

"Rhys," she whispered as he pulled her close enough to brush his lips across her forehead.

"What?" he breathed against her skin. He smelled like his cologne. His hands were strong around her shoulders, moving down her back, her waist. His mouth met hers and Starry was lost inside the kiss for a whole minute before she managed to move her hands up to his chest and push him away.

"Stop it," she gasped. "I hate how you do this to me. I was so angry with you and now you've got me all twisted up in knots. You can't protect me by lying to me. Did you think I'd forget about the equipment? I'm not an idiot. I can go somewhere else, you know." She looked down at her hands and realized they were curled into fists. She was breathing fast and hard.

Rhys took a few steps back, his expression hurt. "I'm sorry," he relented. "You're right, of course, so what do you want me to do? I can't go against your father. It's too dangerous."

Starry narrowed her eyes as she studied Rhys' face. There was something more here than him wanting to protect her, or even control her, but she couldn't put her finger on it. She shook her head in frustration. "I don't know," she grumbled. "You make me so crazy I want to scream."

Rhys smirked and sauntered up to her as if he owned her and the entire world. "Do I, now?" He reached out to run a hand up her hip, but she pushed past him and opened the door. She was too tired to deal with his games.

"I'm going to bed." She was halfway down the hall when Rhys called out goodnight. She ignored him and kept walking.

THIRTEEN

"Snap out of it," a man's voice ordered in Emma's ear.

A hand lightly struck her cheek and she opened her eyes. Everything was a dark blur. The air was frigid. She shivered beneath her thin T-shirt and jeans. She was barefoot, standing on a smooth concrete floor. She opened her mouth to ask the man who had spoken to her what was going on, but he moved out of her line of sight and started speaking first.

"That's it," he said, sounding relieved.

Emma tried to speak, but her lips didn't seem to want to move with the words. All that came out was a groan. She shivered again and wondered what she'd done with her sweatshirt. Last she remembered, she'd been wearing it. Hadn't she? She tried to move her hands, but they were bound together by something cold and hard keeping her upright. Her wrists were numb. Through her blurry vision she could see her arms stretched above her head. They were secured by a chain hooked to the ceiling. The chain looped around . . . handcuffs. Why was she handcuffed?

Panicking, she lurched forward, but the chain stopped her from going more than a few inches.

What is this?

Her brain ached. Her arms ached. And yet she felt numb at the same time. Everything was fuzzy and blank in her head. She didn't know how or why she was here. Or where "here" was. Something about that thought made her want to laugh. Or cry.

Cry. Definitely cry.

The sound of a door opening and shutting echoed through the room, followed by a whoosh of blissfully warm air. It was gone a moment later.

"What the hell is this, Ian?" an angry voice rumbled from somewhere behind her. "Why is she still out of it? It's been an entire day. She was supposed to be ready by now."

There was something eerily familiar about the man's voice, but Emma couldn't put her finger on it.

"I had to give her another dose around two this morning," Ian answered. "She woke up screaming and I was too tired to deal with that shit. It's wearing off quick now, see? She's standing up on her own."

"Barely," the other man sighed. "If it hasn't worn off enough by noon we'll have to get Pearce in here to see what he can do to speed things up. I'm ready to get this going."

The door opened and shut again and the voices went silent. Confused, Emma blinked in an effort to clear her vision and see where she was. The last solid thing she remembered was looking at the couch in her living room. It had been crooked for some reason. Everything about that memory felt ominous, as if the crooked couch was the reason she was in danger now.

"Dad?" she called out in a raspy voice, wondering why he wasn't with her. He was always around when she needed him. "Where are you?"

A deep laugh made her jump. It sounded like the man named Ian. "Sam's dead," he said as he stepped into Emma's blurry view. "I watched him die yesterday." He made a low whistle. "Nasty death, too. I worked him over pretty good back in New York, but that was nothing compared to what Glenn put him through."

Dead? Yesterday?

Grief flooded Emma. A cry left her throat. It couldn't be true. Her father couldn't be dead. She'd just eaten lunch with him, hadn't she? It was a sunny day. The air was warm. She could see him lifting a slice of pizza to his mouth. It was covered in jalapeños.

"No," she choked through her tears. "This can't be happening. Yesterday was Friday. I was just with him eating lunch. Where am I? When did all of this happen?"

"It's Tuesday, kid," Ian said flatly. "Not Saturday. How much did those drugs knock out of your head?"

And then it all came back. None of it was clear, but it was enough to cling to for a moment: Chinese eggs. Paula. Owls. Drugs. Jack. Alex. The fight in the stairwell . . . and then a long stretch of darkness and nightmares.

Adrenaline shot through Emma's body. Her heart pounded. It was such a strong sensation that she could feel it fighting against the effects of the drugs in her bloodstream. She blinked as her vision began to clear. Ian came into focus. Dirty denim jacket. Blond hair. Pretty blue eyes.

Emma almost bit her tongue in horror. She remembered Ian chasing her. There was a needle. Her ribs still hurt from when he'd pushed her down the stairs.

"Looks like everything's coming back," Ian said with a smirk.

"Who are you?" she whispered as her vision went blurry again. "And where am I?" She blinked a few times to bring Ian back into focus, but the moment of clarity was gone. Her mind felt sluggish and slow. Memories came at her like snowballs, slamming against the back of her mind and fading again just as fast.

"You're in LA," Ian answered. "We flew here in a private jet. And it doesn't matter who I am." His footsteps sounded somewhere to Emma's right and moved behind her. "What matters is that you don't disappoint Glenn. He's already in a rotten mood because of Sam."

"Glenn?" Emma asked as a vague memory flitted across her consciousness. "My uncle? Is that who was here a minute ago?"

Footsteps sounded to her left. Ian came into view again, but he was still blurry. "Technically, Glenn is your father," he chuckled. "At least, that's how I understand it. Don't think he'll go easy on you because you're his daughter. He just killed his own brother. You'll tell him everything, got it?"

Emma shook her head in confusion. "I don't understand. *Sam* is my father."

Ian waved his hand. "Either way, Sam is dead."

Emma's tears came even faster. She hung her head. "I never said goodbye. C-can I see him? Is his body still here?"

Ian laughed. "No, you don't want to see him. Trust me."

Gritting her teeth against the pain filling her heart, Emma fought back a scream rising in her throat. Her father was her world. He couldn't be gone forever. It wasn't possible. But no matter how much she tried to reject the idea of her father's death, she knew deep down it was true. And it was her fault. A sadness sharper than anything she'd ever felt in her life squeezed her heart so hard she had to gasp to keep breathing. Tears spilled down her cheeks. A few curled around her lips and into her mouth. They tasted bitter.

"Everything will work out," Ian said smoothly as he touched her cheek and wiped away a few tears. He chuckled, as if the tears amused him. "If you tell Glenn what you know."

Recoiling from his touch, Emma glared at him. "But I don't know anything." She tried to pull farther away from Ian, but he moved his hand to the back of her neck and yanked her forward. Her vision cleared again and she found herself looking into Ian's icy eyes. She remembered looking into them not long ago, right as she'd drifted off into nothingness. The cold air around her crawled up her bare arms like a thousand ants. She shivered.

"Glenn will get what he needs from you," Ian said, his hand still on the back of her neck. He was close enough that Emma could smell cigarette smoke on his breath. "And trust me, the faster you give it to him, the better. Don't be stupid like Sam and resist. That's what got him killed."

"What did my uncle do to him?" Emma whimpered, pushing away the horrific images swirling around in her head. There must have been blood and broken bones and who knows what else.

"Glenn did what he needed to do," Ian laughed. "Just like he's going to do whatever he needs to get what he wants from you."

Emma's knees almost buckled underneath her, but she shifted enough to stay upright. "Please," she whispered. "Please help me. I don't have anything he wants. I don't know anything about what my dad was doing."

"Like hell you don't," Ian snapped, and pushed her hard enough to make her stumble across the floor until the chain pulled her up short. The handcuffs bit hard into her wrists again.

Ian straightened his jacket and then pulled a phone from his pocket. He looked down at the screen, seeming to forget about Emma altogether. Her vision was clear enough now for her to get a look at the rest of the room. It was nothing more than four concrete walls and a metal table screwed to the floor over in one corner and a tall metal cabinet in another. There was a drain in the floor close to where Ian was standing in the middle of the room and a light fixture above him.

Emma squeezed her eyes shut as she tried to push away the very real possibility that she might die in this room. She needed something to hold on to. Some hope. *Anything.*

And then she remembered the last time she'd seen her father. She could almost feel him pulling her into a tight hug.

"*Promise me you'll always stick to what you know is right,*" he had said.

But what did that mean? What was right in this situation? What would he want her to do? She had no idea. Had he done what was right? Dealing drugs, getting himself killed. Right now, she wasn't so sure.

Exhaustion spilled over her. She felt completely drained. Hungry. Thirsty. Cold. Tired. Her knees buckled and she cried out as the handcuffs bit into her wrists again. She was probably bleeding by now. She opened her eyes to look up at her wrists. They were puffy and raw.

"This is hopeless," Ian grumbled as he put his phone back into his pocket and marched past Emma to the door. "I'll be back later. You'd better be more lucid by then."

Emma craned her neck to watch him go. There was no window in the door. No windows anywhere in this room. She cringed as the door clicked shut. A moment later the light went out, plunging the room into absolute darkness.

Emma stood still in the darkness for what felt like hours, her entire body aching as she tried to tamp down her rising panic. It didn't help knowing her father was dead. She kept picturing his last text in her mind: *I love you, Emma. It's a deal.*

She loved him too, more than anyone else in her life. And now he was gone. Even though he'd possibly done bad things, she still wanted to keep the promise she'd made to him. He wanted her to do what was right, and the right thing to do would be to stay strong and true to herself.

But how? Strength seemed impossible right now.

Devastated and angry with herself, she didn't even try to stop her tears. They fell until there were no more, and even then she couldn't stop whimpering. She felt pathetic and helpless. Even worse, as her fuzzy mind finally began to clear, she remembered one more horrible thing: Jack fighting in the stairwell. There was no way he could have survived. Or had they taken him too? Either way, it was a knife in her heart.

Her breathing turned rapid. Her heart wouldn't slow down. She could hardly feel her hands anymore. They were blocks of ice. So were her feet. What if Ian left her here until she starved to death? Or went crazy? Could she die from going crazy? It was so dark. So cold. Ian was going to forget about her . . .

The door opened and Emma bit down on her bottom lip so hard it started to bleed. She squinted when the light turned on.

"Looking a little more awake now," Ian's voice sounded from behind her. "I turned up the temperature a few degrees. You're welcome."

Opening her eyes, Emma saw Ian in front of her. She hated to admit she was relieved to see him after being left in the dark. "Is my friend here too?" she asked, referring to Jack. "Or is he dead?"

It killed her to ask, but she had to know.

A smirk lifted Ian's lips. "Your bodyguard wannabe? You'll be glad to hear I have no idea where he is."

So he could be alive! Emma breathed a sigh of relief. At least there was hope for *something* now, even if she was about to face torture. Or worse.

The door opened again and Emma craned her neck to see a man entering the room. Her stomach sank to the ground. *Glenn.* There was no mistaking him. He looked so much like her father it was uncanny. Same strong nose and chin and broad shoulders. His coiffed hair was going gray, but for some reason Emma couldn't explain this made him look younger than her father. He was so polished. So clean and poised. He was dressed in a three-piece suit the color of sharkskin.

"Emma," he said, his hard gray eyes boring into her as he stopped in front of her. "We finally meet."

Emma noticed his voice had the same timbre as her father's. There was a slight accent, too, just like her father's. It was from growing up on the West coast.

Something about knowing her father had grown up with this man softened the ragged edges of Emma's fear. She lifted her eyes to meet Glenn's intense gaze. She could do this. She could face him.

"You have no right to keep me here," she said with as much courage as she could muster. "Let me go."

Glenn's lips slid into an amused smile as he took a step back and looked her up and down. "Emma, Emma," he said, and *tsked* his tongue. "Do you really think you're in a position to make demands?"

Emma looked up at her hands and cringed.

Ian let out a soft snicker. "Do you want me to get the whip?" he asked.

Whip?

Emma's stomach plummeted. She looked at Glenn and swallowed a growing lump in her throat. "I don't understand," she whispered as every ounce of her courage disintegrated into terror. "My dad never told me anything. I didn't know about the drugs until after he disappeared."

Keeping his eyes on Emma, Glenn waved a hand at Ian. "Yes, bring my equipment," he ordered. "She's awake enough now."

"Gladly."

Ian left the room and fresh tears gathered in Emma's eyes. "What are you going to do?" Her fear was exploding into full-blown panic now. Glenn was going to whip her. She didn't even know how to process that.

It would hurt, she knew that much. She was going to bleed and scream and there was nothing she could do to stop it. Her stomach twisted and turned until she thought she might puke all over Glenn's expensive wingtip shoes.

"Look at you," Glenn snarled as he leaned toward her face. He was so close Emma could feel his moist, hot breath on her skin. "I haven't even hurt you yet and you're falling apart."

She didn't know what else he expected. Her father was dead. She was strung up in a cold concrete room. He was going to whip her for no reason. What did he think she would do? Laugh it off?

Gritting her teeth, she locked eyes with him. The questions in her mind were gathering so fast she couldn't stop them. "Why did you kill my dad? What is all of this about? Please . . . please tell me what's going on."

Glenn's upper lip curled. "Sam took everything from me. He was planning to kill me and destroy everything I love, so don't go thinking he was some sort of saint. I took care of him and he threw it back in my face. He was worse than I have *ever* been."

Emma blinked in surprise. "My dad would never plan to kill anyone. He wasn't like that. You don't know him like I do."

Glenn took a step back and laughed. "Like you knew he was a drug dealer?" He was so confident that Emma had to consider the implications.

It couldn't be true. Her father might have been involved with drugs, but he would never have planned to murder his own brother. It wasn't possible, no matter how horrible of a person Glenn might be.

"Y-yes, I'm sure. He was a good man." But she wasn't one hundred percent sure about that now, and that made her heart break even more than it had when she'd found out her father was dead.

Glenn studied Emma's face as she trembled in front of him. "Sam never deserved you," he sighed, his expression crumbling into an eerie sort of sorrow. "He didn't deserve your mother, either. I should have been the one to raise you. I loved your mother more than he ever did."

Confusion wrapped itself around Emma like a snake. It was so intense her trembling stopped altogether. She remembered what her mother had written about Glenn in her journal entries, how she'd left him because he was on steroids. How did that fit into what was happening now? Why would Glenn say her father never deserved her? He couldn't possibly mean Sam wasn't her real father . . .

Emma opened her mouth to ask Glenn one of the thousand questions on the tip of her tongue, but the door opened and Ian walked in once more, this time carrying a soft nylon case. He took it over to the metal table at the other end of the room and opened it. "Anita said this is the one you use on your smaller subjects," he said as Glenn walked over to the table.

"That's right."

Emma watched in horror as Glenn lifted a coiled whip from the case. He wrapped his fingers around the handle and turned to face Emma. There was a hungry look in his eyes.

Emma sucked in a sharp breath. "Why can't you ask me questions without hurting me?"

Glenn laughed as he approached her. "I have no idea what's hiding in that pretty little head of yours, Emma. There might be some information I need. More importantly, I need to see your true nature before I make any other plans for you. This whip will show me who you really are."

His words cut her deeply. She had no idea if she could give him what he wanted. Her tears came hard and fast as Glenn walked out of her view. She could sense him behind her. Ian stopped in front of her and folded his arms. His expression was a strange mixture of pity, amusement, and fear.

"Let's get started," Glenn said, his voice closer than Emma had anticipated.

"Uncle Glenn, please," she gasped. "Please don't do this."

"Hush. All I want to hear from you now are answers to my questions. Tell me what you know about Sam's syndicate. Now."

His what? Emma stiffened and looked up at Ian as he backed away and sat on the edge of the table. He gave her a hard glare.

"I–I don't know what you're talking about," she answered. "Do you mean the drugs?"

Emma expected to feel a whip slice across her back any second, but nothing happened.

"Yes, the drugs," Glenn said calmly. "Sam was working for me, but he also created his own cute little syndicate without my knowledge. From what I gather, it's not much of a threat, but it must be eradicated all the same. Tell me who he was working with."

"But I don't know anything. You should have asked him," Emma said quickly, and then remembered what Ian had said about her father not cooperating. Why hadn't he told Glenn what he wanted to know? He might still be alive if he had! Or maybe not. Glenn might have wanted him dead no matter what.

"Oh, I did. He gave up some information," Glenn acknowledged. "But not everything. I was planning to torture you in front of him to encourage his cooperation, but he was too far gone by the time Ian got him here." Ian flinched, and Emma wondered if he'd get the whip too. "So now it's up to you. Tell me who he was working with."

Emma quickly searched her memories and stopped on the first thing that came to mind. "Paula," she gasped. "From the antiques store. She was dealing drugs."

Glenn let out an angry sigh. "Paula belongs to me, Emma. She's the reason you're here. That's not what I'm looking for."

Emma cringed as she remembered what Craig had told her the other night. "That's right," she said, thinking aloud. "I delivered my dad's package to Paula. She told you, didn't she?"

Pain sliced across her shoulder blades. The whip cut right through the thin material of her shirt. It happened so fast Emma almost didn't realize she'd been struck. Her back arched. Her breath hitched. A shriek left her throat.

And then it was over and she was left gasping for air as a warm sort of numbness spread across her back.

"You're not allowed to ask the questions here," Glenn snapped. "But if you're dying to know about Paula, then I'll tell you that you delivered Sam's drugs to the wrong buyer. Paula saw the unfamiliar address and reported it immediately, of course, and I sent Ian to track down Sam and question him. So I guess it's your fault he's dead."

Every word out of Glenn's mouth was like a lash across Emma's back. She squeezed her eyes shut and fought back the guilt eating her from the inside. "It was all my fault," she whimpered, and hung her head. "I'm so sorry, Dad."

"Don't give yourself too much credit," Glenn said. "I was bound to find out sooner or later. You can't move that much meth without the wrong people noticing. But enough of that. Tell me who Sam was working with. He must have had friends. Give me their names, even if they seem insignificant. Anyone he knew could be a part of his syndicate."

Emma couldn't wrap her mind around the fact that her father had not only worked for Glenn as a drug dealer, but had also run his own drug syndicate. It seemed impossible. That was not the father she knew.

Glenn cleared his throat and Emma snapped back to the moment. "Alex . . . his friend Alex Sheffield. They worked together at the CPA firm."

"I already know about Alex. He's the one name your father gave up. Ian had a nice, long chat with him. He gave us a dozen other names, but there must be more. Help me, Emma, or I'll have to strike you again."

Emma cringed. Of course Glenn already knew about Alex. That was why Alex was dead. She broke into a sweat as she tried to think of more names, but her mind was blank. "He didn't have any other friends. At least, not any I knew about. Maybe other people he worked with? But I don't know any of their names. I don't know—"

Another lash seared across her shoulders, this one deeper than the first. Emma cried out in pain.

"Who were you with Sunday night?" Glenn demanded. "Who was the boy helping you?"

Emma froze.

Not Jack.

Jack could still be alive. There was no way she could tell Glenn his name. She had already caused her father's death. She couldn't put Jack in more danger, but Ian had obviously told Glenn a boy had been with her, so there was no way around admitting *something* about him.

"H-his name is James," she stuttered. Would Glenn be able to tell she was lying? "I don't know his last name. We only just met on Saturday."

Crack! Another lash. Emma's shriek gurgled in her throat. The lashes were getting worse. It was a slow-building fire and the flames would engulf her if Glenn didn't stop. She could feel her shirt hanging open in back.

"You're lying," Glenn hurled at her. "That tells me we're getting somewhere, but if you keep it up I'll be forced to get out my other tools. You'll be begging for the whip again, understand?"

"Y-yes." Emma glanced up at Ian, who was watching her with a pitying look.

"Now tell me who he really is."

Emma hesitated a second too long.

Crack! A fourth lash.

Crack! A fifth.

Emma's shrieks echoed off the walls, tearing her throat raw. "Tell me!" Glenn yelled.

"His name's Jack." Emma's stomach churned at the idea of betraying Jack. She hoped Glenn couldn't find him with only a first name. "That's the only thing I lied about, I promise. I really don't know his last name. I helped him find his phone on Saturday. That's the first time I met him."

"And did you communicate with Jack on your phone?"

Emma's stomach churned some more. She didn't like where this was going. "Y-yes."

"Ah, good. Ian, go see where Finch is at on getting Emma's phone records. See if he can find any communications with this Jack boy."

Ian nodded and turned to leave.

"No," Emma whimpered. "Please, no. Jack hasn't done anything wrong. He doesn't know anything. His dad's the one who's selling drugs, not Jack."

Ian stopped in his tracks and looked past Emma to Glenn. "I don't know who she's talking about. We never saw anyone else with the boy."

"Go talk to Finch," Glenn ordered. "I'll see what else I can get here."

"Right."

The door clicked shut and Emma's resolve crumbled to the floor. A part of her was overjoyed that Jack was most likely still alive, but now Glenn was going to hunt him down.

Jack could end up right where she was.

Bile rose up her throat. Gagging, she tried to push Jack out of her head. It was no use. She couldn't get past the fact that she'd broken so easily under Glenn's whip. Still, she was sure he would have found out about Jack from her phone records without her help. It didn't matter that she had caved.

"I think I'm gonna puke," she croaked as Glenn walked around to face her. He was still holding the whip, but it was loose in his hands now.

"Don't you dare throw up on me. Tell me who Jack's father is and I'll stop the whipping. For now."

Lowering her eyes to the whip in his hands, Emma swallowed down the bile in her throat. Her back hurt so bad she felt like she might break in half. She was ashamed to admit she would do almost anything to keep Glenn from whipping her again. What kind of person did that make her? Then again, she was sure Glenn would find Jack's father no matter what happened next. She might as well put a stop to her physical pain.

"Craig," she said, choking back tears. "His name is Craig."

FOURTEEN

Emma stumbled away from Glenn as soon as he unhooked her wrists from the chain. She was still handcuffed, her fingers blue in the dim light. Her arms felt numb from the elbow down. Glenn approached her.

"Get away from me," she whispered, backing up until she reached a wall. Pain exploded across her back as torn flesh met cold concrete. She gasped.

"Calm down," Glenn ordered. "I'm going to take off the handcuffs."

Emma shivered as Glenn slipped a key from his suit coat pocket. He lifted her numb hands and inserted the key into one of the metal cuffs. A moment later her wrists were free. She shook out her arms and then quickly wrapped them around herself. Every movement sent shooting pain through her back, but she ignored it as best she could.

Glenn walked to the metal cabinet, opened the cabinet door, and set the handcuffs on a shelf. Then he pulled out a folded blanket.

"Come here," he ordered with a flick of his wrist. "Let me get this around you. You're shivering."

Why did he care if she was shivering? She didn't like the way he was acting, as if he was ignoring what he'd just put her through. She walked to him anyway, her teeth chattering as he shook out the blanket and set it gently over her shoulders. She winced as the soft material brushed up against her wounds, but she'd deal with the pain if it meant getting warm.

"There will be more questions," Glenn said as she stood in front of him and pulled the blanket closer. "But it's clear to me now what I need to do with you. I won't ever bring you in this room again unless you disobey me, understand?"

Emma sniffed and nodded. She desperately wanted to ask what he was going to do with her, but her instincts told her that was a bad idea. She shut her mouth and hung her head. She hated herself for divulging Jack's and Craig's names. She hated herself for everything that had happened in the past few hours. Her father would understand, wouldn't he? He had to. Glenn was too powerful for her to fight.

An intense sadness weighed down on her, a force she had to physically resist. Her knees wobbled and she reached out to steady herself against the wall. She looked up at Glenn. "I want to go home," she pleaded.

Glenn chuckled as he folded his arms. He looked so much like her father in that moment it made her squirm. "You *are* home, Emma."

She shook her head almost imperceptibly. She had to stand still or the blanket rubbed against her stinging back. "My apartment in Brooklyn. That's my home."

"Not anymore. This is your home now, whether you like it or not. And in case you weren't aware, you have a sister named Starry. She's a year older than you. She and I are your rightful family."

Surprise hit Emma square in the chest. *My sister is alive!* She took a step back. "Starry's *here?* I thought she might be dead."

Glenn smirked. "So you do know about her. I should have known Sam lied to me about that too."

Emma shook her head, irritated at his insinuation. "He never told me about her. I found out after he disappeared."

Glenn snorted. "Well, it doesn't matter now. What matters is that Starry is very much alive. You'll meet her soon." He smiled smugly, but there was uncertainty in his eyes.

Emma put a shaky hand to her forehead as the room started to spin. She felt herself falling, and Glenn rushed forward and pulled her into his arms. He smelled faintly of chlorine. "Let's get you to Pearce. He makes everyone feel better."

———⁓———

Dr. Pearce was nothing like Emma had imagined. She had thought he might be like Ian or the huge thug she had seen fighting Jack in the stairwell. Instead, he was thin and dainty. He wore wire-rimmed glasses and was dressed in a pair of slacks and a striped button-up shirt. His blond hair was combed neatly away from his face.

"This is her?" he asked, rushing up to Emma as Glenn led her into a mostly empty room. "She looks terrible. You said you were going to go easy on her."

Glenn let out a low growl as he nudged Emma farther into the room. The dark plush rug was soft and warm against her feet. It was the same reddish-brown as the heavy drapes covering the large window on the far wall. A desk sat near the window, empty except for an open laptop computer.

"I did go easy on her," Glenn said. "I let her keep her clothes on and her skin barely broke. But Ian gave her one too many doses and I think she was exhausted before he took her to begin with. You know what to do."

Pearce came up close to Emma and took one of her hands in his. His touch was gentle and warm. He looked sadly at her puffy wrist before lifting his eyes to Glenn. "Is there a change of clothes for her?"

"I'll have Anita bring some of Starry's. Don't restrain her. Just keep the door locked." He gave Emma a warning look. "She won't try to escape."

Emma swallowed a lump in her throat and looked away.

"Noted," Pearce said.

Glenn turned to leave. When he was gone, Pearce let Emma use the bathroom and then led her across the room to a door she hadn't noticed earlier.

She pulled back as much as she dared. "Where are we going?"

Pearce stopped and let go of her hand. "I need to treat your wounds." He smiled softly. "Glenn pays me to heal people, not hurt them. You're safe with me, I promise."

Searching his face, Emma wondered how much she could trust anyone on Glenn's payroll. But it wasn't like she had any choice. Pearce opened the door and Emma followed him through, surprised to find herself in what looked like a normal doctor's examination room. The lights were blindingly bright.

"Have a seat," Pearce said, motioning to an exam table to Emma's right. "Do you need help getting up?"

Emma hugged the blanket closer to her body and moved over to the table. She could hardly believe Glenn had been whipping her only a few minutes ago.

Now she was being treated like a hospital patient. Nothing made any sense. At least she didn't feel like she was in danger anymore—well, not immediate danger.

"I can do it," she said, stepping onto a little pull-out stool next to the table. The exam paper crinkled loudly as she sat down.

"Let's get you in a hospital gown so you're more comfortable," Pearce said as he pulled open a drawer in a cabinet across the room. He lifted a white gown from the drawer and turned around. "Would you like me to leave while you put it on or would you like some help? You must be hurting."

Emma stared at him like he was crazy. She didn't understand why he was so concerned about her comfort. Then again, she should probably accept his kindness without question.

"I–I don't know," she said, exhausted. A shiver ran through her body and her teeth chattered.

Pearce gave her a worried look as he stepped up to the table and set the gown beside her. "I'll help you," he said gently, pressing his palm against her forehead for a moment. "It'll be okay. Relax."

Slowly, he took the blanket away and helped her remove her torn, bloody shirt. He didn't touch her bra, despite the fact that the whip had sliced through the straps and it was now barely hanging on.

"Put this on and then you can remove that," Pearce said, nodding to her bra as he handed her the hospital gown. "Then lie down on your stomach so I can put something on your wounds."

Nodding, she did as he said. He leaned over to look at her back and muttered something unintelligible. A moment later, a knock on the door made Emma jump.

"Excuse me a moment," Pearce said and walked out of Emma's line of sight. The door opened and a woman started speaking in Spanish. Emma knew enough from her Spanish classes to catch the words "food" and "angel" and something Emma could only translate as, "angry bear."

"*Gracias*," Pearce answered, and closed the door. He came back to the table and smiled at Emma. "That was Anita. She brought you some clothes."

Emma lifted her eyes to a neatly folded stack of clothes in Pearce's hands. There was a black T-shirt on the top. Glenn had said they were Starry's clothes. Something about that thought made Emma's throat swell up. Where *was* her sister? Even more pressing was the question of where she'd been for the past eighteen years. With Glenn? That was a frightening prospect.

"Now, let's have a look at Glenn's handiwork," Pearce said as he set the clothes on a stool near the table. He leaned over to examine Emma's back again, hemming and hawing before clearing his throat. "These aren't so bad. He really did go easy on you. I'll get them cleaned and bandaged. I might put you on an IV too, okay? I think you're dehydrated, and you probably haven't eaten since Ian took you, am I right?"

Emma nodded. She didn't care about anything at this point. Her back stung. Her vision was going spotty. She stared down at the clothes on the chair, focusing hard as she realized something was printed on the black T-shirt. It took her a moment to understand what it said: "CAPS LOCK: Preventing Login Since 1980."

A laugh bubbled up in Emma's throat and Pearce leaned down to look at her, his eyebrows raised. "What's so funny?"

Emma pointed at the pile of clothes. She didn't know why she thought the T-shirt was so funny, but she couldn't stop herself from laughing.

Pearce studied the shirt and shook his head. "All of Starry's T-shirts say things like that."

Emma's laugh died in her throat. "Really? Is she a computer geek?" The thought made Emma irrationally hopeful. It was the first solid detail she'd learned about her sister.

Pearce turned around to the cabinet and pulled open a drawer. "That's putting it mildly." He opened a package and started dabbing something cool and soothing onto Emma's back. "Computers are Starry's life."

Emma kept her eyes on the shirt. "So where is she?" she asked, trying not to sound too eager. "When will I get to meet her?"

"No idea, but I hope she comes back soon. Glenn's been in a pissy mood ever since she left. All he talks about is how Finch can't do half of what Starry does."

Emma scrunched her brow in confusion "So Finch is doing Starry's job?"

Pearce hesitated before answering. "For now."

"Why is Starry working for my uncle?"

"As far as I know, Glenn isn't your uncle. He's your father. I suppose you've grown up thinking otherwise?"

Of course she had, but now Pearce was the third person to suggest Glenn was her father. She clenched her jaw as she thought about her mother's journal entries. They weren't a lie. "Sam is my real father," she whispered. "I *know* he is. And he's Starry's father too."

Pearce shrugged and continued working on Emma's back. "Maybe you're right, but I've learned not to ask too many questions around here."

Emma squeezed her eyes shut as she let everything sink in. If Starry thought Glenn was her real father, did that mean he had raised her? Emma couldn't imagine who else might have raised her. From what Emma had seen so far, Glenn was a horrible, evil man. If he had raised Starry, what was Starry like?

Emma opened her eyes and looked at the T-shirt again. It didn't seem so funny anymore.

FIFTEEN

A patch of afternoon sunlight slid across Starry's face. She rolled over to look at the clock, her growling stomach reminding her how messed up her sleep patterns had become lately.

Yawning, she lifted the covers and got out of bed. Rhys, asleep on his side, didn't even stir. Starry didn't know what time he had finally come to bed, but he had probably followed his usual routine and stayed awake until seven or eight. Starry figured it was too cruel to wake him up now no matter how badly she wanted to talk to him. They still hadn't resolved anything. He was a master at avoiding her, and it was starting to piss her off so much she was about ready to pack up and leave.

Balling her hands into fists, she took a deep breath and tried to push away the anxiety building in her chest. She hated Rhys for lying to her, but how could she continue hating him if he'd done it to protect her? Still, he needed to understand that nothing was more important to her than trust and loyalty. The syndicate was a world thick with secrets and lies and deceit, but those things could not be allowed to taint personal relationships. If Rhys couldn't understand that in the future, then Starry didn't know how she could stay with him. Either way, nothing could be resolved until he woke up.

Turning away from the bed, Starry walked into the bathroom and got in the shower. She was halfway through shampooing her hair when Rhys' phone started ringing. That was weird. He rarely got calls this time of day.

The ringtone stopped and then started up again. Sighing, Starry rinsed out her hair and got out of the shower. Rhys' phone was by the sink, its screen completely fogged up. She grabbed it and swiped away the condensation to see a name flashing across the screen. Mark Anderson, Rhys' new assistant. Didn't he know Rhys was usually asleep right now?

The ringtone ended and Starry set the phone back down. She wrapped a towel around herself and was getting a comb from a drawer when Rhys' phone beeped with a text message. The lock screen lit up with a portion of the message.

MARK: *Hey, man, I know you're sleeping, but you told me to call if that kid looking for Emma showed up again. He's watching the club from the parking lot across the street. What do you . . .*

Starry dropped the comb back into the drawer.

Kid looking for Emma?

Confusion ripped through her, followed quickly by a rush of anger. Why hadn't Rhys told her someone had come to the club looking for Emma? She understood he wanted to protect her, but this was going too far. Way too far.

Marching out of the bathroom, Starry looked at Rhys still asleep on the bed. She pushed down the sudden urge to punch him in the face and instead walked over to the window overlooking the empty parking lot across the street. Sure enough, there was a guy sitting on a concrete divider near a little grove of palm trees at the back of the lot, his eyes trained on the club's entrance. Black hair, tan skin. He looked like he might be eighteen or nineteen. He wasn't exactly scrawny, but he wasn't ripped either. He seemed quietly uninteresting and normal.

Starry kept her eyes on him, wondering why he was looking for Emma. How did he know her? And why look for her at the club? Was he connected to her father somehow?

Her stomach rumbled again and she looked down at it in irritation. She had far more important things to worry about than eating.

———⚬⚬⚬———

"I don't even know who Emma is," Mark sighed as Starry blocked him from exiting his office. "All Rhys told me was to let him know if anyone came around here looking for someone with that name. He was pissed I didn't tell him about the kid earlier, but how was I supposed to know?"

Mark was a tall man, but not even a little bit intimidating. He had uncombed brown hair and the beginnings of a mustache, like he'd been too lazy to shave that morning. Everything about him exuded a sense of mediocrity.

"Describe the conversation for me," Starry demanded. "You know what you talked about, at least."

Mark's shoulders slumped as he looked through the open doorway Starry was blocking. He turned back to his desk and sat down.

"It was last night. Some Asian kid. He insisted he had proof the club was connected to a girl named Emma. He showed me a picture of a package with the club's address on it, but it wasn't the club's name. It was for some antiques store instead."

Starry's eyes widened. She knew what was inside that package: fake antiques filled with thousands of dollars worth of drugs. It was one of the varied ways the syndicate sent merchandise to its runners throughout the US. Starry didn't have anything to do with the actual shipments, but she had been the one to set up the random list of real return addresses. If the package got lost, a real return address was less likely to arouse suspicion than a fake one. Even if the police found the drugs and came knocking on the strip club's door, Rhys and the other business owners whose addresses Starry used kept their establishments so squeaky clean and above-board that the cops would never find anything. They would simply claim someone had used the address as a fake. Which was true, in a way.

All of that meant the guy looking for Emma was intimately connected to the syndicate. She wasn't sure how that changed anything at the moment, but it certainly piqued her curiosity.

"I'm assuming this guy didn't give you his name?" she asked Mark as he started shuffling some papers on his desk.

He shook his head. "Rhys told me if he came around again that I should let him know immediately. So I did." Annoyance flashed across his face. "Not that he's responded. Why don't you go wake him up and tell him for me?"

"Oh, I'll do that," Starry said, rolling her eyes as she walked out of the office. She had deliberately left Rhys' phone in the bathroom so it wouldn't wake him up. She wanted to talk to the guy in the parking lot before he did.

Dressed in her jeans and one of Rhys' hoodies, she went out the back entrance and found a spot in the alleyway where she could see the parking lot. The boy was still sitting on a divider at the back of the lot. Perfect.

She waited for a break in traffic and crossed the street. The second the boy spotted her, he stood up, his jaw dropping as if he recognized her.

That almost made her stop in her tracks. How the hell did he know who she was?

Keeping her eyes on his, she crossed the parking lot and stopped in front of him. He looked her up and down, his jaw still slack. "A–are you Starry?"

She glared and folded her arms. "Depends on who's asking."

"I'm Jack." He stepped forward and stuck out his hand, but lowered it when Starry didn't offer hers in return. "I met Emma a few days ago." He looked hopefully into Starry's eyes. "But you can help me find her now. You—"

"How do you know who I am?" Starry interrupted. "How did you get a package from the club?"

Jack glanced at the club across the street and then pulled a phone from his pocket. A moment later he handed it over to Starry. She took it and stared down at the photo of the package Mark had described. Sure enough, it was the name of an antiques store she had contrived. It was addressed to a man named Sam Coleridge in Brooklyn, New York. It was probably the same Sam her father had been talking to over the phone.

"Flip to the next picture," Jack prompted.

Starry did as he said and saw a girl who looked eerily similar to herself. The girl's hair was straight and sandy blond instead of dark and curly, but they had the same nose and chin, same eyes, even a similar awkward half smile. It was something Starry had always hated about herself in pictures, but seeing it on this girl made it seem okay. Almost pretty, even.

Her hand trembled around the phone as she looked up at Jack. "This is Emma?"

He nodded. "It's from her phone. So was the picture of the package. I showed both of them to the man I talked to in the club yesterday. He said Emma looked like a girl who was dating his boss. Then he said your name and I knew I had to talk to you." He smiled. "There aren't many people named Starry, you know?"

Starry glared at the club. Stupid Mark. He hadn't told her *that* part of the conversation.

"Anyway," Jack continued as Starry returned his phone, "the guy got tired of me asking questions, so he kicked me out and told me not to come back."

"And you obviously didn't listen."

He shrugged. "I thought I might catch you if I waited out here long enough."

"Right." Starry tapped her foot against the pavement. Her mind was filling up with a thousand questions for Jack, but it was probably best if they didn't keep talking in plain sight of the club. "Come on," she said, jerking her head toward the sidewalk. "Let's talk somewhere more private."

Jack looked questioningly at the sidewalk and then back at the grove of palm trees behind him. "What's wrong with right here?"

"If my boyfriend sees me talking to you, we're both in deep shit. Let's go."

Nodding, Jack followed Starry out of the parking lot.

"So tell me what you think I can do to help you find Emma," she said as they walked down the sidewalk. "Because I don't know where she is either."

Jack pushed his hands into his pockets. "Right, he said you probably wouldn't."

"Who said I wouldn't?"

Jack gave her a quick glance and quickened his pace. "Nobody."

Lies. She was so damn sick of lies. If there were more people in on this, she was going to find out who they were and what they were up to. She turned and grabbed Jack's arms, twisting them both behind his back as she shoved him face-first against a chain-link fence along the sidewalk. The fence bulged as she threw her weight against Jack and put her lips up to his ear. "Listen," she hissed. "I want to know *everything* you know. I can beat the shit out of you if you refuse, got it?"

Jack winced against the fence. "Sure, yeah, but can you ease up? You're killing me here." He started coughing and Starry let him go, confused why a little shoving would hurt him so badly.

She looked him up and down. "What is wrong with you?"

Jack peeled himself away from the fence and put a hand to his chest. He was breathing hard, as if he'd just finished a marathon. "I think I have some cracked ribs or something," he gasped, bending forward as he wrapped his arms around his middle. "It happened the other night."

Starry cringed, her emotions switching between a twinge of guilt and a wave of suspicion. Nobody would go to all of this trouble to make her have pity on them, would they? His cough was genuine. His face was white as a sheet.

"Come on," she said. "Let's find a place to sit and then you can tell me everything. But don't you dare lie to me or I'll crack the rest of your ribs."

Jack looked at her, his eyes widening. "You're serious."

"Of course I am. Now move it."

He followed her without question, still wheezing when they reached an abandoned park. The swing set was broken and weeds were crawling over everything. Starry walked over to a bench between two palm trees and waited for Jack to sit down and catch his breath.

"Now," she said, standing in front of him, "first things first. How did you meet Emma? And where?"

Jack squeezed his hands into fists and looked up at her looming figure.

"I met her for the first time in a laundromat in Brooklyn on Saturday. She found my phone and gave it back to me, so I decided to help her out in return. We found her dad's friend murdered in his car and then she was kidnapped. That's how I cracked my ribs. I was trying to save her from the two men who took her." He lowered his eyes to his lap and shook his head. "I don't even know if she's still alive."

Starry's stomach sank to the ground. "Someone *took* her?" She thought about grabbing Jack by the collar, but realized hurting him wasn't going to solve anything.

He hadn't made one single move against her this whole time. "Who was it?"

"No idea. I think they would've killed me or taken me too if they'd had the chance, but the cops got there when I was fighting one of the guys. He pulled a gun and they shot him down. The second guy was already gone with Emma by the time they arrived." He looked up, his eyes filled with regret. "I'm sorry I couldn't save her. I tried."

Starry regarded him skeptically, unsure if his display of affection and regret was completely genuine. It seemed real, but then again, anybody could lie. Including Rhys.

Damn Rhys.

"Who were you talking about earlier?" she demanded.

Jack cringed and looked away. "I shouldn't have mentioned him. I shouldn't have—"

Starry leaned down and grabbed his shirt collar, squeezing and pulling until he was half standing. "Tell me right now or I'll start breaking bones."

He tried to push her away, but she grabbed one of his arms with her free hand and twisted until he cried out and sat back down.

"It's my dad," he said, rubbing his neck as Starry let him go and stepped away. "He doesn't even know I'm here. I'm supposed to be waiting in our hotel room, but I had to try to find Emma. I thought that package's address might lead me to her."

"But that's not why you came to LA, is it? What does your father want?"

Jack held his breath for a moment and then let it out. "He's after a man named Glenn Ramsay. I have a feeling you know who that is."

Starry leaned down to look Jack in the eyes. "Glenn is my father. Why would your dad think he can go after him?"

Jack leaned away from her. "We flew out here early yesterday morning to meet with a man who says he can get to Glenn. Don't ask me who that is because I have no idea. My dad won't tell me. He wanted me to stay in New York, but I refused to let him leave without me." He narrowed his eyes and leaned forward. "Wait, Glenn can't be your dad."

Starry rolled her eyes. "Yes, he can, and he's Emma's dad too. She just doesn't know it yet." Jack gave her a curious look, but before he could say anything, Starry leaned forward and got in his face again. "Tell your dad there's no way he's getting to my dad, no matter who he knows. Do you have any idea who he is? What he does?"

Jack couldn't lean back any farther. "Yes, I do. My dad told me that much, at least. He said Glenn's some big drug lord who runs the whole damn city. He said he might even have Emma, but if that was true, we wouldn't be having this conversation."

Starry stood up straight. It had crossed her mind that her dad might have Emma, but she had pushed the crazy suspicion away because the phone call she'd overheard made it sound like her father didn't want Emma in the same country as Starry, let alone the same city. So why did hearing the idea from another person's mouth change everything? Her father could get Emma if he wanted. Starry had no doubt about that.

But he wouldn't . . . would he?

A chill squeezed her spine as she considered the possibility that maybe he would kill Emma before they ever met each other. But even the infamous Glenn Ramsay wasn't that evil. He wouldn't kill his own blood.

Or maybe he would.

Fear bit into Starry's heart and she flared her nostrils and sucked in a huge breath of warm air. It was obvious now that she was going to have to face her dad soon. She'd be lying to herself if she didn't admit the prospect frightened her. He had hit her once and she wasn't entirely certain he wouldn't do it again—or something worse. She could handle being physically hurt, of course, but being hurt by *him* in any way cut her deeper than she wanted to admit. Either way, she had to confront him and uncover the truth.

"Listen," she said to Jack, "I've gotta leave. Tell me your dad's name and I might not kick your ass if I see you again."

Jack shook his head, his eyes so wide they looked like they might fall out of their sockets. "I shouldn't have told you about him. You're gonna find him and hurt him, aren't you?"

"If he goes after me or my dad, then yes, he's dead. And I'm pretty sure my father will make sure you watch him die. Lots of people want my dad dead, but they're not stupid enough to act on it. If your dad knows what's good for him, he'll stay the hell away from us, understand?"

Jack's eyes got bigger. "Yeah, that makes sense, but I think there's something you should know before you leave. It's about Glenn."

She glared down at him. "What is it?"

Jack dug into his pocket and pulled out his phone again. He navigated to another picture and handed the phone to her. "These are a bunch of pictures that were on Emma's phone. I forwarded them to my phone when I found them. I think you should know the truth."

Starry stared down at the picture, confused. It was a photo of what looked like a journal entry. "What is this?" she asked.

"Just read it. There's more, so keep scrolling over when you're finished with that one."

Starry read, her stomach sinking lower and lower with every passing minute. Her hand trembled around Jack's phone so violently it almost slipped from her fingers. She caught it just in time.

Had her father lied about who he was?

Because it seemed as if Lucy's husband and the father of her children was Sam, not Glenn. And if that was true, then Sam was Starry's real father—her birth father.

But that couldn't be right.

With ice-cold fingers, Starry sent the photos of the entries to her own phone.

"Wasn't what you were expecting, was it?" Jack asked.

She shook her head as the photos finished sending. How could Glenn Ramsay *not* be her father? There were pictures of her with him from when she was an infant. It made no sense.

"If this is true," she said, her shock morphing into anger, "I'm going to kill him. I'm going to slit his damn throat."

She tossed Jack's phone into his lap and stepped away from the bench. She was trembling from head to foot, her skin cold despite the warm breeze rustling the palm tree fronds above.

If her father had lied to her about this, that meant her entire life was one huge lie. It was a slap in the face, and she wasn't sure how to respond. Should she find him and threaten him? Go crying to him and ask him why he'd done this to her? Make him feel guilty as hell? Make him apologize and explain everything? Or simply keep running from him and find the truth herself?

If Sam was her birth father, did that mean her last name was supposed to be Coleridge and not Ramsay? She wondered why they had different last names if they were brothers. Then again, it wouldn't surprise her if her father had changed his name a long time ago.

"Starry?" Jack said, still sitting on the bench as he rested his palms on his knees and looked up at her. "Don't you think it's better this way? It's better to know the truth. I keep trying to tell my dad I need to know the truth, but he won't tell me anything, and I hate it. *Anything* is better than lies. Right?"

"Sure doesn't feel that way right now. What am I supposed to do with this?"

Still trembling, she turned and walked away, her feet pounding the sidewalk leading out of the park.

"Starry, wait!"

She ignored him and broke into a run.

SIXTEEN

"Ow!" Emma cried out as Pearce pricked a needle into her arm.

"I'm so sorry." Pearce pulled out the needle and moved closer to the bed on his short rolling stool. "I've never had this much trouble with an IV before. It's probably because you're so dehydrated. Let me try again." He adjusted his glasses with his free hand and leaned closer to the crook of Emma's elbow.

Emma gritted her teeth and looked away. Her back still ached, but it was better now that Pearce had bandaged up the wounds. He had also helped her put on Starry's borrowed clothes. They fit perfectly.

"Try and relax," Pearce said as he leaned closer to her arm.

She took a deep breath and let it out slowly. She was in a small bedroom next to the examination room. It was empty except for the twin-sized bed where she was sitting, a nightstand with a lamp, and a small desk near the window. The heavy drapes were pulled open far enough to let in a steady stream of sunlight. Emma could see a few palm trees and some blue sky.

She had no idea what time it was, but on a normal day she would probably be sitting in a classroom or her apartment, worrying about things like when her next assignment was due and what she was going to make for dinner, not how she was going to survive as a captive in her terrifying uncle's home.

"Almost there," Pearce said. His latex-gloved hands were warm on Emma's skin.

Emma took another deep breath, wondering how much longer this was going to take. She understood she was dehydrated and the IV would help her feel a million times better, but the last thing she wanted was a needle stuck into her body.

"There." Pearce sat up straight. He grabbed a short, clear tube and snapped it into the piece now sticking out of Emma's vein. "Let me get this taped down and then I'll hook you up to the IV bag, okay?"

Emma nodded, grateful for Pearce's concern and care. He finished taping down the tubes and left the room, coming back a few minutes later with the rest of the IV supplies. "Feel free to lie down," he said as he rolled an IV stand over to the bed. "Unless that hurts too much. How is it feeling?"

"Lots better, thanks." She swung her feet up onto the mattress and looked nervously at the pillows stacked at the head of the bed. Even though she was dressed and the wounds were bandaged, the thought of putting any pressure on her back made her wince. She looked up at Pearce. "Can I be on my stomach?"

"Sure, let me help you." Once Emma was on her stomach, he hooked up some more tubing and started the drip. "Keep your arm turned like this and you'll be fine," he said, gently angling Emma's arm the way he wanted it.

She nodded and looked up at him. "Can I ask you something?"

"Sure."

"Do you know what Glenn is going to do with me?"

Pearce's hands paused in the middle of adjusting the IV bag on the stand. He looked down at her and smiled sadly. "Are you worried he's going to hurt you again?"

Emma cringed as she remembered Glenn's whip slicing across her back. "I guess so, but it's more than that. Is he going to let me go?"

Pearce finished adjusting the IV bag and crouched down so he could look Emma in the eyes. There was so much tenderness in his gaze that Emma wondered how someone like him could work for someone like Glenn.

"I think you should understand something," he said gently as he put a hand over hers. He was still wearing his latex gloves. "I don't know what kind of man raised you or what you've been through, but I have a feeling you don't know what Glenn does for a living, do you?"

Fear trickled into her heart. She didn't know why she was so scared to hear what Pearce was about to say, but her eyes stung with tears. She shook her head. "Something with a drug syndicate?"

Patting her hand, he leaned closer. "Yes, Glenn runs a very powerful drug syndicate. The largest in the US. It's his life and he'll do anything to protect it. That includes hurting people, even family." He paused and looked down at his hand on top of hers. "As far as I know, you're his daughter, Emma. That means he's going to do everything in his power to make you loyal to him and the syndicate."

"What does that mean?"

Pearce lifted his eyes to hers, unblinking. "It means if you do anything to defy him, you'll pay for it. Although I don't understand why you wouldn't want what he has to offer you. You'll be at the top, right alongside your sister. You'll have everything."

Emma didn't know exactly what he meant, but she didn't miss the envy in his voice. "Does making me loyal include torturing me? Does he torture Starry too?"

Pearce let out a surprised grunt. "No, he's never tortured Starry."

Emma nodded, glad to hear her sister hadn't ever been on the receiving end of Glenn's whip.

"But you're new to all of this," Pearce continued. "Do you doubt Glenn's power over you now that you've had a taste of what he's capable of?"

The torture room flashed through Emma's memory, making her heart pound and a few tears break free. "I guess not."

"And that was a very, very small taste," Pearce said, squeezing her hand. "He might not ask me to treat you if he ever tortures you again. He might let you stay in there for days until you wish you were dead. He might decide to do something far more damaging than strike you a few times with a whip. Do you understand?"

Emma met Pearce's gaze and realized he was not as simple as she'd first thought. He was kind and tender, but she couldn't forget who he worked for and where he most likely placed his own loyalties. There was a warning in his eyes now, however gentle it might seem, and Emma's fear returned.

"I understand," she whispered.

"That's good." He stood up. "Try to get some rest. I'll be in and out to check on you."

As soon as he was gone, Emma turned onto her side and curled into a ball even though it made her wounds stretch and burn like mad. She tried to dredge up whatever courage she had left. She was stuck here and there was nowhere else to go. Her father was dead now and she had nobody . . . except for maybe Jack, and he was somewhere she couldn't reach.

Closing her eyes, she thought about her own bed in her own house. The way things were going, she would never see those things again, never cook dinner for her father again, never graduate high school and go to college. She couldn't imagine what was in store for her, but she doubted it was anything good. None of it would be what her father had wanted for her. This was what he had tried to shelter her from in the first place.

"I don't know what's right, Dad," she whispered out loud. "*You* didn't choose the right things."

A cloud shifted over the sun and darkened the room, making Emma shiver. She snuggled deeper into the mattress and wondered what she would have done if she'd discovered her father's drug dealing under less fatal circumstances. She might have turned him in, but she had no idea if that would have been the right thing to do. Was family and loyalty more important than morality and the law? She thought about Jack and how he hadn't turned his father in. Instead, he'd sacrificed all of his own plans and dreams to help him get out of the hole he'd dug himself into. Maybe that was what had happened to her father. Maybe he'd simply gone so deep he couldn't get out. Maybe Glenn had been controlling him.

But where did that leave her?

The room brightened again and she opened her eyes, wondering if her father had known Glenn might try to take her away from him one day. Maybe that was why he'd seemed so intense when he'd made her promise to always stick by what she knew was right. If that was the case, doing what was right probably meant he'd want her to stand up to Glenn . . . and she had no idea if that was even possible.

A loud bang startled Emma awake. Her heart pounding, she pushed herself upright on the bed and looked around. The room was empty and silent and filled with golden light. The sun was lower in the sky now, its rays slanting through the palm tree fronds outside the window. Had she really heard a bang? Maybe she had dreamed it.

Rubbing the sleep from her eyes, she felt a dull, throbbing pain in her arm and looked down to see blood steadily oozing from where her IV had been inserted. It had ripped out at some point, probably when she'd sat up so fast. Whoops. She searched around for the connector and found it on the floor with all the rest of the tubing. The IV bag was empty, so she figured it didn't matter now.

Still, the blood coming out of her arm didn't seem to be slowing. She looked around for something to press against the wound, but the only thing she could find was a pillowcase. It would have to do. She slipped it off the pillow and balled it up before pressing it against the inside of her arm. The wound ached and throbbed, but it was nothing compared to the pain she'd felt earlier in the torture room.

Bang!

Emma jerked in surprise, almost falling off the bed. She scrambled to her feet and tried to calm herself down. She had definitely not dreamed that bang. It sounded like a gunshot. Her heart pounded. Were gunshots normal in a house like this? She looked up at the door, surprised to see a note taped to it. She walked over to read it.

> *Emma, I'm going home for the night. If you're reading this, your IV is probably already finished. Anita will come in before she leaves for the night to remove it for you. I'll see you in the morning.*
>
> *—Pearce*

Emma's heart pounded. It was nice of Pearce to leave her a note, but he felt like her only safety net, and now he was gone. Between that and the sound of the gunshot, she felt claustrophobic. She tried the handle on the door. It turned and she stepped into Pearce's office. The drapes were closed. The air was cooler in here.

She took a deep breath and kept the pillowcase pressed against her arm as she looked around the room. The only piece of furniture was a desk between the windows, but the laptop was no longer there. The exam room door was closed, locked by a keypad on the wall lit up in red. The bathroom door was open. Emma headed straight for it, but stopped when something thudded against the office door.

"Traitor!" a deep voice growled, muffled through the door. It was Glenn, and the cold fury in his tone made Emma tremble. "You've made your last mistake, Chavez. I'm going to destroy everything you love."

Emma heard laughter, weak and bitter. "You already have, you bastard."

Bang!

This time it was so loud it made Emma drop the pillowcase and cover her ears. She crouched down close to the floor, her heart racing.

Bang!

The shot was followed by a thud on the floor and receding footsteps. Then indistinct shouting and more shots farther away. Then silence.

Emma stood up, her legs shaking. She turned in a circle. There was another thud against the door and she backed away toward the bathroom, her hands out

217

in front of her. What if Glenn came for her again? What if he was angry that she wasn't on the bed where Pearce had left her?

She turned toward the bedroom just as the office door swung wide open. A suited man with a bleeding gash down the side of his face burst into the room. Spotting her, he headed straight for her.

A little cry of surprise escaping her mouth, she ran into the bathroom and tried to close the door, but the man was too fast. He was inside the bathroom and had her in a choke hold from behind before she even knew what was happening. His breath was hot against the side of her face.

"Calm down, I'm here to help you. Let's get out of here, okay?"

Her knees wobbled. She had no idea who this man was. Was she supposed to believe he was here to save her? Not that she had much choice. He released her from the choke hold and grabbed her hand. She ran with him out of the bathroom and through the office, nearly tripping over a body in the hallway. It wasn't Glenn.

Her rescuer kept a tight hold of her hand. He looked behind his shoulder at her, but didn't say anything. Lamps in the hallway had been knocked to the floor. A mirror was broken. Emma dodged some glass, not wanting to cut her bare feet.

And then there were footsteps behind her.

Whipping her head around, she caught sight of another suited man running after them, but he was slow, almost hesitant. He looked disoriented. "Andrews, stop!" he yelled before glancing behind his shoulder at the open doorway from which he'd come.

Andrews doubled his speed and Emma fought to keep up with him. They burst out the front door and ran down a few steps and a curved walkway before they reached two dark sedans parked next to each other. Andrews let go of Emma's hand and shoved her toward one of the cars. "It's open. Get in."

Emma hesitated, wondering if she was jumping out of the fire and into the frying pan.

"Now!" Andrews yelled, already on the other side of the car. He yanked open his door and slipped inside.

Emma looked behind her just as the other man from the hallway burst out onto the porch, his eyes immediately catching her. She fumbled with the front passenger door, managed to get it open, and slipped inside before the man had even cleared the walkway. Andrews had already started the engine and put it in reverse. The car squealed backward down the driveway and out the open wrought iron gates as the other man stopped, his expression murderous. He glanced back at the house.

"He's too worried about Glenn to follow us," Andrews laughed nastily as he reached the street and whipped the wheel around to straighten the car. The sudden movement forced Emma to lean back against the seat and she cried out in pain at the pressure on her wounds. "I hope that bastard bleeds to death," Andrews said. "But if he doesn't, Craig's men will finish him off."

"How do you know Craig?" Emma gasped, assuming he was talking about the same Craig she knew.

He gave her an annoyed look. "He's the one running this whole operation." He shook his head. "Not that it's any of your damn business."

Emma reached for her seatbelt as Andrews jerked around another corner. He was driving like a maniac and the last thing she wanted was to die in a wreck when she'd just managed to escape. She'd have to deal with the pain of leaning against the back of the seat.

She looked down where the IV had ripped out of her arm. The wound was still bleeding, but not nearly as much. "Where are we going?" she asked as she clicked her seatbelt in place and put a shaky hand over the inside of her elbow.

"I'm taking you to Craig. He's waiting for me, but I need you to call him on my phone." Andrews gripped the steering wheel with one hand, smearing blood across the leather, and dug into his suit coat pocket with the other. "Tell him I found out Glenn was keeping you at the house when I was there. Tell him he owes me more money if he wants me to hand you over."

Emma's eyes widened. Maybe it hadn't been a good idea to leave the house with this man . . .

"Do it!" Andrews yelled, holding his phone out to her.

Breaking into a sweat, Emma let go of her elbow and wiped her bloody hand on Starry's jeans before taking Andrews' phone. "It's asking for a fingerprint. How do I—"

Andrews grabbed the phone from her with his clean hand and pressed his thumb against the screen. It lit up green and unlocked the screen before he handed it back. Emma found Craig's number and put the phone to her ear.

"Andrews?" Craig's voice spoke through the phone.

"It's Emma. Andrews is driving."

There was a short gasp. "*Emma?* You were in New York. How . . ."

She repeated what Andrews had told her to say and Craig sighed with relief. "I'm so glad you're okay. Can you put the phone on speaker?"

"I think so." She lowered the phone and pushed the speaker key. "Okay," she said, glancing nervously at Andrews as she set the phone on her thigh. "Go ahead."

"What happened, Andrews?" Craig asked. "Is the job finished? How did you find Emma?"

Andrews glanced down at the phone. "Glenn filled us in on everything before we made our move. He mentioned he had Emma at the house. Flew her here yesterday morning. Sam too. So I figured I'd rescue Emma as a bonus once we took care of Glenn. You *do* want her, right?"

"Of course, and yes, I'll pay you extra. But what about Sam? I thought for sure he'd been killed in New York."

"Nope, Glenn killed him yesterday. Can you believe Sam held out to the very end? Never told Glenn about me and Chavez, or you, apparently." He grunted. "Anyway, I want my money before I hand Emma over. And to answer your question, no, the job isn't finished. I shot Glenn, but the bullet didn't kill him. He's injured, though. That's better than nothing. The backup team should be able to take him out."

"Where is Chavez? And why the hell did you wait to call in the backup team until two minutes ago? If things weren't going as planned, you should have called them in earlier."

Andrews scowled at the phone. "Things *were* going as planned. The house was practically empty. Only the guards and two housekeepers. None of them were expecting us to turn on them, so it was easy as pie to get in and bring 'em all down. We did it so quiet, Glenn didn't suspect a thing. But then Rhys showed up, almost like he expected something to be wrong.

Bastard knows how to fight too. I couldn't even take him out. Now Chavez is dead. Glenn killed him."

Craig swore again. "Who is Rhys?"

"One of Glenn's underlings. Nobody important. Or, at least, I thought he wasn't until today. I still don't know why he showed up right then. Maybe someone tipped him off."

"Okay, okay. We can sort everything out when you get here. Emma, you're okay, right? Jack's been worried sick."

Jack! Emma jerked forward in her seat and lifted the phone up to her ear. "He's with you? Is he okay?"

There was a pause and some shuffling. Emma turned off the speaker phone.

"Emma?" Jack said. "Please tell me that asshole hasn't hurt you."

Emma didn't know which asshole he was talking about. All she cared about was how sweet Jack's voice sounded. She gripped the edge of her seat with her free hand. "Jack," she whimpered, tears stinging her eyes. "I thought they were going to kill you."

"They cracked my ribs, but they didn't kill me. Are *you* okay?"

"I-I'm a little injured, but I'm all right. How did you get away?"

"Injured? How much?"

"A few cuts on my back, but I'm fine, I promise. What about you?"

Jack cleared his throat. "I called the police when I found the dead cop in his car outside your complex. They showed up right after that other guy got away with you, and shot the guy I was fighting." His breathing sounded labored. "Anyway, Dad's telling me we should get off the phone now. Tell Andrews to hurry and bring you here safely or he won't get paid."

"I'll tell him. Goodbye, Jack." She hung up the phone and glanced at Andrews. There were scars on his hands. The smooth, powerful way he moved made Emma shift closer to the door. "He said you should get me back there safely or you won't get paid," she said.

Andrews took the phone from her and gave her a sly glance. "Don't you worry, love. You're worth too much money for me to hurt you."

SEVENTEEN

Starry crumpled up her trash and tossed it onto the passenger seat of her car. Groaning, she put a hand to her stomach and stared at the fast food restaurant where she'd been parked for the past hour. Maybe eating two cheeseburgers and half a sack of French fries hadn't been such a good idea. Now she felt sick.

But she hadn't eaten all day and she needed some sort of strength to gather her courage.

She finally felt ready to face her father.

Maybe.

Groaning again, she squeezed her eyes shut and fought off angry tears. Her worries came crashing back down on her, popping up in her head one after the other so fast she could hardly grasp any of them. She couldn't make sense of what she had read in the journal entries Jack had shown her, and it made her want to squeeze the life out of everything in sight.

But maybe none of it was real. Maybe Sam or someone else had forged those journal entries for some reason. But why?

She would find out. She would face her father and make him tell her the truth, and when that was done, she would decide what to do.

Her heart sank a second later. If he'd lied to her for her whole life, then nothing would stop him from lying again. She might not be able to tell the lies from the truth, but she knew for a fact how much he cared about her. He couldn't possibly have faked *that* her whole life. She also knew for certain that she loved him and always would, no matter how bad things got. That was what made his lies hurt so damn much. That was what had made her drive to the closest fast food joint instead of straight back home to face him.

She had to de-stress and get a grip somehow. Eating obviously hadn't helped.

"*Just go,*" she hissed to herself. "You're strong. Show him you're strong. Stop putting it off."

A few minutes later she was on the road to her house, the late afternoon sun bright in her eyes. Stopping at the front gate, she reached up to punch in the code and realized the huge wrought iron doors were already hanging open. That was odd. Her father's security guys always made sure the gate stayed closed and locked.

Backing up, she parked her car on the street and got out. She walked through the open gate and swept her gaze across the front of the house, peering into the lengthening shadows for anything else amiss. Nothing looked wrong. Yet. She reached into her back pocket and pulled out the knife she always carried with her. Flipping it open, she kept to the shadows as she approached the house, her heart pounding with a small burst of unexpected fear. She knew the fear came from feeling caught off guard, and she pushed it away as she passed the front fountain, alert for any vehicles she didn't recognize. There was only one car in the driveway: a dark gray Audi with a license plate that read STRIPIT.

Rhys.

Her feet stilled, her apprehension returning. Shouldn't he still be asleep? She looked at her watch. It was a quarter to five. Okay, so he could have woken up a little early, but how did he know which house her father was using right now? He was high up on her father's list of trusted men, but he had never been part of the inner circle as far as she was aware.

She moved up the walk and entered the front door security code. The entryway was silent. Her tennis shoes made no sound on the floor as she shut the door and made her way into the sitting room. Nothing.

Nobody. Where were the guards and the afternoon staff?

Stopping in her tracks, she held her breath and listened. Something was very wrong. She could sense it in the too-quiet atmosphere, like a scream waiting to be released.

Then she heard it. A muffled cry. Then there was a thump, as if something had fallen onto the floor. She rushed down the hallway toward the sounds, freezing in place when she caught a glimpse of a man-shaped lump near one of the sofas in a secondary sitting room. Her throat closed up. The man looked as if he'd been kneeling down and then fallen over.

Starry moved toward him, her knife at the ready. He was about the same build as her father.

No, no, no. It can't be him.

She breathed a sigh of relief as she caught sight of the man's face. He was one of her father's security guards, his head twisted at an unnatural angle.

Her heart pounded. Perhaps *all* of the guards had been killed. It seemed the only likely explanation for the emptiness of the house.

Sweeping her eyes across the room, she saw another lump over by the window and moved toward it. It was Anita, one of their most trusted housekeepers, also with a broken neck.

Straightening, Starry put a hand to her forehead, her confusion and curiosity almost overwhelming. She left the room, keeping a sharp lookout for any movements or sounds. Whoever had made the sound earlier was now deathly silent. She didn't like that. She didn't like any of this. She felt unprepared, uncertain, and far too naked without a decent weapon.

Making her way to the weapons room farther down the hall, she punched in the code and noted that it didn't appear as if anyone had been inside recently. She pocketed her knife, loaded two pistols, strapped on a double shoulder holster, and stuffed some extra loaded clips into one of the holster pockets. She kept hold of one pistol and left the room as quietly as she had entered.

Whoever was in the house was going to have to deal with her, and if that person was Rhys, she would face him head-on and find out what the hell was happening.

She started in the direction of her father's office where she thought the thump had come from earlier. She didn't get far. She jerked to a halt when Rhys rounded the corner, a man slung over his shoulder.

Starry snapped her gun into position. The man over Rhys' shoulder was her father, bleeding and possibly unconscious.

Rhys' eyes went as wide as quarters. "Starry!" he gasped, his knees buckling as he stumbled to a halt. Starry caught a glimpse of her father's face. It was dangerously pale. He was breathing, but his eyes were rolled back in his head. Starry's heart sank to the ground. She had never seen her father so helpless.

"What did you do to him?" she demanded, aiming her gun between Rhys' eyes. She didn't want to have to shoot him. Despite hundreds of hours at the shooting range and training with her father, she had never shot anyone in her life, let alone someone she had been sleeping with. But if Rhys had hurt her father she would blow his head off.

Rhys' eyes narrowed at her question and a look of pure confusion washed over his face. "I didn't do anything to him, Star. I'm helping him. We have to get out of here before anyone else shows up. Andrews already took off with Emma, but I'm pretty sure it's your dad he was after."

At the mention of Emma, Starry's finger trembled against the trigger. "Emma? So my dad *did* have her? How long has she been here? And how long have you known?"

Rhys rolled his eyes and took a bold step forward. "There's no time for this. I'll explain later, but for now—"

Starry re-aimed her gun. "Tell me why you're here." She stepped back as Rhys moved forward. "How did you know about this house?"

Rhys grimaced as he looked down the barrel of the gun. "It's such a long story, and I'd love to tell it to you, but I . . ." He gave her a desperate, pleading look.

"I have to get your dad out of here. He was shot in the shoulder and it won't stop bleeding. We've got to get him to a doctor. Fast."

Starry lowered her gun. The facts before her were irrefutable. Her father was unconscious and possibly dying from blood loss and she wasn't about to waste precious seconds trying to figure out what was going on.

Letting out a sigh, she tucked her gun into the holster and straightened her shoulders. "Get him to the garage and keep pressure on the wound. I'll grab a med kit."

Rhys nodded and took off down the hallway as fast as he could. Starry went in the opposite direction, her hands shaking as she rushed downstairs where they kept the emergency medical supplies. A small, frightened whimper left her throat as she whipped open a cabinet door and searched for a decent med kit. Why the hell was she frightened? Was she afraid to lose her father even after all of the lies he'd told her?

Yes, yes, of course she was, more than she wanted to admit. She hated his lies, his possible betrayal, the very idea that he might not even *be* her father. At the same time, she couldn't bear the thought of losing him like this.

Tucking a kit under her arm, she raced back up the stairs and met Rhys in the hallway. His gray dress shirt was blood-soaked from his right shoulder all the way down the front of his chest. Her father's blood.

"Time to go," he said. "I heard someone outside the garage as I was putting your father in the SUV. They must be surrounding the house or looking for a way in."

Starry stopped in her tracks, her thoughts tangling into a knot. Every inch of her didn't trust Rhys. There were too many unanswered questions. She'd have to look past all of that, though, because she needed his help to make her father safe.

"Let's get out of here before they make it inside," she ordered. She motioned for Rhys to take the lead so she could keep an eye on him. Her father's SUV was an armored vehicle, so making it out of the garage and past anyone surrounding the house, armed or not, wasn't an issue. Rhys was an issue. And her father. If the two of them were in on something together, that entailed a whole slew of betrayal she couldn't even begin to sort through.

Rhys glanced over his shoulder as they crossed the living room. "Listen, Starry, there's something I need to—"

But he was interrupted by three men bursting around the corner. The first man aimed his rifle at Rhys, but Rhys rammed into him and they both crashed to the floor. Starry dropped the med kit and whipped out one of her pistols, her heart hammering in her throat as she aimed at the second man turning

232

toward her, his rifle at the ready. She pulled her trigger before he could pull his. Her bullet hit him square in the chest. She put another bullet in his heart and he collapsed to the ground near her feet.

A strange sensation flowed through Starry, sweet and powerful.

Then something hard punched into her—the third attacker. She flew backward into an end table, a sharp corner digging into her hip before she hit the floor and then rolled onto her side. She jumped to her feet just as another blow slammed into the side of her head. *Son of a bitch!*

Her vision spinning, she crouched into attack position and swiped an arm against the back of the man's knees, bringing him halfway to the ground. Before she could raise her gun and shoot him too, Rhys was behind him and emptying two rounds into his head. He crumpled the rest of the way to the floor.

Starry looked to the other end of the room where the first attacker lay on the floor, his head turned at an angle that could only be achieved with a broken neck.

So Rhys was apparently a serious badass when it came to killing people. Were all of her father's money launderers trained killers?

"What the hell?" she gasped at Rhys, looking from one dead man to another.

Rhys wiped a sheen of sweat from his brow as he lowered the gun he'd taken off the man he'd killed.

"I'll tell you everything, but right now we have to leave. There could be more of them outside."

Starry looked at the three dead men and heaved a sigh. She didn't recognize a single one of them. "Yeah, yeah, yeah." She found the med kit on the floor, scooped it into her arms, and followed Rhys out of the room.

"I'm glad you're okay," Rhys said over his shoulder as he opened the door leading out to the garage. "Really, Starry, if anything happened to you . . ."

Starry gave him a dirty look as she stepped up to the SUV and yanked open the passenger door. Rhys had laid her father across the back seat, and from what Starry could see his shoulder was still bleeding. She had to stop the blood flow immediately.

"If anything happened to me, then what?" she snapped as she climbed into the car and squeezed into the back with her father. She pressed her hands firmly against the bullet wound, blood smearing across her skin. "You'd die of a broken heart? You *lied* to me, Rhys. You've been lying to me for who knows how long. And so has he!" She jerked her head toward her father. "I sure as hell hope it's for a good reason, because if it isn't, I swear I'll kill both of you."

The softness in Rhys' eyes hardened into disappointment just before he slammed the door shut.

EIGHTEEN

Starry folded a long strip of gauze and used it to keep direct pressure on her father's wound, but it was clear the bleeding wasn't going to stop. She leaned down to get a better look. The wound looked savagely deep. They had to get him to Pearce soon.

"Go as fast as you can," she said to Rhys as she stripped off her shoulder holster and set it and both pistols on the floor of the car. The guns were heavy and in the way. "Pearce lives over on—"

"I know where he lives. It's only a few minutes away from here." Rhys cleared his throat as he smoothly switched lanes. "I sure as hell hope we can trust him, Star." He kept glancing in the rearview mirror, but Starry doubted he could see much.

"Why wouldn't we trust him? He's been with the syndicate from the beginning."

Rhys snorted. "Andrews and Chavez have been with your father most of their lives, too, but that didn't stop them from trying to kill him today."

Starry froze as Rhys' words hit her. She stared down at her hands now covered in her father's blood. "That's right, you said Andrews was the one at the house." She gritted her teeth and leaned harder on her father's shoulder. This was all her fault. She was the one who had kept Andrews and Chavez's impending betrayal a secret from her father. "Well, in that case," she said, "maybe we shouldn't go to Pearce. Andrews and Chavez would know he's the first man we'd run to if someone's hurt."

"And again, maybe we can't trust Pearce. Your father thinks someone hired Andrews and Chavez to kill him. If that's true, then we shouldn't trust anyone."

Starry squeezed her eyes shut. Who would hire Andrews and Chavez? From what she had found, they were working alone and didn't have any desire to actually hurt her father. They just wanted more money, maybe. Or more power. No, she had to focus on the immediate problem.

"We can trust Pearce," she declared firmly. "He helped raise me. He's practically family. Plus, he's at the very top of my dad's payroll. There's no way he would betray the syndicate." She opened her eyes and glared at the back of Rhys' head. "So get him on the phone and find out if there's somewhere we can meet him where Andrews and Chavez or whoever the hell is trying to kill us won't be able to find us."

"Give me a sec, then." Rhys picked up his cell phone.

Starry watched him closely, surprised he had Pearce's number in his phone at all. Something was very off. She moved her gaze out the window and watched the sun sinking lower in the sky.

"And by the way," Rhys said as he waited for Pearce to pick up. "Chavez is dead. Your dad killed him during the fight."

"Okay, fine, but why would either he or Andrews or whoever hired them want Emma? Is that what they were after?"

"I already told you they were after your father, not Emma. She was an afterthought," Rhys sighed, and then turned his attention to his phone. "Pearce, we've got an emergency."

As Starry listened to Rhys and Pearce figure out where to meet, her mind ran in circles. So her father really had taken Emma. The question was what was he planning on doing with her?

"Okay," Rhys said, ending his call. "Pearce checked his own security and hasn't seen anything fishy around his place, but he agrees we should meet somewhere else. One of his assistants lives ten minutes away from here. Pearce will probably beat us there, depending on traffic."

"Which assistant?"

"Last name Blaire or something like that."

"That's his nephew. He's fine." Starry looked down at her father. His lips were so pale they were practically colorless. She leaned forward and spoke in his ear. "Come on, Dad, you can pull through. Hang in there for a few more minutes, okay?" A moment later, she looked back up at Rhys. "So how much do you know about Emma being at the house?"

"Your father had her flown here from New York yesterday morning."

Starry glared at him. "So you've known everything that's been going on with her?"

Rhys winced. "Kind of. It all happened so fast, Starry. I knew he was planning on bringing her here, but I didn't know he actually had her until I showed up at the house and he mentioned her before he passed out. I'm sorry. Your father knew you were staying with me. I had to give him regular reports. It was his way of keeping an eye on you until you calmed down."

Shock hit her in the gut. Her hands started shaking. "Regular reports? You told him *everything*?" She shuddered at the thought of Rhys spying on her, lying to her, sleeping with her . . . all for her father. "*None* of this relationship has been real?"

"What?" Rhys gasped, his voice rising in pitch. "No, Starry, that's not it at all. It just worked out that way. Your father was going to reunite you with Emma, but he said he had to make sure she was clean before that happened. Your staying with me was a convenient way to—"

"Make sure she was *clean?*" Starry shrieked.

Clean was a term used in the syndicate to specify a member's standing. If you were clean, that meant you had no affiliations with any other syndicates or rival organizations. If someone's cleanliness was questioned, intense, brutal torture was one way to determine their standing. That often led to their death and the deaths of anyone else the person cared about. It was one of the reasons every member higher up in the syndicate tried so hard to maintain their status as one hundred percent loyal.

"Do you know if he tortured her?" Starry asked.

"All he said was that he'd made sure she was clean. When I saw her leaving the house with Andrews, she was healthy enough to be running on her own two feet, at least. That's something, right?"

"Oh, sure, that's something." Starry's chest grew tight as she glared down at her father's face. There were cuts and bruises across his cheekbones and he was even paler than before. How could she hate this man so much and yet fear to lose him just as much? She had never once feared for his life until now. He was her rock.

Her hands shook on the gauze she was pressing over his wound. She wanted to pull it away and let him bleed out and die. She wanted to punch him in the face and add to the bruises already there. She couldn't do either of those things. All she could do was glare down at him, her pulse pounding in her head like a hammer. She had never felt so much anger and fear in her life. It mixed around inside like an angry cocktail waiting to explode. She wasn't sure how long she could keep it contained.

The SUV came to a stop and Starry looked up to see a small but expensive house. She recognized it from some of her surveillance in the past. It was Blaire's home. It looked vacant, but Starry knew better.

"Pearce is here," Rhys said, and opened the driver's side door.

Pearce opened the back door and Starry turned to look at him. It only took one brief glance at his shocked expression for her to see she could trust him just as she'd said. He had taught her so many things, from stitching up a wound to how to kill a person in less than two minutes with no mess or brute force involved.

He gave Starry a saddened, almost panicked look. "Let's get him inside. I'm sure it looks worse than it is."

Rhys helped Pearce haul her father's limp body to the house. Blaire was at the front door holding it open, and Starry followed everyone inside and down a hallway toward Blaire's surgical room. He was as serious about medicine as his uncle.

"Starry, you should wash up," Pearce said as he glanced at Starry's bloody hands. "Bathroom's there on your right."

She nodded and went into the bathroom. She took her time, worried that if she followed Pearce to the surgical room, she'd completely lose her cool and do something stupid—whatever cool she had left, anyway. She needed to breathe and get back to a place where she could think and control her emotions.

As the hot water rushed over her skin, she looked at herself in the mirror. She was pale. No makeup. Her hair was a mess. There was blood splattered on her hoodie. She didn't know if it was from the men she and Rhys had killed or if it was her father's. She didn't care. All she wanted was for her father to wake up so she could yell at him. And then she wanted to pound on Rhys' face until he passed out. She couldn't wake up her father, but she could at least find Rhys.

She left the bathroom and found Pearce coming out of the surgical room.

"How is he?" she asked, peeking over Pearce's shoulder as the door closed behind him.

He peeled off a pair of latex gloves. "He'll make it. I've got to grab a few things." His eyes flicked down to her bloody clothes. "Do you want to clean up a little more? Blaire's got some clothes you can use." He jerked his head down the hallway. "First room on the left. Take whatever you need."

"Thanks." She looked at the closed door again. "Is Rhys in there?"

"Yeah, Blaire needs a hand so he's playing surgical nurse. Let me know when you want to come in. It's kind of crowded, but I'll kick Rhys out if you want."

"No, I'm fine for now." Starry moved to let Pearce pass, deciding it would be best to let him and Blaire and Rhys do whatever they needed to do to help her father without her getting in the way.

She found the room Pearce had mentioned and rummaged through a closetful of Blaire's shirts. She pulled on a clean hoodie and sat down on the bed to look at her phone. When she couldn't stand waiting anymore, she went back down the hallway to the surgical room. It was a bedroom converted into a sterile medical environment. Nothing too fancy, but enough space to perform emergency procedures if needed.

When she opened the door to peek inside, Rhys was not in the room. Blaire was over in the corner writing something on a pad of paper. Pearce stood over her father, who was lying on a small operating table next to an IV stand and a monitoring station. Color had returned to her father's face, and the monitor beeped his steady heartbeat. Relief rushed through Starry, making her relax for the first time in hours.

"He'll be fine, Starry," Pearce said as he picked up a tiny pair of scissors from a surgical tray. "He woke when we brought him in here, but I've sedated him. It'll be awhile before you can talk to him."

"It's okay. I'll let you finish." Backing away from the door, she let it shut softly before she went searching for Rhys.

Rhys was in the kitchen. He was sitting at the bar, his back to the doorway. He had changed into a clean T-shirt, probably one of Blaire's.

Approaching him as silently as a cat, Starry tried to make out what Rhys was doing, but all the blinds and drapes were closed and only the light on the stove was on. Lifting something to his mouth, Rhys took a big bite.

"How can you eat right now?" Starry asked, her hands balling into fists at her sides.

Rhys spun around. There was a spot of mustard at the corner of his mouth. If all he could think about was his stomach at a time like this, he deserved a punch in the face.

Infuriated, Starry raised her fist to hit him, but he was faster and grabbed her arm. She twisted it away and decked him with her other fist. He teetered on the stool and regained his balance by planting his feet on the floor and leaning against the counter. He touched his cheek and looked at Starry with widened eyes.

"What the hell?" he snarled. "I told you we'd talk about this. Does that have to include hitting me?"

"Yes it does. Think about it, Rhys. I've been sleeping with you for days, and this whole time you've been in league with my dad . . . I'm seriously . . . I don't even . . ." She threw another punch. Her knuckles slammed against his nose and a trickle of blood rolled down to his lip. He hadn't tried to stop her this time.

"Are you finished now?" he asked calmly as he touched the blood dripping from his nose.

"For the moment." Starry rubbed her sore knuckles. "That was for the lies. I'm sure there will be more reasons for me to hit you in a few minutes."

"Can I clean up first? Shit, Starry. I thought you'd be hovering over you father right now, not hunting me down to beat me up."

"You thought wrong." She stepped far enough away for Rhys to slip off the stool and walk around the counter to get to the sink. He washed the blood off his hand and found a paper towel to press against his nose.

"Well, in case you're curious," Rhys said, his voice nasal, "Pearce said your father should be okay, but if we'd waited much longer he probably would have bled to death."

Starry caught sight of a white bandage wrapped around Rhys' elbow and her mouth dropped open. "Did you give blood?"

Rhys tilted his head down as he squeezed his nose with the paper towel. "Yes, I'm the universal blood type."

"I see." Her eyes drifted down to the bandage around Rhys' elbow and then to the sandwich on the counter. "I guess that's why you're eating something."

"Blaire told me to help myself to anything in the fridge." He leaned across the counter to grab the sandwich. "So if you don't mind." He lifted the sandwich with one hand and took another big bite. He kept his eyes on Starry as he chewed, his body swaying a little until he rested his hip against the counter.

Starry shook out her still-throbbing fist, not regretting in the slightest her decision to hit Rhys. He deserved it, but she had to at least acknowledge what he'd done for her father. "Thank you for giving blood," she said with a slight nod, and then raised an index finger and pointed it at Rhys' chest. "But it doesn't excuse any of the shit you've done."

"Maybe we should call it even."

"Maybe we shouldn't."

They stared each other down, and after a full minute, Starry blinked. "So what happened?" she asked as Rhys took another bite of sandwich. "With Andrews and Chavez? With Emma?"

Rhys chewed slowly and then swallowed. Starry could tell he was sorting through what he wanted to tell her. She decided to beat him to the punch with the biggest piece of information she wanted cleared up. "I know Emma's father is my birth father. At least, that's what it looks like from what I've seen. How much of that story do you know?"

Rhys' eyes widened. "What the hell are you talking about? You mean Glenn's not you real father?"

Grinding her teeth for a moment, Starry pushed down her need to get *all* the facts and decided to focus on what Rhys did know. "Never mind. That's obviously something I'll have to discuss with *him*. Tell me about Andrews and Chavez. What happened at the house?"

His brow furrowing, Rhys turned and opened a cupboard. It was full of plates, so he shut the door and tried another. When he found a glass, he filled it with water at the fridge and sipped at it for a few seconds before meeting Starry's eyes. She tapped her foot as she watched him.

He lowered his glass. "From what I've pieced together, and from what your father told me before he passed out, Andrews and Chavez arranged a last-minute meeting with him. He told them to meet him in one of the torture rooms where he was busy teaching Ian never to make a mistake again. When they arrived at the house, they took down the security guards outside. From there, they went inside and killed the two housekeepers and the other guards. They must have done it quick and silent because no alarms were tripped and your father didn't know anything was off when they knocked on the torture room door. He took them into his office, and everything seemed normal to him during the meeting until they attacked him and tried to tie him to a chair. Glenn said they were going to torture him before they killed him. That's when I showed up.

"Chavez tried to run and Glenn grabbed a gun from his office desk and went after him while I was trying to figure out what the hell was going on. Andrews came after me and we got into it, but then we heard shots and Glenn came back. That's when Andrews pulled a gun and shot Glenn in the shoulder. I managed to kick the gun out of his hand, and he knocked me down and ran off. I thought he'd gone for good until I heard him and Emma leaving the house. You showed up a minute later."

"And exactly why did you show up when you did?"

Rhys sighed and rubbed lightly around the bandage on his elbow. "That was all you, Star. You were gone when I woke up and I couldn't find you anywhere. I asked Mark and he told me about your conversation. I called Glenn to see if you'd gone home, but he'd turned his phone off so he could deal with Ian uninterrupted. I went over to look for you and give him my report on what's been going on."

Starry nodded. "Do you think we should send someone over to let Ian out of there?" she asked.

"I'm sure he's dead by now, and it'd be too risky anyway. He's not worth it."

She shifted her feet. "Well, I'm done here, then." She had a lot of reasons not to believe any of Rhys' story, but as she watched him sip at his water and dab at the blood still dripping from his nose, she couldn't help but believe him. He looked absolutely pathetic.

That didn't mean she forgave him for any of his previous lies.

He looked up at her. "Starry, let's not let any of this ruin—"

She put up a hand. "No, Rhys. Don't think for one second that anything is fine between us. I'm going to figure out who's behind all of this. I'm going to fix it, and then you and my dad are going to apologize for treating me like shit instead of an equal." She leveled her gaze at Rhys and he looked back at her with a hurt expression. "I'll decide at that point if I'm ever going to speak to you again. You were never trying to protect me, were you? It was all a cover-up so you could keep an eye on me for my father and keep me from Emma."

Before Rhys could respond, she turned and left the room, her ego deflating as she headed to a quiet room where she could sit down and rest. She knew she would eventually find whoever was trying to kill her father. She already suspected Jack's father, whoever the hell he was. It could literally be anyone else too. Either way, thinking about how Emma might be linked to whatever was going on wasn't pleasant. She wasn't sure she was ready to face what she might find. What if Emma was a threat? Why would Andrews take Emma if she didn't have something to do with what was going on?

Starry thought back on all the times she'd watched her father torture people—and the times she'd helped too. It was one thing to hurt people who worked for you. It was quite another to hurt those connected to you by blood or friendship. Unless they were trying to hurt other people you loved. Then it was nothing but a huge, disastrous mess. Unfortunately, Starry had a feeling that was exactly what she was headed into.

NINETEEN

It took over an hour to get through rush hour traffic. Andrews kept cursing and touching the angry red skin around his cut. The bleeding had stopped, but his suit coat and shirt collar were soaked red now. He looked like a car crash victim.

Emma looked down at her elbow. The pressure she'd been keeping on it seemed to have stopped the bleeding. Her back was throbbing. She looked up at Andrews again. "Does it hurt?"

"Like a bitch." He turned a corner and they pulled into a quiet hotel parking lot. "We're here. Stay put. We need to wait for Craig to get down here."

"Okay."

Andrews put his phone to his ear. "We're here in the lot. There's nobody coming or going down here, so bring a wet towel or something so I can clean up. I've been bleeding all over the damn place."

Emma cleared her throat as Andrews ended the call. "Are you really only doing this for money?" she asked.

Andrews rolled down his window and pulled out a pack of cigarettes from his suit pocket. "It's a lot of money," he said, giving her an annoyed look. When she didn't respond, he stuck a cigarette between his lips and pulled out a lighter. "I've been working for Glenn most of my life, but he's never appreciated what I do for him. He's killed too many people I care about, even if they did deserve it. He's a greedy, self-absorbed bastard and now he's gonna pay for it." He laughed and let out a puff of smoke. "It's a good thing Craig's got money or I would have left the second I heard Glenn found out what Sam was up to."

"But where is Craig getting so much money?"

The smoke from Andrews' cigarette swirled out the open window. "You don't have a clue what Sam was doing, do you?"

Emma shook her head.

Andrews' expression filled with a kind of sadness Emma had no idea a man like him could feel. He took a long drag on his cigarette and then turned his head to blow the smoke out the window. "Sam contacted me six months ago and made me an offer I couldn't refuse. It's a shame he's dead now." He looked Emma in the eyes, the gash on his face glinting wetly in the setting sun. "You should do everything you can to help Craig. It's what Sam would've wanted."

A knock on her window made Emma jump. "Emma!" Jack said, his voice muffled through the glass. "Open up. It's locked."

Letting out a sigh of relief, Emma scrambled to unlock the door, but Andrews grabbed her arm and yanked her hand away. "Oh, no you don't. You're mine until I'm paid, pretty girl." She struggled against him until he held the burning end of his cigarette close to her face. "Don't make me do it."

There was no doubt in her mind he would burn her. She stopped struggling just as Craig appeared at Andrews' window. "Let her go," he ordered.

Andrews slowly lowered the cigarette from Emma's face. "I'm not handing her over until I get my money."

The two men glared at each other. Shifting his feet, Craig folded his arms and took a deep breath. The anger in his face melted away. "We can't decide anything down here," he declared, and pushed a wet towel through the window. "Clean up and let's go upstairs. I just got a call from what's left of the backup team you thought you didn't need to wait for. We lost three of them. Glenn got away, so we've got to figure out what the hell we're going to do."

Andrews cursed under his breath and tossed his cigarette butt out the window. Snatching the towel from Craig, he pulled down the sun visor and started cleaning up the blood on his face and neck.

"Emma?" Jack said, still standing on her side of the car. "Are you okay?"

She nodded as she backed as far away from Andrews as she could. Trapped with the smell of his blood and cigarette smoke, she needed some fresh air. When he finally finished cleaning up and got out of the car, Emma unlocked her door and got out too.

Jack pulled her into a loose hug. Emma noticed he was careful not to touch her back.

She gently wrapped her arms around him, but even that small movement made pain shoot across her back. Still, she didn't want to let go of him. She felt like she'd slipped off the edge of a cliff and he was catching her. Tears spilled from her eyes. "I'm so glad you're all right."

"Mostly." Jack backed away, choking and wheezing as he cradled his ribs. "Sometimes I can't breathe."

Emma glanced worriedly at Craig as he and Andrews came around to her side of the car. "Is there anything we can do for him?"

Craig shrugged. "Not really much you can do for cracked ribs. We've kept ice on them. He'll be fine if he takes it easy."

Emma nodded. Even though Jack was pale from pain, he still looked good. His big brown eyes, his messy hair. She already wanted to hug him again.

"Let's get upstairs," Craig ordered.

"Fine idea." Andrews grabbed Emma's arm and she winced under his tight grip.

Craig's hands balled into fists at his side. He turned on his heel and they all followed him. Jack glanced back at Andrews' hand on Emma's arm, but didn't make a move to intervene. Emma was glad. She didn't want him hurt more than he already was.

They all walked into the lobby and headed for the elevators. The concierge gave Emma's bare feet a disapproving look and then glanced away when Craig caught his eye. At this point, it wouldn't surprise Emma if Craig had paid the lobby staff not to ask any questions.

They hurried into the elevator and a few moments later they were standing in front of a hotel room door. Craig swiped a card through the reader and stepped inside. He held the door open.

Andrews finally let go of Emma's arm and pushed her inside the room. It was a large suite with a hallway and two bedrooms. There was a small kitchenette and a living room space. Emma turned around to look at Andrews, hoping he wasn't staying.

Jack came up to her and leaned close to her ear. "He and Chavez booked the suite next door because their places are under surveillance or something," he whispered, "but I guess Chavez is dead now?"

Emma shrugged and squeezed her eyes shut as she remembered seeing the man shot on the floor. She had seen way too many dead bodies in the past few days.

"I want my money now," Andrews said as he ripped off his suit jacket and turned toward a mirror near the door. He grimaced at his reflection. "And not just for Emma. I want to be paid for the job too. I've taken enough risks."

"One thing at a time," Craig said as he walked farther into the room. "Emma, are you okay? Andrews didn't hurt you?"

Andrews threw his suit jacket onto the sofa and spun around to face Craig. He looked positively feral with the gash and blood-soaked shirt. "Can't you see she's fine?"

Craig lifted a hand, nodding calmly. "I'll pay you, don't worry." He flashed Andrews a dark look. "Even though you technically haven't accomplished anything we agreed on."

Andrews' lips curled against his teeth. "How did the backup team fail? You said those men were reliable. Glenn was already injured, so it shouldn't have been difficult for them to take him down. Rhys is strong, but he couldn't have fought off all of them on his own."

Craig nodded. "Let's sit tight. The survivor is on his way here so he can fill us in. Either Glenn is harder to kill than we thought or something else has happened." He looked nervously at Jack before turning back to

Andrews. "I don't think this is the reason you or the team failed, but you should know Jack met with Starry this afternoon when I specifically told him not to go anywhere. He mentioned me, but didn't give her my name. He knows nothing that would be helpful to her."

Emma sucked in a sharp breath at the mention of her sister and Jack, but knew now wasn't the time to start asking questions. It was the time to talk. She opened her mouth to tell everyone that she had divulged Craig's and Jack's names, but couldn't quite get the words out of her mouth.

Andrews glared at Jack. "What did you meet her for?"

Jack looked at the ground. "I was trying to find Emma, but I swear I didn't tell Starry anything that could have interfered with your plans." He shot a dirty glare at his father. "If I had known what you were planning I never would have gone looking for Emma until it was all over. I don't know how you expected me to hang around here doing nothing."

Craig raised a hand and nodded. "I know, I know, and I'll fill you in later, okay? For now we need to figure out what Glenn might know and how it will affect us."

Andrews muttered some curses under his breath and kept dabbing at his wound. "I *told* you it would be hard to kill Glenn. You think nobody's tried this before?"

"Not from as high up as you, they haven't."

"That's because anyone as high up as me knows the rest of the syndicate will kill anyone who turns on Glenn. They don't tolerate traitors. That's why I'm getting out as fast as I can when this is finished."

"Exactly," Craig sighed. "Your killing Glenn was the perfect way in for Sam. He spent nearly two decades getting to this point and you botched it."

Emma tried to make sense of what the men were discussing. She needed more information, but she also knew she couldn't keep to herself what she'd given up during her torture.

"There's something you all should know," she said shakily. Everyone turned to look at her. She looked at Craig. "Glenn tortured me this morning . . . at least I *think* it was this morning . . . and I ended up telling him your name and Jack's. He probably would have found your information in my phone records, anyway, but I still feel bad about it."

Craig's eyes widened. "He tortured you? What did he do?"

"He whipped me."

Jack turned to her. "He *what?*"

Andrews grunted and kept dabbing at his wound. "Glenn was still trying to dig up a last name when we met with him. Craig's done a good job of keeping his and Jack's phone records secure, so there's no way Glenn could have connected us that fast. Besides, he didn't suspect us of anything before we attacked him. I think it was Rhys who was tipped off, not Glenn."

"Emma," Craig said, stepping closer. "You didn't give Glenn a last name?"

She shook her head. "I don't even know your last name."

"Then it should take him a while to find us. We've got tonight and maybe tomorrow."

"Either way," Andrews said, "let's go get my money."

"Fine, fine. But you're not getting the full amount until the rest of the job is completed."

Andrews followed Craig into the kitchen area, still bickering about money.

Breathing hard, Emma sat on the edge of the sofa. She buried her face in her hands. When she looked up again, Jack was kneeling in front of her, his eyes filled with worry. He touched her knee so softly she was sure he was afraid she might break any second.

"You're safe now," he said. "I'm going to find out what's going on and I'm going to make sure you stay safe. Andrews will leave once he's paid."

She nodded and looked down at his hand. In a world falling apart around her, he was the only person she could count on. "Thank you, Jack. I don't know how I'd get through this without you. Glenn was horrible. He . . . he . . ." Her voice shattered into a sob.

Jack stood up. "I'll get you a drink of water. Try to relax, okay?"

She nodded and watched him walk into the kitchen. She could see a small dining table covered in a surprisingly large array of computer equipment. She remembered Jack saying his dad worked as a white hat hacker. Now it seemed he'd been using those skills all along as part of his plan to kill Glenn. She shuddered. Her father had wanted to kill Glenn too. His own brother . . .

Jack walked out of the kitchen with a water bottle. Emma gulped down half of it as soon as she had it in her hands. "Thank you. I didn't realize how thirsty I was."

Jack sat next to her on the sofa, but he wasn't close enough to touch her. He glanced at her nervously, as if he didn't know what to do next.

Emma smiled. She didn't know what it was about Jack, but simply being near him made her feel better. She scooted closer to him, her knee brushing against his. "I still don't like that you lied to me, but I'm not mad at you anymore, just so you know."

A smile brightened his face. "I kinda figured that when we kissed each other."

She blushed. "Well, yeah, but I'm even less mad at you now." She hoped he could see how serious she was.

"Not any guy would fly all the way across the country looking for a girl he just met."

Jack met her gaze with a half-serious, half-joking expression. "Well, I told you I was a nice guy."

A little laugh escaped her throat. "Yes, you did tell me that, and I believe you now." She glanced over at the kitchen. "Just . . . just promise you won't leave me. I don't think I can handle being left alone with your dad or Andrews."

Smiling, Jack rolled his eyes. "There's no way I'd ever leave you alone with either of them. They're both nuts."

"Why are they trying to kill Glenn, do you know?"

"No, but we'll find out, don't worry." He looked down at his knee touching hers and leaned forward to look her in the eyes. He took in a sudden sharp breath, his eyes widening in pain as he put a hand to his chest. He started coughing.

Emma watched his trembling shoulders, wanting to help but afraid to touch him. Her heart ached at the thought of him in any sort of pain. He'd done so much for her in the past few days and she cared about him more than she would have ever thought possible. "What can I do?" she asked. "Seriously, you seem more in pain than I am."

"It'll . . . pass," he gasped, and caught his breath before he looked down at the dried blood smeared across the inside of her arm. "What happened? Is that Andrews' blood or did he hurt you? I swear if he—"

"It's from an IV," she explained. "Glenn's doctor put it in and I ripped it out on accident. The bleeding's stopped, so it's fine."

"Why were you on an IV?"

"I was dehydrated."

"Oh . . . right . . . I guess that makes sense. Why was Glenn torturing you in the first place?"

She looked down at her lap. "He thought my dad might have included me in whatever he was doing with the drugs. He said my dad was running a drug syndicate behind his back."

Jack looked over at the kitchen. Emma could hear Andrews speaking, but his voice was too hushed for her to make out what he was saying. "A drug syndicate, right," Jack said. "That must be how my dad was involved with your dad. I guessed it was something like that. So how hurt are you?"

A lump formed in Emma's throat. "You can lift up the back of my shirt and see, but it's all bandaged."

Jack gently lifted up her shirt, his knuckles grazing her skin. He took in a sharp breath and then lowered the shirt. Emma tried to look him in the eyes, but couldn't quite do it. "I-I had to tell him your names. The whip hurt so bad and he wasn't going to stop and I—"

"Emma, look at me."

She lifted her eyes to his, her heart pounding so hard she was sure it was going to burst. "I'm so sorry. That could have been why—"

Jack put a finger to her lips. "Andrews said it wasn't you who tipped them off, so stop feeling bad about it. It easily could have been my fault too."

Emma nodded. "You mean because of your meeting with Starry? How did you find her in the first place?"

"Remember how you lost your phone when we met with my dad?"

She nodded.

"Well, my dad picked it up. He hacked into it and found all of your pictures, including the one of your dad's package. I went to the address from where it was shipped and Starry was there. She wasn't happy when I showed her your mom's journal entries. She ran off. I think she was going to confront Glenn, but maybe she decided to ask that Rhys guy for help. She easily could have tipped him off that someone was going after Glenn, so don't blame yourself, okay?"

"I guess so. I don't know anything for sure right now." She took a deep breath and moved even closer to Jack, surprised at how unemotional she was. Exhaustion had sunk in.

"It'll be okay." Jack slipped his hand in hers and squeezed. "No matter what happens, I'm sticking by you. I'm never leaving your side again unless you want me to."

Warmth filled her heart as she looked down at his fingers entwined with hers. "Thanks, Jack." She looked up when Andrews and Craig walked into the living room, their expressions twitching with irritation.

"What's going on?" Jack asked.

Craig ran a hand over his buzzed head. "Andrews has some ideas about what we should do, but I'm not sure I agree."

Andrews scowled at Craig. "Fill them in on what's going on and we'll talk about it when I get back. I'm gonna go get a drink." He marched out of the suite and the door shut behind him.

Jack faced his father. "Will you tell me what's going on now?"

Craig let out a long sigh. "I suppose it's time."

TWENTY

Craig paced the room for a moment before motioning Emma and Jack into the kitchen. "Let's talk in here," he said. "I need a drink worse than Andrews."

Jack looked down at their entwined hands and then stood up from the sofa, gently tugging her up with him. "You ready for this?"

Emma looked at Craig, who was already disappearing around the corner into the kitchen, and shrugged. "I've been ready for a long time."

Jack nodded. "Okay, then here goes." He led her to the dining table covered with computer equipment.

Craig was already standing by the fridge with an open beer bottle in his hand. He paced in front of the table while Jack pulled out two chairs and sat down next to Emma.

Emma took a deep breath as she looked through a large window with an impressive city view. They were at least ten floors up. The blinds were mostly closed, but

Emma could still see some of the sky. It was a purplish orange as the sun sank deeper toward the horizon.

Craig set his beer on the table. "I've kept all of this from you for so long," he said to Jack. "Please understand it was for a good reason." He turned to Emma. "Same goes for Sam. He never meant to hurt you."

Anger and confusion swelled in Emma's chest. She knew she shouldn't be angry with her father, especially now that he was dead. Calming herself as best she could, she looked up at Craig. "So exactly how long was my dad planning all of this?"

Craig glanced at Jack. "About eighteen years."

"My entire life," Emma muttered, and shook her head. "He's wanted to kill his brother my entire life. Why?"

Craig took a deep breath and held it for a moment before unclasping his hands from behind his back. "It's a long story, but let's start with the basics. First of all, we only kept this from you for your own protection." He nodded his head at Emma. "Obviously, you've had a taste of what Glenn is capable of. If you had known too much about Sam's plan to kill Glenn, you probably wouldn't be here right now. Glenn would have killed you. Am I right?"

Her heart pounding at the memory of that morning, Emma unfolded her arms and looked down at her lap. Craig was right, of course. She had no doubt that if Glenn had thought she was any sort of threat to him, even just from knowing too much, he would have killed her.

"Yes, that's right," she said and then looked up at Craig, the anger in her chest still swelling. "But Dad raised me to be a good person and do the right things. How is running a drug network and planning a murder the right things? How can I ever know who my dad was now?"

Craig folded his arms and looked at the floor. "I know, Emma, I know. I'm sure Jack feels the same way." He lifted his eyes to his son.

Jack looked as angry as Emma felt. His jaw was set tight and his hands were balled into fists. "Yeah, just a bit. We were doing fine for so long, even after Mom died, but then you got so obsessed with the drug stuff and I didn't know what to do. I've given up so much to help you, but if I'd known you were doing something on this scale I would have left a long time ago. There's no way I can fix any of this."

Craig lowered his eyes again. "I know, and you're right, you can't fix any of it." He looked at Emma. "But we have a chance with Andrews' help now, even if he did fail the first time. He was one of Glenn's top lieutenants. He knows things nobody else knows. He's our only chance."

"And how exactly are you paying him?" Emma asked, narrowing her eyes. "Do you make *that* much money? He's got to be asking for a lot."

Craig shook his head. "It's Sam's money. He saved every cent of it specifically to pay off someone to help him bring down Glenn in just the right way. It took us years to find Andrews. He was bitter and angry and vengeful—all the right weak points we needed to bribe him. Six months ago, Sam finally reached out to him and made him an offer." He gave Emma a pained look. "Everything was falling into place until you delivered that package. Andrews told me Glenn's men hunted Sam down and tortured him. They got Alex's name and found the others from there. Most of the network was taken out in less than a day."

Emma looked away, guilt pressing down on her.

"Why didn't Glenn come after you too?" Jack asked. "You're a part of Sam's network, aren't you?"

"Alex didn't know about me. Nobody in Sam's network knew about me. I've always been the backup plan if it all went sour. Everything is up to me now."

"And that's the whole reason we're here?" Jack asked. "To make sure Andrews kills Glenn? Why hasn't someone done it before this? I mean, it can't be that hard to take the guy out with a sniper rifle or something, right? Wouldn't that be easier than all of these complicated plans?"

Craig laughed. "You'd think so, but no. Glenn's too well guarded and connected. I had to scrape the bottom of the barrel just to find enough mercenaries crazy and desperate enough for money to take this job."

Jack nodded. "Okay, then what about prison? Wouldn't it be easier to let the police take over? Can't *they* dismantle the syndicate?"

"Prison can't hold Glenn," Craig explained, clasping his hands behind his back. "Even if we did manage to get him in there, he knows too many important people who could get him out. There's a chance to break down the syndicate, but only if Glenn is dead."

"So my dad didn't just want to kill Glenn," Emma said, surprised with this new information. "He wanted to bring down the entire syndicate." She turned back to Craig. "But how? Isn't it huge?"

"That's the problem," Craig said. "We have to be able to step into Glenn's position ourselves in order to break it down. We know Starry is the one who will take over the syndicate if Glenn dies, but Sam's plan was to step in ahead of her, or at least beside her. He fully believed Starry would allow him to do that once she found out the truth about her past. He planned on convincing her to help him bring down the syndicate from the inside."

"But why *did* Glenn raise Starry instead of my dad?" Emma asked.

"Sam never told me why. He only told me Glenn took her from him when you were both just babies."

Emma nodded. So that was one reason why there were no other pictures of her sister in that box.

"Wait," Jack said, getting up from his chair to stand face to face with his father. "You are the only person left to carry out this crazy murder scheme? Everyone else is dead?"

Craig nodded. Emma saw what was coming, but she still hadn't put all the pieces together. Starry didn't seem the type to let a complete stranger like Craig take over the syndicate that was rightfully hers.

"But you're not Sam," Jack said, voicing Emma's thoughts. "How do you expect to step into Glenn's place with Starry in the way? You're not blood family. You're not her birth father. That plan can't work now. We should all just walk away."

"I know," Craig interrupted. "But I haven't been working toward this for eighteen years to give up now. There still might be a way to carry out Sam's plan."

"Wh-what is that?" Emma asked, her heart pounding with dread.

Craig took a deep breath. "Well, Emma, with Glenn out of the picture, you'd be Starry's only family. If you joined the syndicate right beside her, you could be the one to eventually bring it down." He gave her a nasty smile. "If you're strong and brave enough to do that. No offense, but I'm pretty sure you aren't. So now we've got to figure out something else."

Emma opened her mouth to say something, but she couldn't put her swirling thoughts into words. She wasn't going to join a drug syndicate, not even to bring it down.

"I don't understand why you're doing any of this in the first place," Jack growled. "What was your payoff going to be if Sam took over the syndicate? Were you going to be a part of it too?"

Craig nodded. "I was going to work beside him, yes."

Jack's jaw tensed. "But *why?* Why not just keep all of Sam's money for yourself and walk away from all of this? You said nobody knew your name or your part in the plan. Why are you still involved?"

Craig looked hard at Jack. "Because when I say I'll do something, I do it. You know that better than anyone."

Jack stared at his father for a few moments before turning away, silent.

Emma stood up from her chair, her hands shaking as she faced Craig. "Speaking of that money, how much did my dad save to pay off Andrews?"

"It's got to be millions," Jack muttered.

Craig stared hard at both of them and then looked away with a huff. "None of this is about money or power. I thought you knew me better than that."

Jack rolled his eyes. "I guess not."

Craig's phone started ringing in his pocket. He pulled it out and gave Jack a threatening look. "I think we've talked long enough for tonight. I've got to take this call."

When he had left the room, Jack turned to Emma and pulled her into a loose hug. "I'm so sorry. We should run away from all of this, but I have no idea how to hide from people like Glenn and Starry, or even my dad."

Emma rested her cheek on Jack's shoulder, savoring the feeling of being with him. He felt safe to her, even if everything else around her was falling apart. "We have no money, Jack. We wouldn't get very far. They wouldn't even have to look hard." She lifted her head and looked into his eyes. They reflected the warm light of the sunset. "Do you think Glenn will come after us if Andrews can't kill him?"

Jack looked away. "I don't know. It's possible. I doubt my dad could walk away now if he wanted to. Glenn's going to find out who he is and then we're all screwed." He gave her a half-smile. "Well, maybe not you. Glenn might not kill you, right?"

Emma thought about what Dr. Pearce had told her earlier. Her heart thudded in her chest so hard she was sure Jack could feel it as she leaned against him. "Don't count on it. I wish there was a way for us to disappear.

With all of my dad's money, we should be able to do that, right?"

Jack sighed. "You'd think, but something is stopping my dad from doing it, and it's gotta be more than him wanting to follow through on a promise. I don't understand why he's so loyal to your dad's plan when it won't get him anything in the end." He tightened his arms around her. "Whatever happens, we'll get through it together."

Emma nodded. That was all she could ask for.

TWENTY-ONE

Two hours passed before Pearce came into the room to tell Starry her father was awake. She was curled up in the corner of a large sofa, her eyes droopy as she watched a TV show on her phone. Rhys had brought her a piece of toast and a glass of milk an hour earlier, and out of spite she'd left them untouched on the end table next to her.

"Is he in any condition to talk?" Starry asked as she turned off her phone and stood up from the sofa. It was almost nine o'clock, and since her body hated her for recently trying to adjust to Rhys' insane nightclub schedule, she felt tired and awake at the same time. It was annoying and put her off-balance.

Pearce shrugged. "He's cranky as hell, but other than that, he's fine. He's in the guest bedroom down the hall."

Starry slipped her phone into her back pocket and thanked Pearce before brushing past him. The bedroom was dim, lit only by two lamps on the bedside tables. Her father was in the bed, propped up by a mound of pillows. His arm was in a sling, the type that immobilized the entire shoulder. He looked up as she closed the door and approached the bed.

"I'm glad you're here," he said, his speech slightly slurred from the drugs Pearce had used to sedate him earlier. His expression was sad and hurt. He was crazy if he thought this meeting was going to be filled with tears and apologies—on either side.

Folding her arms across her chest, Starry stayed near the door. She couldn't quite glare at her father after he'd almost lost his life, but her expression wasn't exactly warm, either. "You have a lot of explaining to do. And if you keep lying to me, I'll kill you myself."

Her father sniffed and looked down at the quilt pulled up to his waist. "I understand why you're upset, but we need to get to the safe house as soon as possible. Rhys is packing the car as we speak."

Starry's nostrils flared. "I am not going anywhere with either of you until I know the truth. Is Sam my birth father? And don't lie. I've seen my mother's journal entries, so unless those are fake—"

"Journal entries?" Shock spread across her father's face, his eyes growing so wide they looked as if they might bug right out of his head. "How? I took all of

Lucy's possessions after she died. There was no journal." He clenched his jaw. "Sam must of have hidden it from me. That's probably how Emma found out. How did you get your hands on it?"

"Are you my father or not?" Starry demanded. Tears stung her eyes as she watched her dad's shock wither into fear and then anger. She figured Pearce would be pissed if he knew she was in here stressing out his most valuable patient so soon after surgery, but she didn't care. The more stressed out he was, the more vulnerable he was to spilling information.

"You are *my* daughter," her father said, his angry expression easing into his usual calm demeanor. His voice leveled out into a more composed tone. "You always have been, and you always will be. I love you more than Sam could have ever loved you."

Starry had to hold herself back from charging across the room and punching him in the nose. "Then it's true."

"Yes."

A few tears leaked out of Starry's eyes and she brushed them away with the back of her fist before they had a chance to fall. "I can't believe it. So you really are my uncle."

Her father nodded again, unblinking. "Sam didn't want you. That's the truth. You were too much for him after Emma was born. When I stepped in to help him, he was happy to give you up. You were a difficult baby."

Fury roiled inside of Starry. She paced a few feet across the room as her heart pounded harder. "So you're saying my birth father didn't want me because I was *difficult*? What the hell kind of explanation is that?"

"It was so much more than that. Listen, Starry, I don't think either of us are in any condition to get into this right now."

"Oh, hell no," Starry snarled, whipping around to face the bed. "You're going to tell me every piece of the truth, even if it kills you. You did not raise me to take this kind of shit, so why do you expect me to stand back and let it slide?"

Raising his good hand, he gave her a curt nod. "You're right, of course." He slowly peeled the blanket off his body. "Let's get out to the car and I'll explain on the way to the safe house." He sat up a few inches and then closed his eyes before falling back against the pillows, his chest heaving.

Starry moved forward a few feet and then stopped. "Maybe we should stay here until you've rested some more. You're going to pass out again if you get up too fast."

"No, we can't stay here a minute longer. We can't trust anyone, not even Pearce and Blaire."

Starry stared at him, open-mouthed. "They just saved your life. I'm pretty sure we can trust them."

"For now, maybe, but Rhys must have told you I suspect someone is controlling Andrews. Until I know who that is, we have to lay low."

Starry watched him try to catch his breath. "You're right," she agreed. "Stay there. I'll get Rhys and we can help you out to the car."

"Thank you, Starry. Rhys told me how you showed up and took charge."

Starry's hand froze around the door handle. She looked over her shoulder at her father. Her *uncle*. Everything was upside down. Nothing was what it seemed. The only thing she could trust was the fact that she loved him like a father, not an uncle who had raised her. Nothing could take that away, and that only made the lies cut so much deeper.

"I'll be back in a minute." She yanked open the door and stomped down the hallway, torn between bursting into tears and slamming her fist through the wall.

The safe house was twenty miles from Blaire's home, tucked away in a quiet, elite neighborhood outside the city. It was a place Starry and her father had kept secret from everyone for almost two years now. Starry had overseen everything, from installing the security system herself to hiring a regular indoor cleaning service and lawn maintenance crew. It had one more year to go before she and her father would replace it with a different safe house in another location. As her father always said, you could never be too careful. A safe house was essential. She suspected he had another one somewhere that not even she knew about, which pissed her off and impressed her at the same time.

"Stay on this road for about five miles," Starry told Rhys as he pulled out of Blaire's neighborhood. "I'll tell you when to turn."

Rhys nodded and gave her a soft smile. She turned away in response.

"Can I get a little help?" her father asked from the back seat as he lifted a water bottle he had been trying to open one-handed.

Starry reached back between the seats and grabbed the bottle. She had insisted he sit in the back seat so she wouldn't have to stare at the back of his head the entire trip to the safe house. She wanted to look him in the eyes as he spoke to her.

Twisting off the cap, she returned the bottle. "Now talk."

He took a long swig of water. "Where do you want me to start?"

"At the beginning. Sam is your brother. Start there."

He leaned back against the headrest. "Sam *was* my brother. He's dead now, which complicates everything."

Starry's breath stopped in her throat. "He's *dead?*" For some reason, it hurt her inside to find out her birth father was gone. She didn't understand why. She'd never even known the man.

Her father lowered his water bottle and shrugged. "None of this is how I planned it. Emma delivered a package to Paula on Friday, but it didn't belong to our syndicate. Paula reported it immediately, and Sam was taken and questioned. Ian got one name out of him: Alex Sheffield. Ian found Sheffield and got the names of an entire syndicate Sam was building on his own. I had those people eliminated, but I suspect there's more. Ian flew Sam and Emma here yesterday morning. I tried to get more information out of Sam, but the bastard had the gall to die on me. I thought he'd be tougher than that."

Starry took a deep breath through her nose in an effort to calm herself. Not only had Sam died, but it was her own father who had killed him. She had so many questions, but she had to start at the beginning. "So Sam was working for us?" she asked.

"Yes, when I took you all those years ago, I also hired him as an Elite in order to keep him tethered to the syndicate—and under my control."

An Elite. That meant Sam was sent consistent shipments of the highest grade drugs at the lowest cost. The money he'd make selling those drugs was significant, to say the least—especially if he'd been doing it for the last eighteen years. Working as an Elite also meant Sam had to stay clean inside the syndicate, as well as steer clear of the law. Elites often became dependent on the healthy income their drug shipments provided. Apparently Sam had wanted more.

But now he was dead.

And the way things were going, Emma could end up dead too.

Starry gritted her teeth. She had never met Sam or Emma, but she was still unsettled by the thought of losing them so suddenly. Her blood. Her family. Now she would never know what her birth father had been like, what traits she might have inherited from him. If she could find Emma, there was still a chance to connect with something she might lose otherwise.

"Like I said," her father continued. "I didn't mean for Sam to die so soon. I got out of him that he was planning to infiltrate the syndicate to bring me down from the inside. He'd been saving all of his personal profit from my drugs and his own syndicate to carry out his plan. Bastard always did have it out for me, even after he swore his loyalty to me. I let him keep Emma. I let him live his own damned life, and I foolishly trusted him. He owed me so much, but I should have known better and killed him eighteen years ago." He shook his head angrily. "I wasn't the same man back then as I am now. I was softer. Weaker."

Anger flared up inside of Starry. "What do you mean you *let* him keep Emma?"

Her father looked off to the side. Starry knew him well enough to know she'd caught him in some sort of lie.

"I thought about taking her too," he admitted, "but when I realized what that would do to Sam, I backed off. He'd just lost Lucy. He wasn't . . . stable. Besides, letting him keep Emma gave me more power over him. He knew I would take her away from him if he ever fell out of line."

"You're still lying to me," Starry growled. "You told me in the beginning that Sam didn't *want* me, and now I'm getting the impression you took me against his will. Which one was it?"

Her father looked exhausted. "Does it matter?"

"Yes, it matters." Starry slumped against the edge of her seat and looked over at Rhys. He was intently focused on the road, as if he wanted to stay as far out of the conversation as possible. She couldn't blame him, and told him to take a right at the next light.

Turning back to her father, she said, "I need to know everything, so *please*, for God's sake, stop lying to me."

He sighed. "I'm not trying to lie to you, Starry. It was so long ago, and I honestly haven't thought about the details in years. Sam really was having a difficult time with you back then, and I really did want to help him out—for Lucy's sake, and for yours and Emma's. And he really didn't fight when I said I was going to take you. I hated him for that. He didn't deserve you."

Starry rubbed her temples, feeling a headache coming on. She still wasn't sure if she could trust a word out of her father's mouth, but figured she would have to give him a little slack when it came to recounting details from eighteen years ago.

"Fine," she relented. "Let's move on. So you killed Sam, and then what? What did you do with Emma?"

She gritted her teeth as she prepared herself for what was coming. If Sam had betrayed her father, it was possible Emma was part of that betrayal.

Her father's expression remained emotionless. "It only took a minute for her to break under my whip. I figured I wouldn't have to go far, and I was right. She's so soft. Not like you. Five lashes and she completely fell apart. It's obvious she was never a part of Sam's plans."

Starry's shoulders relaxed. She had imagined the worst, but five lashes was nothing. Or was it? Her father's whip could do some real damage if he was using all his strength. And of course he would use all his strength to get the information he needed, even if it was out of his own niece. He would cut off his right hand if it betrayed him. That sort of ruthlessness had never been a problem for Starry. Until now. She shuddered. If she was bothered by her father's actions, did that mean she was weak?

She squeezed her hands into fists. Of course it meant she was weak. The problem was she didn't know how to sever her emotions from things that cut too deep. Her father knew how, and she admired that ability more than anything.

"But Emma did give up two names," her father continued. "Craig and Jack, a father and son who may be the ones backing Andrews. I'll leave that to your expertise to figure out."

"Yes," Starry said. "I know about Jack and his father. Don't worry, I've got enough information to figure out exactly who they are and where to find them. And I'll find Emma too."

"I know you will."

The confidence and pride in his expression warmed Starry's heart. But she still didn't know the whole story. "So," she said. "Why did you and Sam have a falling out in the first place?"

Her father looked up at the roof of the car. "It goes way back. Sam and I used to be inseparable, despite our differences. He was a math whiz and good with computers, and I was captain of the football team."

"You played football?" Starry had never seen him even watch sports. Ever.

He shrugged with his good shoulder. "It was my life."

Starry narrowed her eyes. It was a rare thing for her father to talk about his past. All he'd told her before was that his parents had died in a car crash when he was fifteen and he'd spent a few years in foster care. He'd never once mentioned a brother or football or high school. She nodded for him to go on.

His expression grew pained as the city lights lessened and the inside of the car grew darker. There was a soft blue glow across his face from the radio console.

"Lucy stepped into our lives near the end of my senior year," he said. "We both fell in love with her, but I was the one she liked the most. Sam took it hard and decided to get back at me by exposing my steroid habit." His eyes turned icy as he looked at Starry through the dim light. "I had a scholarship to Ohio State. I was going to play pro. It had always been my dream, and Sam ruined it. Lucy left me for him. She wouldn't talk to me after that and it broke me apart. I lost everything."

Starry furrowed her brow. "Steroids? But you've never used drugs." She paused for a split second as her mind spun. "And why would you lose *everything*? Universities don't take away scholarships just for using steroids. Players get away with that all the time."

Her father looked out the window. "It wasn't just the steroids. A few other guys on the team used them too. Sam waited to expose me until I was caught up in a nasty mess that involved one of the players dying from an overdose. It was too much for any university to ignore." He took another sip of water. "After that, I was moved to another foster home, and then another, away from Sam, away from Lucy, away from anything stable. Sam married Lucy when they graduated, and ten years later they had you. They always said they wanted children right away, but it took them that long to get pregnant."

Starry held her breath as the information sank in. It was difficult to imagine what her birth parents were like, but hearing that they had tried for ten years to have her said a lot. "Back up a sec. You said Sam didn't fight you when you took me because I was too much for him."

"That's right."

Starry jutted out her jaw. "Why the hell would he not fight to keep me when he'd waited ten years to have me? That makes no sense."

Her father deflated, his shoulders drooping. "Because Lucy's death changed everything."

"You told me she died right after having me," Starry said. "But I guess that was after she had Emma, not me?"

"That's right. I had to lie to you about that. I couldn't tell you the truth without telling you about Emma."

Starry's eyes fluttered up to the roof of the car. Of course he'd *had* to lie to her, as if he'd had no choice whatsoever. She looked over at Rhys, who was still staring hard at the road. He was just like her father, convinced lying to her was the only way to protect her. Well, they were wrong and she was proving it.

"Go on," she ordered.

"Lucy's death left Sam with two babies and more debt than he could handle. He was severely depressed. Suicidal, even. I stepped in and saved him." He looked up at Starry, his face filled with so much pain that Starry wanted to punch him in the jaw just to get an honest reaction. Was he putting on a show to manipulate her emotions, or was he actually hurting?

She looked over her shoulder to catch a glimpse of where they were. "Turn left at the next light," she said to Rhys, and turned back to her father. "So you took me after that, and then you took all of my mother's stuff away from Sam and Emma. Why would you do that?"

He narrowed his eyes. "Because I never wanted you two to know about each other. I wanted you for my own so I could raise you the way I needed to. How else can I hand over the syndicate to someone when I die? It has to be blood. It has to be you."

286

Starry's mouth dropped open. He *had* to be joking. "That's what all of this is about?" she barked, firing the words at him like bullets. "You took me as a replacement to carry on your legacy? Why didn't you just knock up some woman and raise that bastard as your heir?" She spun around to face the front of the car and leaned forward as her chest grew so tight she could hardly breathe. "I have to get out of here," she gasped. "I'm nothing but a pawn in this whole sick game. I'm nothing but—"

"Starry, shut the hell up and listen to your dad." Rhys pressed on the gas and passed a slow car.

Starry shot him daggers as she leaned back in her seat and pushed her feet hard against the floor. "Where do you get off ordering me around? This has nothing to do with you."

Rhys snorted. "As long as we're together, it has everything to do with me. I don't want you doing something stupid to ruin your chance to get what you really want." He pushed even harder on the gas. Traffic was light along this road, and the bright city lights off in the distance whipped into a blur in the corner of Starry's vision. She squeezed her eyes shut and rubbed at her temples again.

"We are not together," she said. "I don't even know why we're talking about this. We should be talking about the fact that my entire life has been one huge lie. We should be—"

"I don't know why you're so upset," Rhys interrupted. "Don't you *want* the syndicate? Your father is handing it to you on a silver platter when he's ready to pass it on. How is that a bad thing?"

Starry opened her eyes and caught Rhys' confused expression. Maybe he was right. She had always wanted to be an important part of the syndicate. It was her life. Her father had made it that way. Would she want it if Sam had raised her instead?

She leaned forward and pressed her face between her knees. She was overreacting to trivial things. It didn't matter what might have happened differently in the past. The present was *now*, and what she wanted now was the same as it had always been.

"I don't want to be left out of any plans," she said, sitting up and turning around to face her father. "I want to make decisions *with* you, not behind you. No more lies. No more secrets. Is that too much to ask?"

Her father swallowed the last of his water. "No, it isn't. I'm sorry I've lied to you, but can you blame me? I found out a long time ago that I can't have children. Even if I could, they wouldn't be *you*. They wouldn't be Lucy's. You know how hard I've worked to build the syndicate. I want to leave it in the hands of someone I love and trust implicitly. You're more than that, Starry. I've spent eighteen years trying to show you how much you mean to me. Please don't let all of this stuff about Sam wipe that away."

Starry realized he was truly opening up to her. He didn't want to lose her as much as she didn't want to lose him. At the same time, there was something inside her that felt tight and wound up, like a big ball of elastic. It made her uneasy, and the longer she looked at her father, the more it made her squirm. He had lied to her for so long.

"I'm still angry as hell," she said. "I'm going to figure out who's trying to kill you, but that doesn't mean all of this tension between us is going to disappear."

Her father nodded calmly. "I understand."

Turning around, Starry shot Rhys a cold look before telling him to turn at the next street. Both he and her father were far too calm for her liking. She was a mess, as if she'd been shaken up and left in a million broken pieces. She would never be able to fit them back together.

TWENTY-TWO

The nightmare of Glenn's torture wouldn't leave Emma alone. It was sharp and clear, as if it was happening over and over again. Terror slammed into her as the whip sliced through the air, the sharp sound swallowed up by her screams.

Sitting up with a start, Emma's breath caught in her throat as pain stabbed her upper back along the five lashes Glenn had given her. They still stung even with the tender care Dr. Pearce had given them. She didn't know if he had put any pain medication in her IV, but she seemed to be in a lot more pain now than she had been earlier. Maybe it was because she had rolled onto her back while she was sleeping.

Slowly letting out her breath, she looked over at the clock on the end table. 2:30. The sun was still high in the sky. A window across the hotel room displayed the warm, sparkling skyline. No wonder her back hurt if she'd been lying on it for so long. She vaguely remembered standing in the kitchen with Jack, her tears turning into uncontrolled sobs after awhile. She had finally calmed herself and asked for a sleeping pill. There was no way she could function or make any decisions without sleep. And it had helped. Aside from the pain in her back, her mind felt clearer.

Pushing back the covers, she moved her feet to the floor and slowly stood up. Pain shot down her back and she gritted her teeth. Maybe Jack or his dad had some pills she could take to dull the pain. She made her way to the door and pulled it open. It was dark in the hallway, but not silent. Voices drifted from the sitting room around the corner.

"It's too risky!" Jack was saying. "Why would Starry agree to that if Glenn's still alive? I'm guessing they don't work separately from each other."

"They've had some sort of falling out," Craig answered. "Andrews said she'll want to meet with her alone."

Emma rounded the corner and stood in the doorway. Craig was on the sofa, his legs stretched out. Jack was pacing the floor, his hands behind his back, his expression furious.

They both looked up as she entered the room. "Do you have any pain meds?" she asked as Craig got to his feet and Jack turned toward her, his eyes wide. "My back really hurts."

"You're awake," Jack sighed, walking up to her. He gave her a small hug. He smelled clean.

"I'll find some pills," Craig said, standing up from the sofa. He gave Jack an intense look before leaving the room.

"Here, come sit down." Jack led her to the sofa.

She did as he said, suddenly aware of how dirty she felt. She probably looked like a drowned rat. "Sorry for sleeping so long," she said, putting a hand to her forehead. "Has anything happened?"

Jack shook his head and leaned over to sweep some hair from Emma's face. "My dad and Andrews have been hatching a new plan. They've got it mostly nailed down, but you're a big part of it so they need you on board. It's all crazy, but I don't see what other choice we have. I'll be right back, okay?"

She nodded and stared down at her lap, wondering what Andrews and Craig could possibly want her to do. A moment later the door opened and Andrews walked in, his face as stony and harsh as Emma remembered from the night before. Seeing him immediately put her into panic mode. She stood up and backed away from the sofa, her heart pounding.

"It's about time you woke up," Andrews growled as the door closed behind him. He was dressed in jeans and a button-down shirt. The gash down the side of his face had crusted over now. "We need to get moving on our plan."

Emma took another step back as he approached her. "What is it you want me to do? Because there's no way I'm joining that syndicate."

"I've thought of a way you won't have to. It'll help us get to Glenn, at the very least." He came up so close that Emma could smell the cigarette smoke on his breath. He narrowed his eyes. "You look so much like Starry. Let's hope you can play just as dirty as she does."

Emma tried to take another step back, but ran out of space as her back hit the wall. She winced in pain. "I don't know if I want to help you."

Andrews' icy eyes swirled with anger. "You don't have a choice, Emma."

"Get away from her." Jack came into the room and marched up to Andrews.

Andrews shook his head and walked into the kitchen.

"Here," Jack said, dropping two pills into Emma's hand. He handed her a water bottle next and she swallowed the pills as quickly as she could.

She squeezed her eyes shut and took a deep breath. "If all of Glenn's top people are like Andrews, I don't want to be anywhere near the syndicate."

"I hear you, and with this new idea they've got going, you won't have to be."

"How?"

Jack brushed a few stray hairs away from her face. "They'll explain."

"Jack and Emma, get in here!" Craig called out from the kitchen.

Jack took Emma's hand and they walked into the kitchen. Craig was sitting at the table, his eyes fixed intently on a computer monitor as Andrews stood next to him. Craig glanced up at Emma. "We talked with the survivor from the backup team. He said Starry and Rhys are the ones who killed the rest of the team. They left with Glenn, which means if we can find Starry, we'll find Glenn."

Emma tightened her grip on Jack's hand. "*Starry* killed them?" she gasped, her mind trying to wrap around the idea of her sister taking down a team of trained assassins. That wasn't how she'd imagined Starry at all.

Andrews rolled his eyes at her. "Of course she did. She's a tough little bitch. You think after being raised by Glenn she'd be afraid to get her hands dirty?"

Emma wanted to argue with him, but he was right. She shouldn't be so surprised, especially after everything she'd seen and experienced since Friday. This was the world Starry lived in every day of her life. It was violent and brutal and only the strongest survived. The thought wasn't a pleasant one and she decided to switch subjects. "How is it any easier to find Starry than it is to find Glenn?" she asked.

Craig flashed a smile at Jack. "Thanks to my disobedient son, we have a way to contact her."

Emma looked at Jack. "What did you do?"

"Remember how I told you I showed her a picture of you and your mother's journal entries?"

Emma nodded.

"Well, she forwarded those pictures to her phone. It's a number not even Andrews has access to, so it's not something we could have found otherwise."

Emma looked down at all the equipment on the table. "So you can find her with the phone number?"

Craig shook his head. "I can't hack her GPS location, but we can send her a message."

"And then what?" Emma asked, worry creeping into her heart. She knew something was coming up that would involve her, and even if it didn't mean joining the syndicate, she was sure it wouldn't be pleasant. "What happens when you contact her?"

"*You're* going to talk to her once we get her attention," Andrews said before Craig could answer. "And if we can get her to agree to a meeting, you'll have the chance to convince her to bring down the syndicate like Sam always wanted."

Emma turned to look at him as a threatening smile crept across his lips. "I—*what?*"

"It occurred to me a few hours ago," he explained. "I've known Starry her whole life. You're her true family and that means everything in her world. She'll risk anything to meet you, and possibly risk anything to keep you in her life, especially if she's as angry with Glenn as I think she is. You're innocent and vulnerable, and I'm willing to bet she'll want to protect you, especially after Glenn hurt you. You won't even have to join the syndicate. Play her right, and you'll be able to push her in any direction you want."

Emma shifted her feet. "You really think she'll go for that? I don't know how I could possibly—"

"Don't complicate it, Emma," Andrews snapped. "Right now, let's just worry about setting up the meeting. Getting you two together will get her out of hiding, and that will give me an opportunity to track her back to Glenn so I can finally kill the bastard. That is, unless Starry goes for your proposition and wants to kill him herself. She just might. Craig's promised I'll get the rest of my money either way."

Emma slipped her hand from Jack's and put her hands on her hips. "So it's a trap? Don't you think she'll see right through that?"

Andrews shrugged. "I think she'll be willing to take the risk. Just watch, you'll see."

"And what happens if she meets with me and doesn't let me leave?"

"We'll set those terms before the meeting," Craig said nonchalantly. "It will be a public place."

Emma rolled her eyes. "What if she doesn't go for it? What if I can't convince her of anything?"

Craig gave her a dark look. "Sam believed she'd want revenge on Glenn when she found out the truth."

"That's right," Andrews chimed in. "And I personally believe there's a lot of stock in that. She loves Glenn, but the man goes too far and she knows it. Let's hope she's willing to make him pay."

Emma held her breath, worry creasing her brow. "And if she's not?"

"Then I'll kill Glenn, and you and Craig and Jack can fend for yourselves with what's left of the money. I don't care."

"And if you're not *able* to kill Glenn?"

Andrews let out a mirthless laugh. "Then I'll probably be dead, and you'd all better run like hell."

TWENTY-THREE

Starry loved hitting punching bags. She loved the sound of her gloves smacking the stretched leather, the *thwack* of each jab, uppercut, and hook rippling through her body, her breathing perfectly synced with each hit.

Moving her feet in a shuffle around the hanging bag, she started on some kicks to give her arms a rest.

It had been thirty-six hours since the attack on her father and she was nowhere close to finding Emma or Andrews or anyone else. This safe house had less than adequate equipment and software and she didn't have her laptop, but she had at least been able to dig up some info on Jack and his father, Craig. She'd found out their last name was Mihashi. They lived in New York. She dug into medical records, employment and apartment rental information, school records on Jack, a death certificate for Craig's wife. But Craig had obviously been covering his tracks, because a lot of her research led to dead ends, especially when she went back more than fifteen years, and nothing she dug up led her closer to actually finding him here in LA. She tried to hack into Jack's GPS, but it was secured too tightly and there was no way she would get in without better equipment. Right now she was waiting for Rhys to bring it to her. It was tricky since her dad couldn't go through any of his connections himself, let alone leave the house. It was risky for Rhys too, but he had insisted.

Starry hit the punching bag again. She was already tired and she'd barely begun. She hadn't slept very well last night after a full day of unsuccessful searching, but she kept going with the workout until sweat poured down her neck and shoulders. It was useless. Nothing was going to ease her endless store of anger and anxiety. Giving the bag one last kick, she marched out of the small workout room less relaxed than when she had entered.

"Starry!" Rhys called out from the front of the house. "I've got your equipment!"

She yelled back that she was getting in the shower and he should leave it in her room, figuring she could avoid seeing him as much as possible that way. She was grateful to have the equipment, but that didn't mean she was ready to patch things up.

There was an unopened bag of Doritos by the equipment Rhys had left on Starry's desk. She rolled her eyes. As she toweled off her hair and got dressed, she remembered the night Rhys had licked Doritos cheese off her fingers. Idiot. He had probably been thinking how gullible she was to fall for his lies.

She grabbed the bag of Doritos and threw it across the room where it hit the far wall and dropped to the floor. He might have been physically attracted to her, but how genuine were his feelings for her beyond that?

Enough of him. She started putting together the equipment and installing and rewriting software, and then finally settled in for a long hacking session. Her stomach rumbling, she gave in to the Doritos and ripped the bag open. She tried hacking into Jack's GPS again, but either he or Craig was just as good as she was at securing equipment. Calling Jack's number might open up a few possibilities, but she wouldn't resort to that yet.

Sam was next. Maybe there was information on him that would lead her in a good direction. When she found a picture of him she stared at it for a full five minutes. He looked a lot like her father, but Sam was physically smaller, with hair that wasn't graying yet, and his eyes were softer and less angry.

She dug further and discovered he worked at a well-known CPA firm in Manhattan. Then she found a list of his clients, one of which didn't surprise her at all: Craig Mihashi. She dug some more and found credit card statements with dates and addresses for dining establishments. Phone calls lasting an hour or more. She started looking into the other names her father had given her from Alex Sheffield's interrogation and found similar trails. Her father had killed all of those people. He'd made sure to kill anyone remotely connected to Sam and the network he'd built up, so how had Craig slipped under his radar?

"I got your favorite," Rhys said when Starry entered the kitchen hours later, her stomach aching from hunger. It was close to nine o'clock now and all she'd eaten was the bag of Doritos. Her head hurt from all of her research, and she still hadn't nailed down who had hired Andrews. She suspected Craig, but had no solid evidence.

Rhys held up a little white box with bright red Chinese symbols stamped across the side. Starry stopped for a full two seconds before she ripped her gaze from the takeout box and headed for the fridge. He was crazy if he thought he could tempt her with her favorite food.

Her stomach growled and the sound seemed to echo through the sparsely-decorated kitchen and adjoining dining area.

"I heard that," Rhys called out to her from the dining table. When she glanced over at him, he was taking a big bite of one of the pork buns, a playful smile on his lips.

Her stomach growled again and she yanked open the fridge. It was as bad as Rhys' apartment: bread, eggs, milk, pickles. She looked in the freezer next. Frozen waffles.

"Starry," Rhys said through his chewing, "don't ignore me anymore, please. I can't take it. I got these just for you."

"Then why are you eating one?" She reluctantly pulled out the waffle box.

"In an attempt to lure you over here to take it away from me."

That made her lower the box. He had to be kidding. The freezer door closed and she was left standing in the middle of the kitchen, waffle box in hand, as Rhys turned around in his chair to look her in the eyes. It was the first eye contact she'd had with him since their trip to the safe house, and it sent a strange shudder through her—a mixture of fear, anger, and attraction. He looked so good dressed down in a T-shirt and jeans, his hair messy, his jaw scruffy, his chalky blue eyes filled with hurt and regret.

"I can't trust you," she whispered, unable to take her eyes off him. "I want to so much, but the lies you told me, how you acted . . . it was all so . . . I mean, I bought into it, and you let me . . . and I don't know how I can—"

"I know, I know." He swallowed a mouthful of food. "I know."

"If you know, then why are you bothering me? I need time."

"I know that too, but you haven't given me a chance to explain everything. Just let me talk to you, okay?"

Looking down at the waffle box, she nodded. He had a point. There were facts she was missing, but she hadn't been in the mood to hear them, let alone deal with them. She would be stupid to put it off any longer. "Fine."

"Great, now come eat some real food. You haven't had a decent meal since we got here."

He was right about that too. All she had eaten yesterday was a bowl of cereal and a slice of cold pizza. Putting the waffles back in the freezer, she walked to the dining table and sat in the chair opposite Rhys. She snatched the small box away from him and opened it up. The sweet scent of barbecue pork and dense bread wafted up to her nose. "You got the char siu bao again." She looked at the other takeout boxes, their lids still closed. "Garlic shrimp?"

Rhys tossed her a pair of chopsticks and smiled. "Of course. It's the exact same order as before."

She closed her eyes and fought back her mixed emotions. How could she hate and love someone in the same moment? "I've fallen hard for you, Rhys," she said, plucking a bun out of the box and taking a big bite. "But nothing is ever going to be the same now that I know you lied."

"I know that."

She swallowed. "Where do I fit? Is my father first, or am I?"

He lowered his eyes. "Your father saved me, Starry. There's not a lot I can—"

"Saved you from what? All you've told me was he cleaned you up and gave you a job. You're not one of his Top Eight. You're not a dealer or even anyone that important in the syndicate. If you really wanted out, he'd let you out. I know you don't want to keep running that strip club. That much wasn't a lie. So why are you here? Why does he trust you so damn much?"

Rhys slowly spun one of the takeout boxes around and around on the table. He kept his eyes lowered. "I need to start a few years back, so please bear with me. My dad abused me when I was a kid. Not only me, but my mom and my sister, even my two brothers.

Eventually, my brothers got old enough to leave, but they didn't bother taking me with them. My sister ran away when she was twelve. I stuck around. I was my mom's favorite and I couldn't leave her alone with my dad. So I stayed."

As much as Starry wasn't in the mood for a sob story, she couldn't help but feel sorry for Rhys. She kept her face neutral and looked down at the table. "Keep talking."

"Then my mom left."

Starry looked up, glowering. What kind of a mother did that to her son? Then again, what kind of a father gave up his child to his brother? She didn't like that Rhys was sucking her in already. "Why didn't she take you with her?" She straightened her shoulders in an attempt to shake off her growing empathy.

Rhys kept pushing the takeout box in circles. "She was too scared, I guess. I don't know. So it was just me and Dad. He had me in his grip so tight there was no getting away from him. I guess I was the reason my mom could leave. If he had at least one person to control, he was happy. Anyway, I finally left when I was eighteen. Took all of Dad's cash and drugs that I could find, and ran." He stopped pushing the box. "It was the hardest thing I'd ever done."

So maybe he was getting somewhere with all of this. Starry nodded for him to go on.

"I made it here to LA, but I was a wreck. I had no idea how to work a job, how to survive outside of my father's abuse. I ended up on the street. Got into more drugs than I was already into. I gave up. It was a coward's way to end it all, you know? I mean, what's the point of that kind of life? I thought if I stuck to the drugs long and hard enough, they'd finish me off for good. And if your dad hadn't come along, they would have."

Starry forgot about finishing the pork bun and waited for Rhys to continue.

"I ran out of money, so I asked my supplier if there was a way I could sell like he did—anything so I could keep using. It was the only thing that mattered. He said he'd set me up, and that was good for a while until I ran into trouble and ended up in some rough fights. In one of those fights, I accidentally killed my supplier, and that was bad because he was one of Glenn's favorites. I ended up in one of Glenn's torture rooms, but not for information. All he wanted to do was make me pay. I knew he was going to kill me when it was over. He cut me a few times, stressed all the pressure points, broke some fingers, sliced me pretty deep along my ribs and let me bleed until I was barely conscious. It bothered him that I didn't care, but I was done, you know?"

He looked at Starry again, who realized she had been so sucked into Rhys' story that she was on the edge of her seat. Her father was ruthless. She'd watched grown men completely fall apart under his torture methods.

"Why didn't he kill you?" she asked. "It's not like him to go that far and not kill you in the end."

"Like I said, it bothered him. He kept asking me why I wasn't begging for my life like everyone else. I told him how I ended up where I was. It didn't seem to faze him, but he slowed down. He kept talking to me, said he was intrigued by how fast I'd worked my way up in his system and how well I was taking his torture. He said he needed a manager for one of his clubs and asked if I was up to the job. He said it would include a place to live, good pay, and he'd clean me up from the drugs so I could actually function. I don't know why he decided to do all of that, but it sounded okay at the time. I should have known it came with a heavy price."

"Of course it came with a heavy price. If he saves you instead of killing you, you can't ever leave or he'll finish what he started."

"It was like that . . . at first."

Raising an eyebrow, Starry slid her chopsticks out of their paper wrapper and broke them apart. "At first?"

Rhys took his hands off the takeout box and looked up at her. "He's treated me with more kindness than anyone ever has. Except for the torture, but I earned that. Business, you know? So I can't blame him there. He became the father I should have had, if that makes sense. I don't *want* to leave him, Starry. I care about him, and I don't want to hurt him. Ever. Would you?"

She rolled her eyes, but knew exactly what he meant. In the past few days, she had wanted to kill her father more than anything, but she had always known deep down that she'd never be able to follow through with it. "He has a way of making people loyal," she sighed, "and it makes sense. He's a father figure to both of us."

Rhys nodded. "Yes, exactly. When he cleaned me up, it was hard. He was ruthless, but I got clean, and it was worth it. It wasn't just the drugs. He put me through therapy for my father's abuse and my abandonment issues with my mom and the others. He spent time with me. We bonded like father and son. I was his pet project and he grew protective of me, more than any of the other men in the syndicate. It always seemed like it was even more than that. He really cared. He still does, and nobody's ever cared for me like that, Star. Nobody except him and you. That's why I'm here. He loves me like family, like blood, just as much as he loves you."

A few of the broken pieces inside Starry snapped together and astonishment rushed through her. "It's making sense now," she said, her eyes widening. "I've always been the most important person to him. Always. Maybe that's why he kept his attachment to you a secret. He didn't want me to be jealous." She looked up and met Rhys' eyes. "Unless there's more you're not telling me."

Rhys shook his head. "I promise I've told you everything."

Studying his desperate expression, Starry decided to believe him. She closed her eyes, trying to focus. "But why wouldn't he tell me about you after all this time? He must have seen how much I was falling for you. He must have . . ."

Her heart nearly stopped as a realization hit her. She opened her eyes and drilled them into Rhys, who folded his arms and sat back in his chair. "What?" he asked.

"My father is all about blood ties, so us falling for each other is all so *convenient*, don't you think? I'm wondering if he's been planning this all along, with you and me permanently together."

"Maybe."

Starry leaned forward. "Think about it. If you and I stay together and have children, the Ramsay blood stays in the syndicate. That sort of thing, am I right? It makes sense. It's what he would want most of all for the future."

Rhys nodded slowly. "You're right. He hasn't ever said it out loud to me, but he's hinted at something like that. I don't think that was his original idea when he took me under his wing, but you have to admit it's an intriguing plan."

Starry gritted her teeth. "*Intriguing plan?* He's setting us up!"

Rhys shrugged and Starry wanted to slap him. "But it makes sense, like you said. And what's wrong with being set up if we want to be together anyway? Everybody wins." He cleared his throat and looked down at the table. "If you can forgive me, that is."

If she had ever wondered what it might feel like to be thrown into an arranged marriage, she didn't have to look any further than how she felt in that moment. Her father had orchestrated things perfectly. He had probably made sure she met Rhys at a time when she was unattached to anyone. He had probably made sure she was the one who would work on installing Rhys' surveillance system so they would get to spend time together. If that hadn't worked out, she was sure he would have found another way to throw them together. What frightened her was how well he knew her. She and Rhys clicked in all the right ways. Even now when she was pissed as hell at him for lying to her, she couldn't deny her physical and emotional attraction to him.

She glanced at the adorable little freckle under his bottom lip. "My dad has a way with people," she said. "I'm sure that's how he's managed to run the syndicate so well for so long."

"I'm sure you're right, but he and I both should have thought about what we were doing to you." He reached across the table and Starry backed away from him. "I'm sorry we hurt you, Star."

She narrowed her eyes. "You might be sorry, but you're always going to choose my father over me, so what does it matter?"

He blinked, but didn't say anything. His eyes filled with regret so intense Starry almost reached out to grab the hand still stretched out to her.

"I fell for you too," he said as he slowly withdrew his hand. "I know you don't trust me right now, and I know my words mean nothing to you, but I need you to know what I feel for you is not a lie. I've never felt it with anyone else before. It's real, and I will do anything to make this right—when you're ready."

She locked her gaze on him, certain he was trying to manipulate her on some level. She was not ready to back down. "No," she said, scooting her chair away from the table. She picked up the two takeout boxes she'd been eating from, and stood. "I can't trust you, Rhys. I can't. And now all of this with my father's sick plan to make all my decisions for me . . . I'm just . . . I'm done. I can't talk to either of you until I've decided how the hell I feel about any of it."

"I understand." Rhys looked down at the table.

A part of Starry wanted to feel bad for him, but the other part wanted to punch him in the throat. "Thanks for the food," she said, forcing her voice to stay even and calm. "I'm going to bed."

She turned and left the room before he could respond. As she sat down at her desk and dug into the garlic shrimp, she grabbed her phone to see that a new text message had come through hours ago. She must have been too occupied with her hacking to notice it earlier. It was Jack's phone number. She was confused for a moment about how he'd gotten her number until she remembered forwarding those journal entries to her phone from his. That hadn't been the smartest thing ever, but it didn't matter now. She was probably going to contact him at some point anyway. She opened the message.

JACK: *I have a proposition for you.*

She narrowed her eyes and typed her reply.

STARRY: *Proposition? What the hell is that supposed to mean?*

JACK: *It has to do with Emma – a way for you to meet with her.*

STARRY: *But you didn't know anything the last time I saw you. What could you possibly propose . . . unless your father has finally let you in on his dirty plans?*

JACK: *No, nothing like that. We have her. We have Emma.*

Starry's mouth dropped open. If Jack had Emma, that meant he and his father were definitely the ones working with Andrews. That solved the mystery of who to track down and kill. But if they had Emma . . .

Starry rubbed at a spot between her eyes, her heart pounding. If there was one thing her father had taught her, it was not to jump at a dangling carrot. She would have to play this carefully.

STARRY: *Talk to me.*

TWENTY-FOUR

"Perfect timing," Craig said when Emma came into the kitchen. "I've been in touch with Starry. She said she can video chat for exactly two minutes."

Emma froze in the doorway. She had just taken a hot shower and her hair was still wet. A few drops of water trickled down the back of her neck. "Oh," was all she could say. She darted her eyes to Jack standing near the refrigerator with a can of Coke in his hands. He set the can on the counter and met her gaze, his eyes questioning whether or not this was what she really wanted.

"You sure this is safe?" he asked, turning to his dad.

Craig looked up from the computer monitor at the table. "Yes, I've masked our IP address. It should have her looking for a while. If we're only on for two minutes I doubt she or I will get far trying to find each other."

Swallowing a lump in her throat, Emma nodded confidently despite the growing tightness in her stomach. It would be a two-minute conversation to convince Starry to meet with her, that was all. She could do this. She had no idea *how*, but she would try.

She walked over to Craig and watched him pull up some windows then sit back as a ringtone sounded through the speakers.

"You two are going to listen?" Emma asked, her stomach clenching tighter. She had imagined a private conversation. This was, after all, the very first time she would ever see and talk to her sister.

"No, we'll leave," Jack said, giving his dad a crusty look.

Craig got up from the chair and motioned for Emma to sit down. "I'd like to stay. It'll be better for Emma if we're here."

"No." Jack grabbed Craig's elbow and practically yanked him to the living room area. "Give her some privacy."

Surprisingly, Craig didn't fight his son, and before Emma could think about how odd that was, the ringtone ended, followed by a muffled click.

"Hi, Emma," a confident voice sounded through the speakers. "How are you?"

The video window was still black, and Emma narrowed her eyes. "Uh, fine . . . uh . . . hold on a second." She moved the cursor around the screen in search of something that might show her Starry's video feed. "I can't see you."

"Oh, that's some technical difficulties on my end," Starry interrupted casually. "Don't worry about it. I can see you just fine."

Emma glanced down at the bottom corner of the screen where her end of the video feed was working. She cringed at her image. Her wet hair looked stringy and her skin looked pale under the kitchen light above.

"Okay," she said, a little irritated that she couldn't see Starry. It seemed unfair.

Craig appeared around the corner, his face concerned as he tapped at the watch on his wrist. He was behind the camera so Starry couldn't see him.

Flustered, Emma looked at the elapsed time on the screen and cleared her throat. "So, uh, Starry, I was hoping we could meet each other. Craig told me . . . I mean . . ."

She was botching the entire thing. Her hands started to sweat and she wiped them on her jeans. They were Starry's jeans, and they fit perfectly, meaning Starry was the same size as her. What else was the same? *Please, oh please let Starry be somewhat normal like me*, she said to herself. *Please let us have something in common besides the same birth father and pants size.*

316

"What did Glenn do to you?" Starry asked before Emma could spit out anything else. "He told me he whipped you. How bad was it?"

Emma's mouth went even drier than before. Why hadn't she thought about getting a glass of water before this? "I'm fine," she answered flatly.

"He didn't strip you down, did he? I swear, if he did I'll rip his throat out. He's sick, but not that sick."

Emma squeezed her eyes shut against sudden memories from the torture room. "No, he didn't, but it . . . the whip . . . it hurt so much."

Starry let out a string of swear words that would fill the Swear Jar to its brim. Finally, she let out a heavy sigh, the sound of it crackling over the speakers. "Are you crying?" she asked.

Emma swiped away a few tears and bit back the rest of her emotions. She was supposed to keep it together, play it cool, be professional and levelheaded so she could entice Starry to meet with her. Not fall apart like a helpless coward. At least Starry seemed angry with Glenn, just as Andrews had said.

And that's when it occurred to her that Starry was reacting exactly the way Andrews had said she would. She was acting protective of Emma's innocence and vulnerability. Maybe there was something to his idea after all.

Not that it mattered at the moment. Time was going by too fast, and her emotions were too intense

317

for her to think too much beyond wiping away her tears.

"I don't know how to do this," she said, sniffing. She didn't want Starry to see her cry, but her entire body felt cold and alien, as if she had no control over what was going on. And maybe she didn't. She stared at the black video screen and tried to imagine her sister's face there—someone with kind, understanding eyes. No matter how hard she tried, she couldn't picture it. Starry was completely foreign to her.

"I don't know how to tell you what I'm feeling," she said. "I'm not sure how I'd act if we met. You . . . you scare me, Starry. Glenn scares me. Everything that's happening scares me. I should be better at this. I should be stronger, like my dad tried to teach me to be."

A few more tears fell down her cheeks and she pushed back the sudden desire to get up and leave. When she lifted her eyes, Jack and Craig were in the doorway, both of them looking at her with shocked expressions. Craig glanced at his watch, his eyes widening.

The elapsed time on the timer read 2:15 and counting.

"I need to go," Starry said after a long pause. "But I want to meet you, Emma. Tell Craig I'll message him in a minute."

The audio feed went silent, and Emma lifted her eyes to Craig, who was smiling. "Good work," he said. "You knew exactly how to play her."

Emma screwed up her face, her tears finally stopping. "I wasn't 'playing' her," she said acidly.

His smile faded. "Oh, of course you weren't."

Emma stood up, and Jack pulled her into his arms and squeezed her gently. "I'm sorry. That must have been hard."

Nuzzling into his neck, she soaked him in. "Meeting her in person will be even harder. What if she hates me?"

Jack rubbed his thumb in little circles on her shoulder. "Have some faith in yourself, Emma."

TWENTY-FIVE

Starry tiptoed down the hallway, avoiding the spots where the floor creaked. She had already disabled the security system so she could leave quietly.

Checking her watch, she rounded the corner to the back sliding door, carefully unlatched the lock, and slipped out onto the deck. She turned to close the door, only to see a tall, dark figure staring back at her, his hand curled around the door to keep it open.

She let out a small gasp and jumped back.

"Going somewhere?" Rhys asked, his eyes glinting in the semi-darkness. The moon was bright. Starry shot it a dirty look before turning back to Rhys.

"How the *hell* did you—"

"You must have eaten that entire box of garlic shrimp," he laughed. "I could smell you when you stuck your head in my room."

Cringing, Starry lifted her hand to her mouth and sniffed her breath. Yeah, it was strong, even after she'd brushed her teeth. Damn garlic. She had passed Rhys' bedroom on her way through the house and poked her head in to make sure he was asleep. Apparently he hadn't been completely out. Either that or he hadn't been trying to sleep in the first place. He had probably heard her moving around long before she'd checked on him. She hadn't been able to sit still since talking to Emma.

"I didn't even hear you following me," she said as she lowered her hand from her face. "When did you learn how to do that?"

He shrugged. "Moving silently was kind of an essential survival skill back home."

She looked out across the backyard, frowning. Her plan was ruined now, so she might as well give up.

But . . . *no.*

Grabbing Rhys' wrist, Starry pulled him out onto the deck and gently shut the sliding door. Rhys didn't resist. He folded his arms as she stepped up to him. She looked him square in the eyes. "This is something I have to do, and my dad can't know about it. If he finds out, I'll be in deep shit. Either that or he'll do something stupid and screw us all over."

Rhys tilted his head and looked her up and down. She was dressed in dark jeans and the black hoodie she had taken from Blaire's closet. She had rimmed her eyes in heavy eyeliner, and her hair was pulled into a tight ponytail. Rhys glanced at the backpack she carried. "What's in there?" he asked, eyes filling with hurt. "Are you leaving for good?"

She peered through the glass doors. "No, I'm coming back. I'm bringing a few precautions, that's all."

Rhys looked confused. "Where are you going? Spit it out."

She did not owe him any explanation, but there was really only one option at this point: take him with her. If she left him here, he'd probably tell her father she was gone.

She gave him the dirtiest look she could muster. "You'll have to come with me." She looked down at his bare feet. "Let's get your shoes."

Rhys snorted. "What, are we going behind your dad's back to get Emma? Should I pack one of the sniper rifles from the weapons closet just in case? Seriously, Starry, are you *nuts*? What possible reason could compel you to leave your father like this?"

Starry ground her teeth together and decided she wasn't going to keep any secrets from Rhys. She was stronger than that. "I've found the connection between the mysterious Craig and Sam. I think he's the one who hired Andrews to kill my dad."

Rhys tilted his head. "What kind of connection?"

She shrugged. "He was one of Sam's CPA clients. And his son is totally hung up on Emma. You can't tell me that's a coincidence."

"No, of course not." Rhys rubbed his chin and gave her a skeptical look. "But is that enough for you to rush into something like this?"

She steeled herself, knowing Rhys would try his best to talk her out of it. "They have Emma."

Rhys' eyes narrowed into slits. His folded arms tightened over his chest, the muscles in his biceps bulging. "*They have Emma?* And you're not informing your father?" He lowered his arms to his sides and stepped close to Starry, his face inches from hers. She could smell his stale cologne and aftershave. "Starry, that's why we're in hiding—so we can give you time to find the threat. And now you've found that threat and you're sneaking out to take care of it on your own? If you don't get killed doing this, I'm pretty sure your father will kill you when you get back."

"Thanks for the vote of confidence, but it's not what you think. I want to meet with her away from my father. They promised they won't try anything."

Rhys looked like he wanted to strangle her. A vein in his neck bulged. "You talked to them? How?"

She rolled her eyes. "Through secure channels, don't worry. I talked to Emma over a video feed. I could see her, but she couldn't see me."

Rhys angrily shook his head. "This is a trap. Unless you're planning to ambush them and take *them* out all on your own? Is this about killing Craig because he's after your father? Or is it about Emma?"

"I don't want to kill Craig." It was the truth. "At least, not yet. I don't have enough information. And I don't want to hurt Emma. They promised to tell me more about what they want, and I figure if they're playing this sort of game, none of it's what we were anticipating."

"I don't buy that. Andrews and those other men clearly wanted your father dead, which means Craig wants him dead—and probably you too. This feels like a trap to me. It's too easy."

Yes, of course it was too easy. She leaned back against the deck railing and crossed her arms. The moonlight fell across Rhys' strong, angry figure, making him look like an eerie sort of ethereal guardian. He'd told her he would do anything to make things right between them, and she supposed that meant protecting her at all costs. Unless, of course, her father came into play. The syndicate and her father always came first.

A hollow sensation crept up on her, and it surprised her. It almost felt like loneliness. "I need to meet Emma," she explained, her voice cold and strong as she tried to push back her emotions. "I need to see if meeting her changes things. I don't know if that makes any sense, but now that Sam's dead and gone, she's it, you know? I'm tired of my father manipulating me. If it's true he wants me and you together, that's just one more thing he's got his hands in. I want to meet Emma on my own, without him there, without him pushing things around where he wants them. I want control of this one thing. If I can show her I won't hurt her like he did . . . if I can get her on *my* side . . ."

She stopped when Rhys raised an eyebrow. "I thought you and your father were on the same side."

She shook her head and blinked back a few tears as the loneliness returned and nearly consumed her. "I'm not sure we are anymore. Ever since he hit me, things haven't been the same."

Rhys was silent and Starry looked up to see his eyes filled with empathy. It was then that she felt a few tears roll down her cheeks and she quickly swiped them away, irritated at the weakness they showed. It was the last thing she wanted Rhys to see.

He slid up so close to her that she could feel his breath on her face. "I'll come with you," he said, inching an arm around her to pull her closer. "I can see there's no talking you out of this, and I can't let you walk into it alone. I still think it's beyond stupid."

She didn't have the will to pull away from him. He felt too good. He smelled too good. "You'll do that?" she asked, leaning against him. His shirt smelled like Chinese food and the laundry detergent the cleaning service used to wash the sheets. Starry had been the one to schedule those services. She was the only one who managed this secret house. Her father entrusted that to her. He entrusted her with a lot of stuff, but she was about to go behind his back on this, and she wasn't sure that was a bad thing. A lot of things were starting to fall apart for

Starry, all thanks to Emma. She hoped she didn't regret her decision when it came time to meet her face to face.

"Sure, I'll do it," Rhys answered softly, no trace of sarcasm in his voice. "If this is what it takes for you to realize how much I want to fix things with you. If Jack and his father have a problem with me coming along, we'll figure out a solution—or we can make sure they don't know I'm there." He ran a finger down her neck, playing with a bit of hair that had fallen out of her ponytail.

And just like that, something inside of her broke. She wrapped her arms around him and buried her face against his chest. For a brief moment, she let herself want him, accept him, trust him. She squeezed him closer to her body, her breaths quick and soft as his warmth surrounded her. She wasn't alone. She was connected, and it was a feeling she never wanted to lose. How could it last?

Her arms went slack and she pulled away a fraction of an inch. Accepting Rhys back into her life meant she'd always have something to lose. He made her weak in so many ways. Maybe he was worth it, even if his jumping at the chance to help her was a little suspect. She'd have to keep an eye on him.

"Okay," she said, letting him go and backing away. She met his eyes and gave him a steely look. "Let's do this."

He nodded as he turned and quietly slid open the glass door. "I'll grab my shoes. Where are we headed?"

Starry let out a quiet laugh and looked down at his jeans. "You might want to change once we get there. We're meeting at the club."

Rhys spun around. "Why?"

"It's open late, and it's a public place I know I won't have a problem getting into. I figure if Jack and his dad want to hurt me, they're a lot less likely to do it somewhere public. I think it's a good sign they agreed to meet there in the first place, and if we need somewhere more private, Ginger can get us one of the VIP rooms or put us in your office."

"Thanks for including me in the plans," Rhys said sarcastically. "You didn't think someone would try to call me and tell me you'd been there since I've ordered them to report anything unusual?"

Unruffled, Starry gave him a self-satisfied smirk. "I thought that through. I made it so your calls are routed through my phone and won't go through unless I approve them." She tightened her jaw when he shot her a death glare. "I'm sorry, but would you expect any less from me?"

Shaking his head, Rhys stepped into the house with silent footfalls. "With you, Starry?" he whispered. "Never."

TWENTY-SIX

The strip club smelled like sweat and men's cologne. Emma held onto Jack's hand as they walked behind Craig into the main area.

There was a lot more skin on display than Emma particularly wanted to see. Several women dancing on raised platforms in the middle of the room were almost naked. Emma guessed it wouldn't be long before the rest of their clothes would be on the stage floor.

"Have you ever been in a place like this before?" Emma asked Jack as she looked around, shocked. When Jack didn't answer her, she turned to see him gazing at the raised platform where a striking Asian woman was contorting her naked body around a pole.

Emma elbowed him in the arm. "Hey!"

He jumped and tore his attention away from the stripper. "What?" he shouted over the extra-loud music, turning to look her in the eyes as they passed the platform and walked around a crowded dance floor. "It's kind of hard *not* to look." He gestured to a seating area where several scantily clad women were giving men lap dances on sofas. "It's everywhere."

She shrugged. "I know . . . it's just . . ."

Just what? Jealousy? And why was she worrying about something like that when they could all die in the next few hours?

"Hey," Jack said, squeezing her hand. "If it bothers you, I'll close my eyes and you can lead me to wherever my dad is headed."

"It's fine," she muttered. "Seriously, it's not a big deal. I'm worried about meeting Starry, and I'm on edge, and we could die if I screw this up, you know?"

Her voice kept getting higher the more she talked. Jack tightened his grip on her hand. "Let's sit down and try to relax."

They followed Craig to a corner of the seating area and sat down. Almost immediately, a woman dressed in red fishnet stockings and a black leather teddy approached their sofa, her eyes sliding over the three of them and then stopping on Craig. Her lips lifted into a seductive smile as she sauntered over to him, her sharp red nails sliding up her hips.

Craig shifted into position to welcome her on his lap.

Emma glared at the two of them, disgusted. It was creepy how comfortable Craig seemed in a place like this.

"Hey, handsome," the woman cooed as she settled onto Craig and lightly dragged her nails over his buzzed head, down his neck, and into the collar of his button-up shirt. Emma noticed the tiny, flesh-colored earpiece in Craig's left ear. It was something anyone could miss unless they were looking for such a thing. She had watched him put it in back at the hotel room while Andrews did the same. It allowed the two of them to communicate as Andrews waited on standby in a rental car outside. That didn't put Emma at ease.

"Want a private room?" the woman on Craig's lap asked, leaning close to his ear. She didn't seem to notice the earpiece, or didn't care. "I can entertain multiples if you want to bring your friends." Her eyes roved over Jack, and then Emma, who squirmed.

"We can't give you any business tonight," Craig said, nudging her away from his ear, "but you can have this for your trouble." He pulled a fifty-dollar bill out of his pocket and tucked it deep into the woman's left bra cup, his fingers lingering inside for a few seconds before he nudged her off his lap.

She shrugged and sauntered off. Jack let out a soft grunt. "I thought we were going to have to sit here and watch."

Craig cast him a sideways scowl. "I don't want to draw attention, Jack, and I don't want to piss anyone off. Play it cool like we talked about."

Jack breathed heavily through his nose, but didn't say anything. It was then that Emma realized she'd dug half-moon indents into his arm. He slowly pried her fingers away and gave her a shaky smile. "You need to relax. We're all nervous, but it's going to be okay. Starry's going to meet us and you'll be fine. Just be yourself, like you were on the video chat. That got us here, didn't it?"

She relaxed her fingers. "I guess so. All I did was break down and freak out, but sure."

Craig folded his arms and glanced at her. "Don't underestimate emotional manipulation. Sam was a genius with that, which means you've got it in you too."

Emma blinked, simultaneously horrified and eager to hear more about this side of her father. "What do you mean?"

"How else do you think he recruited his crew? Money alone doesn't inspire that kind of loyalty. You've got it in you to convince Starry. Dig deep. Trust your gut."

Jack turned to his dad and cocked an eyebrow. "So is that how Sam got you on board? He manipulated your *feelings?*"

Craig narrowed his eyes. "Now's not the time."

Jack let out an annoyed sigh and leaned back into the sofa. He nudged Emma to follow, and she leaned against him, wishing she could stay right next to him forever, even if it was in a strip club. Starry had told them this was the only place she was willing to meet them, and Emma could see why. It was private, but public at the same time. And loud enough to have a conversation without anyone eavesdropping. She didn't feel like anyone had even looked at her besides the woman Craig had sent away.

"Starry's here," Craig said, nodding his head toward a corner of the room by the bar.

Emma followed the direction of Craig's nod and saw a slender woman about her size leaning against the bar with a bright orange drink in her hand. She took a sip and nodded as the bartender said something to her.

"Yep, that's her," Jack confirmed.

Just then, Starry looked across the room, her eyes landing on Emma and staying there. She jerked her head, as if to say, "I'm ready, let's do this," and Emma dug her fingernails into Jack's arm again.

He pried them away once more. "Go on. If she tries to leave with you, tell her you want to stay here. You know we're here if you need us. We're not far away."

She swallowed a lump in her throat and nodded. Her heart was going a million miles an hour. This was it. She was going to convince her sister to betray one of the most dangerous men in the city, or Western Hemisphere, for all she knew.

"Okay," she said, and turned to face Jack before she stood up.

He looked hard into her eyes and held tightly onto her hand. "I know you can do this, Emma."

She nodded curtly and pulled her hand away. As she walked toward Starry, she felt more out of place than she ever had in her life, especially decked out in an extremely short, too-tight dress and thigh-high leather boots that had made Jack do a double-take when he first saw her in them. Craig had bought the outfit for her, insisting she had to be dressed a certain way to get into the club.

She reached Starry, who set down her drink and motioned for Emma to sit on a stool next to her.

"You're prettier in person," Starry said. She glanced at Emma's outfit. "But I'll bet you normally don't dress that way, do you? You look like you want to run away and hide."

"I kind of do," Emma admitted so quietly the loud music drowned it out.

Starry was dressed in a black skirt and lacy camisole that seemed to show more skin than hide it. Her curly dark hair reached down past her shoulders, and even though she was only eleven months older than Emma, she looked as if she could be eleven years older. Her eyes were rimmed with black eyeliner, her cheekbones high and pronounced, a nose ring curled around her right nostril and a smaller ring poised perfectly at the edge of her left eyebrow. Her lips were a deep red. They lifted into a smirk as Emma sat staring at her, astonished. It was as if she was seeing a possible version of herself—a dangerous version.

"Am I not what you expected?" Starry asked, a laugh bubbling up from deep in her throat. She picked up her glass, slung back the last of her drink, and licked her lips without marring her perfect lipstick.

"I don't know." Emma straightened on the stool. She had decided before coming in here that she would keep a backbone through the whole ordeal, but she could already tell it was going to be difficult. Starry was her sister, her blood, a secret Emma had finally uncovered, and she had to remember above all that her father had believed he could turn her away from Glenn. If he had lost his life believing that, Emma would accomplish what he'd set out to do. Or die trying. Backbone or not.

"You're not exactly what I expected either," Starry said as she touched Emma's hand resting on the bar.

Relief spread through Emma as she looked down at Starry's fingertips touching hers. In that moment she knew that no matter how Starry had been raised or who she had become, nothing would change the undeniable connection between them. They were sisters. It was a force binding them together, despite everything.

"Eighteen years," Starry said as she moved her hand on top of Emma's. "Can you imagine what it would have been like if we'd lived together all that time? I mean, what kind of music do you like? Do you love Chinese food as much as I do? What was our dad like?" She let out a nervous laugh. "There's just so much I want to know about you, about us, about what it's like to have a sister. You know?"

Emma's mouth dropped open as she realized she was catching a glimpse of the real Starry. Beneath her tough exterior, she was warm and attentive. Emma liked that. A lot.

She smiled and looked Starry in the eyes. "My favorite band is Fleetwood Mac—don't judge—and I don't know if I love Chinese food as much as you do, but it's definitely at the top of my list. I love lo mein noodles best. And our dad . . ." Her voice faded as tears filled her eyes. "Our dad was the kindest man I've ever met. He worked so hard to make me happy."

A soft smile lifted Starry's lips. "I'm glad he made you happy." She squeezed Emma's hand before letting it go. "It makes me wonder if I would have been happy with him too. Where would we both be in that situation? Would we be different than we are now, do you think?"

Emma frowned as she thought about the question. She didn't doubt that she'd still be herself, but Starry might be completely different. First of all, her tough shell probably wouldn't exist. Did Emma have the courage to say that to her?

"I don't think you'd be where you are," she finally answered. "And I don't think you'd be as confused about what you want or who you want to be."

Starry's faint smile faded. She glanced across the room at Jack and Craig, who were watching them closely with hopeful expressions. "Did they tell you to go for emotional punches?" she asked.

Emma blinked, worry seeping into her heart as she realized the real Starry had retreated back into her shell. "What do you mean?"

Starry glared at her. "Oh, come on, I'm not stupid. The way Jack and his father played this, it's obvious it's a trap. So what do they want you to do? How are they using you?"

Already feeling exhausted from her effort, Emma slumped on her stool and stopped herself from looking over her shoulder at Jack. This really was going to be difficult. How was she supposed to accomplish her task if Starry had already caught on? Then she remembered Craig's advice to follow her gut. What did that even mean? All she wanted to do right now was talk to Starry long enough to really get to know her—even if what she learned scared her. How far did Starry's toughness really go? Emma had caught a glimpse of someone warm beneath the cold exterior. That was the person she had to appeal to and manipulate, as Craig had said her father did so well. She shuddered.

"You're right," she relented as Starry turned to her again. "They are using me. *Craig* is using me. Jack is here because he doesn't want to leave me."

Starry cocked her head. "So you two are together?"

Emma nodded. "I think so. We haven't really discussed it, but I don't know what else it could be."

"Well, he is kind of hot. Good job."

Emma didn't know if she should laugh or not. "Thanks."

Starry waved a hand in the air, dismissing the subject. "So Craig's using you. Tell me what he wants you to do and maybe I'll stay a bit longer. Otherwise, I'm out of here."

Emma's heart sank, followed by a jolt of fear as she grasped for the most emotional card she could play. She didn't care if Starry knew what she was doing. She had to at least try.

"You'd leave that fast after just meeting me?" she asked, widening her eyes dramatically. She felt like a complete fool, but kept the expression going. "I thought you'd want to spend a little more time—"

Starry's eyes narrowed and she cut Emma off. "Tell me what Craig's planning."

Emma stiffened. "I'll tell you everything he wants, but you have to promise not to hurt us if you don't agree. That means keeping all of this from Glenn."

Starry laughed so loud people looked around to see what was so funny. Leaning forward, she lowered her voice. "I promise not to hurt you or your friends, Emma, but it's obvious Craig wants me to lead him to my dad so he can kill him. You think I'm going to keep that from my father? Craig must know I'll take my father's place if he does manage to kill him, so he'd come after me next. What could he possibly offer to make me shoot myself in the foot like that?" She flicked her hand at Emma. "Are you the prize I'm supposed to snatch up? What makes him think he has any right to offer you up like that, anyway? You're not his prisoner. You said you're with Jack, so unless he's a complete dick, I doubt he or his dad are really *making* you do anything. Am I right?" She sat back and folded her arms, waiting for an answer.

A sense of awe and frustration at Starry's insight filled Emma. "There is no prize." She lowered her gaze and wondered how this would ever work with Starry punching holes in all their stupid plans. She looked back up. "And they're not making me do this. Yes, Craig wants to get rid of Glenn, but he doesn't want to hurt you. This was our dad's plan, Starry. If Glenn hadn't caught him and killed him, *he'd* be sitting here with you right now instead of me, and he'd be asking you to do this, and he'd probably be doing it a lot better than I am."

For the first time, Starry looked surprised. Her arms fell to her sides and one of her high heels slipped forward on the bottom of her stool. "Sam's plan? What did he want to ask me to do?"

Emma straightened her spine and took a deep breath. There was no way around it except to tell the truth. "He was going to ask you to betray Glenn and take over the syndicate so the two of you could dismantle it from the inside."

Starry's expression twisted into confusion. Her jaw clenched as she looked off to the side near the front entrance at a man dressed in a suit. His eyes were tired but forcefully alert as he caught Starry's gaze and frowned. Emma thought he looked vaguely familiar, and that planted a seed of suspicion deep in her gut. Starry had promised to come alone.

"Dismantle the syndicate?" Starry said as she turned back to Emma. "Why would he want to do that? And don't tell me it's because he thought it was evil and wrong. He ran his own syndicate, you know. He might have been a kind and loving father, like you said, but that doesn't make him a saint. There's no way he would pass up the opportunity to run a syndicate as powerful as my father's."

Emma blinked as she remembered Craig telling her about the plans he and her father had made for the syndicate. As much as Emma wanted to believe her father would have dismantled the syndicate, a part of her wondered if that had really been his goal. It didn't matter now that he was gone. All that mattered was finishing what Craig said was set into motion.

"I don't know what his reasons were," Emma said, thinking out loud. "Maybe it was so he could get rid of everything Glenn ever built. Revenge or something. Whatever the reason was, he planned on you wanting to destroy it all when you found out Glenn wasn't your real father." She paused for a long moment, trying to envision how the syndicate really worked. It had to be an incredibly complex network, each path paved with lies and drugs and money. And Starry was the crucial path leading to Glenn. She was the only one who could open the door to destroy it all.

"The syndicate is evil, Starry," Emma said. "What Glenn is doing. The lives he ruins. You must know it's wrong. Don't you? I guess this isn't even about what our dad wanted anymore. It's about doing what's right."

This was it.

Starry's reaction would foretell everything to come.

A long moment passed. Starry looked as if someone had punched her in the gut, her face contorting with pain until finally she opened her mouth. "Do you even hear what you're asking?" she hissed. "You want me to betray my father. You want me to lead him to his death, and then you want me to step into his shoes and destroy everything he's spent a lifetime building." She leaned forward, her lips drawn into a tight, angry slash across her face. "The syndicate is *everything* to him. If I destroyed it, it would be like desecrating his body after he's dead. Nothing could make me hate him that much. Not even you. Not even what he did to you."

Emma was surprised at how Starry could love a man as evil as Glenn. "But he's not your father," she fired back, pulling the words deep from her gut. Her voice trembled with resolve and a fierce need to make her sister see reason. If there was any decency left in Starry at all, she had to see how evil Glenn truly was.

"If you knew your real father," she continued, "you'd know he would never give you up willingly. He kept a locked box with your baby pictures in it. Why would he keep those if he never wanted you? Why would you stay loyal to Glenn when you know he's lied to you your entire life?"

"*Everybody* lies," Starry growled. "When I found out my dad was keeping you a secret from me, I was so pissed I thought I'd never go back to him. I thought I hated him. Now I've learned he kept even more from me and I think I hate him more. But I don't think I could ever hate him enough to hurt him like you're asking me to do. Could you have ever hurt Sam that way, Emma? Even if it was the right thing to do?"

Emma looked away, her heart sinking in despair. Of course she could never have hurt her father. "No," she said.

Starry nodded. "Okay, then. So what do we do now? I want to get to know you better. You know, be your sister and all that shit. Unless the only reason you're here is because of them." She nodded at Jack and Craig.

Emma's heart split wide open with panic. "They aren't the only reason I'm here. I wanted to meet you."

Starry clenched her jaw. "I wanted to meet you too. In fact, I don't want to let you leave, but I have to. I didn't come here to backstab Craig after I promised not to hurt any of you. I'll meet with him if he really wants, but that's not going to go the way he hopes. Now that I know his intentions, I want to slit his throat. If he gets anywhere near my father, that's exactly what I'll do."

So Starry really was a killer, and not just in self-defense. Emma inched away from her. "Craig's going to be angry when he finds out I couldn't convince you. Maybe it's better if we all leave."

Starry glared at Craig. "He'd better not lay a finger on you or I'll make him beg for death." She leaned forward and wrapped her fingers around Emma's wrist. "I know my dad hurt you, but I promise you he will never do it again if you come back with me." Her expression bordered on pleading. "Let us be your family, Emma. We can protect you forever."

Go back to Glenn? Willingly? Emma swallowed a lump in her throat, anguish ripping through her. Nothing could entice her to join Glenn, even if refusing meant never seeing Starry again. She shook her head. "No," she said, tugging her hand away. "I have Jack now, and I don't want to end up like . . ."

She let her words trail off before Starry's angry expression turned into pure fury. "Like *me?*" she hissed, pushing Emma's wrist away.

Emma pressed her lips together. She had to say something to fix what she'd implied. She didn't want to hurt Starry. That was the flaw in this entire plan. If asking Starry to betray her father ended up hurting her, Emma realized she couldn't push it any further than she already had. Craig and Andrews should have seen that from the beginning.

But something inside of her refused to quit trying.

"There's more to you than what you're showing me," she said as the music in the room pounded around them. "I can see it, Starry. You're tough, like Glenn, but you're so much more too. I hope you realize that someday. I do want to be like you. I want to be strong, but I don't want to hurt other people. What Glenn does hurts other people, and if you're with him in that, I can't see you again."

Emma watched Starry carefully, her heart banging with increasing fear. What if she pushed Starry too far the wrong way?

Emotion filled Starry's eyes, but Emma couldn't tell if it was anger or disappointment. Probably both.

"You're like everyone else," Starry snarled. "You want to know why I'm still loyal to my dad? It's because he accepts this side of me. This *is* me, okay? I don't bend. I don't give in. I don't take shit. And nobody but two people in my life can handle that." She stopped for a moment, her angry expression melting into confusion. And then something sparked in her eyes. Understanding. "You know, I didn't realize it before, but I think that's why I've wanted to meet you all this time. I was hoping you wouldn't care that I'm like him, that you'd accept it, but now I see I was an idiot to think you would be any different. Sam was mistaken. I never would have gone along with what he wanted. He wasted his time planning all of this. He was a fool."

Emma expected to feel anger, fear, guilt, shame, anything but the heartache consuming her as Starry spoke. It shuddered through her like the deep bass pumping from the speakers. There was no hope for Starry. She was who she was. Glenn had raised her to be like him, and he had succeeded. That could only mean one thing.

"It's time for me to go," Emma said as she stood from the stool. She had to end this now or everything would fall apart. "I'm sorry, Starry. I'm sorry we can't be friends, and I'm sorry I asked you to do something impossible." She glanced back at Craig and Jack now standing up from the sofa, concern in their expressions. Emma looked back to Starry still sitting on her stool with a deepening scowl. "I'll do my best to talk Craig out of hunting down Glenn. I don't think it'll get him anywhere but killed anyway."

Starry's bottom lip trembled before she bit down on it and looked away. "Leave before I change my mind and kill all of you. This is the only chance I'll ever give you."

Emma waited for Starry to look at her again, but it was obvious her sister had said her last goodbye. It seemed like the meeting had been such a waste. Or maybe it hadn't. At least she knew what Starry was like now.

Giving her sister one last desperate look, Emma headed back to Craig and Jack, assuring herself everything would be okay even though she had failed on every possible level.

TWENTY-SEVEN

Starry watched Emma walk away. How dare she come in here thinking she could ask her own sister to betray everything she lived for? It was ridiculous. It was insane. Maybe Glenn Ramsay wasn't who Starry had always believed, but he had never, ever asked her to do anything as crazy as what Emma had just proposed.

"Another St. Clements, Miss Ramsay?" the bartender asked.

There was a downside to picking Rhys' club as a meeting place. Most of the staff knew her on sight. It made her antsy that word might get to her father about her going behind his back, but she'd taken a few precautions, at least. Before she had left, she'd made sure his phone would re-route calls and messages to her phone, just as she had for Rhys. She checked her phone, but so far nothing had come through. That alone put her on edge. Plenty of people in the syndicate should be trying to find him right now, even this late at night.

Something was wrong.

"What can I get for you, Miss Ramsay?" the bartender asked her again.

Her answering glare was enough to make him shut his mouth and leave her alone. What she really needed was some hard liquor after that meeting with Emma, but full-nude strip clubs didn't allow drinking. Damn California zoning laws. Why couldn't Rhys run one of her dad's bars or restaurants instead?

She shifted on the barstool as she watched Craig and Jack stand up to meet Emma. It was obvious Craig was uncomfortable. He had probably tried to come in with a gun or a knife and the bouncers had taken it away from him. No weapons for the other team. The last thing she wanted was some sort of ambush where she didn't have the upper hand. She was armed, of course.

But things were winding down now. Rhys had several people ready to keep an eye on Emma and her friends for the next few days, just in case they tried anything stupid.

Heaving a sigh, Starry slid off the stool, eager to get home before her father woke up. She didn't know what she was going to tell him now. He would kill Emma if he knew what she had asked of Starry, and as furious as

Starry was with her long-lost sister, she didn't want her dead. She was blood, after all.

Grumbling to herself, Starry headed through the crowd toward Rhys. He had been standing near the entrance all this time. She caught his eye and then stopped abruptly.

Two bouncers were rushing past him. Starry knew the looks on their faces. They were intent. Driven. What were they after?

Starry turned, her heart nearly stopping as she saw Craig, Jack, and Emma heading for the entrance. The bouncers were about to intercept them. What the *hell?* Starry had given Rhys explicit instructions to let the three of them leave safely unless she ordered otherwise. Had he misunderstood a gesture of hers?

Charging toward him, she caught his eye once again and felt a lump rise in her throat. He hadn't misunderstood anything. It was written all over his angry, frustrated expression. He wanted the bouncers to grab Emma and her friends.

"You son of a bitch," she hissed as she came up to him. "You're backstabbing me? What the hell is going on? Are you in contact with my father?"

Rhys let out a heavy sigh. "I can explain, but first I have to . . ."

He took off in the direction of the bouncers now chasing after Emma and her friends toward the back entrance. Starry stared after him, too confused and shocked to follow.

Bastard! Had he lied to her *again?* He'd had no communication with her father—unless he'd gotten around her phone hack. Or maybe he'd used another form of communication, or her father had another phone she wasn't aware of. There were too many possibilities. She had to find out what was going on.

She balled her hands into fists and took off after Rhys, wishing for steel-toed boots instead of the six-inch heels she'd put on to fit in with the club crowd. Whatever. She could do plenty of damage in heels too.

An alarm sounded, and Starry stopped. The sound was barely audible over the loud music, and cut off a few seconds later.

Emma and the others must have gone through the emergency exit.

Turning around, she headed for the front doors. They had to be somewhere around the back. She would cut through the alleyway and help them there. She wasn't going to let Rhys break her promise to let them go. She pulled off her heels, keeping them in her hand. She was two feet away from the door when someone stepped in front of her.

It was Ginger. Her bright blond hair fell in waves down to her shoulders. Her lipstick was a vicious red. "Hello, Starry," she said in her usual sweet tone. "Leaving so soon?"

"Not now, Ginger." Starry stepped to the side to brush past her.

But Ginger held her ground. She folded her arms and narrowed her eyes. "I can't let you leave." Her voice was almost sad.

"What the hell are you doing?" Starry was about to shove her out of the way, but hesitated. Ginger was a friend and clearly upset in a motherly sort of way. "Let me out."

Ginger's sad expression hardened, though there was a hint of regret in her eyes. "I can't let you leave. Glenn wants you to stay here."

Glenn? Starry's grip on her shoes tightened. "*What? My dad . . . you . . . what?*"

Ginger frowned. "You should never trust anyone. Especially when your father's in charge."

A fierce, hot burst of anger exploded inside of Starry. Her father manipulated *everyone*—even kind, thoughtful Ginger who normally wouldn't hurt a fly. Had he paid her? Or had he threatened her? Either way, it didn't matter now.

Looking into Ginger's eyes, Starry fought off a wave of disappointment. She had thought of Ginger as a friend, but now that was over. She should have known it could never last, not with her father involved. Just like Ginger had said. Her disappointment faded, replaced by a fresh burst of anger. She squeezed the shoes in her hand. "Is he here?" she asked through gritted teeth.

Ginger's frown twitched. "Of course he is. He said the stunt you pulled with his phone was cute, but he's not stupid enough to keep only one."

Starry cringed. Of course he had more than one phone. *She* was the stupid one.

Oh, hell, there was no time for this. Ginger was still talking when Starry lifted the shoes in her hand and struck them heel-first at the woman's face so hard and fast that she had no time to react. The heels raked two shallow cuts across her forehead and cheek. She shrieked, and Starry grabbed the back of her neck, pulled her forward, and swiped a leg against her knees, bringing her face-down to the ground.

"Bitch," Starry growled, and stepped over Ginger to the front door. As she grabbed the handle, something hit her head hard, bringing stars into her vision. She tried to assume a protective stance, but was so disoriented from the blow to her head that everything was spinning and all she managed to do was stumble around. She grabbed for the gun holstered on her left thigh beneath her skirt, but several pairs of hands grabbed her arms and forced her up straight. She caught a glimpse of one of her father's grunt men, and then her father's face as he approached from the direction of the VIP rooms. He was speaking with

Rhys, who nodded once and then turned around and walked away without even a glance at Starry.

"Take her into Rhys' office," her father ordered, meeting Starry's eyes as he came up to her. He looked like he was going to kill her, and that was as good as a punch to the stomach. She opened her mouth to say something, but the man who had a hold of her was three times her size and strength and yanked her wrists behind her back so hard she nearly bit her tongue. He forced her into the quiet hallway leading to Rhys' office.

Kicking and struggling, she nearly broke free, but he was too strong. "If I ever get out of this I'm going to rip you to shreds," she hissed.

The man laughed and stopped in front of Rhys' office door, which was flanked by two equally large men Starry had never seen before. Was her father recruiting muscle without telling her?

"Play your cards right, Starry, and you'll have a chance to rip a lot of people to shreds," her father said from behind her. She tried to look over her shoulder, but couldn't see past her captor's broad chest. One of the men at the door came forward to frisk her. His meaty hand slid up between her legs, and he smiled smugly as he ripped her pistol out of her thigh holster. The other man opened the door and she was shoved inside, her father coming in behind her. The office was empty. The door closed and she spun around to face her father, nostrils flaring.

"What the *hell* is going on?" she yelled into his stony face. "You had Ginger keeping an eye on me too? Did Rhys know?"

Her father's blank expression didn't change. "Ginger wasn't in on this until yesterday," he said nonchalantly. "I paid her very well to tell me if Rhys showed up doing anything suspicious. You know I can't trust anyone completely, not even you and Rhys, apparently." His eyes narrowed as he grabbed her wrist and squeezed. "Imagine what I thought when Ginger told me *you* came here with him tonight. Imagine how that made me feel knowing you two went behind my back to fix things on your own without my approval. Imagine what I want to do to you right now. You're supposed to be loyal to me above everything and every*one*. This is not your syndicate to run yet."

He squeezed her wrist so hard she was sure he was breaking blood vessels. She kept her face as straight as possible. She could hold her own too, and she would prove it.

"You're the one who kept Emma away from me," she said calmly. "She's my sister. I needed to meet her without you around. Interfering."

All of that was true, at least.

"Because you want to shift your loyalty," her father accused, anger finally spreading across his face. His grip on her trembled. He was still wearing his sling.

"No, I don't. I wanted to meet Emma because I needed to see if she changed how I felt. Do you know what she wanted me to do, Dad? She wanted me to take your place and bring down the syndicate from the inside. And you know what I told her?" His grip on her wrist loosened and she ripped away from him. "I told her I would never hurt you like that. *Ever*. If that means nothing to you, then I don't even know why I'm still here."

His angry expression faltered, mixing with confusion and hurt. "Just now, Rhys told me you made an agreement to meet Emma and two men. He said you found proof that Craig Mihashi is the man who paid Andrews. I don't recognize his name, but why would you meet with him? Why didn't you tell me when you found him?"

She tensed and took a step back. "I was going to tell you about him. First I wanted to know what Craig was planning and how Emma fit into it."

"And now that you know?"

She looked back up, her fists tightening. "I already told you I can't hurt you like that. I thought maybe— *maybe*—I hated you enough to betray you, but when Emma asked me to do it, I realized that I—"

She met his eyes, tears swelling her throat and cutting off her words. She didn't want to cry, but she couldn't help it. As much as she tried to fight it, she loved her father more than anyone. More than Rhys. More than her sister. She knew that now, and while it made her angrier than she had ever been, it also made her admire him even more for how he had managed to get her right where he wanted her. He was unequivocally ruthless. He would slit her throat if it meant saving his own skin, but she couldn't blame him for that. He had to be that type of person to do what he did. It was how he had risen so high and how he would continue to survive. Lies. Deceit. Betrayal. It was all part of the game.

It was how she would survive too.

And he knew it.

If their trust in each other hung on one thing, it was knowing they were able to sacrifice anything for the good of the syndicate. Even each other. Maybe that was what he had been trying to teach her all along.

"Tell me one thing," she said as she swiped away a few tears that had escaped. "Have you told me the entire truth about me and Sam? Did he really give me up to you or did you take me from him?"

Her father's angry expression finally melted away. He stepped forward and gathered her close with his good arm. He smelled like his usual spicy cologne and soap. "I told you already, it was like everything else. I suppose you can say I made him believe he wanted to give you to me."

She took a deep breath. "Like you manipulate everyone, including me."

He nodded and squeezed her a little tighter. "You're learning what it takes to run this business. I don't ever want to lose you, Starry, but you're no exception to the rules. I live by them. Everyone lives by them. If we break them, everything falls apart. I can't let that happen, even if it means losing someone I love as much as you."

She closed her eyes and nodded. "I understand."

She really did understand—no matter how much it sucked.

Her father loosened his embrace and planted one hand on her shoulder as he looked her in the eyes. "Good, because I need you to prove your loyalty."

Her forehead scrunched. "Refusing Emma's offer isn't proof enough?"

He chuckled, his hand tightening on her shoulder. "No, it isn't. You have so much to learn, Starry, but I don't doubt you have what it takes to fill my shoes one day." He shook his head and looked down before meeting her eyes again, this time his expression so cold it sent a shudder up her spine. "I wanted things to work out with Emma, for her to join us as family, but that's clearly not going to happen now. Still, don't you think it's wonderful how this is playing out? It allows you the perfect opportunity to not only prove your loyalty, but cement your position in the syndicate forever."

An iciness she had never felt before seeped into her heart. She straightened, eager to meet her father's challenge. She could handle anything he asked of her. "What is it?"

His lips twisted into a smile. "I want you to kill Emma."

The words pounded into Starry like a wrecking ball, smashing the resolve she had built up. The pieces flew every which way, leaving fear and confusion behind them.

Kill Emma. Her own sister. Her own flesh and blood . . .

She didn't agree with Emma's proposed betrayal, but that didn't mean she wanted to *kill* her. If anything, she wanted to steal Emma away and mold her into someone who could love and understand her like her father did.

He seemed to understand her a little too well at the moment.

She took in a long, slow breath and then let it out. Killing Emma *would* cement her place in the syndicate. Permanently. How could she possibly emerge from something like that unscathed? She had to prove her loyalty. It was the only option because the syndicate and the power it promised were far more important than anything else. Even Emma.

She could see that clearly now.

She thought back to all of her physical training through the years—martial arts, boxing, mastering a wide range of weapons. She thought about the countless hours her father had spent teaching her the ins and outs of the drug trade, his future plans to expand his syndicate beyond its current borders, about the hundreds of cartels he was with and against, and how to keep the syndicate at the top of that particular power chain. It was so complex, it was beautiful. It gave her a rush just thinking about controlling all of that one day.

So it made no sense that she would question any of that now just because of a sister she had never known. A sister who wanted to destroy it all.

Which meant Emma had to die, blood or not.

Looking into her father's eyes, Starry straightened her shoulders and felt a surge of fire whip through her. "Okay. I'll do it."

Starry followed her father down a set of concrete stairs to the basement of the strip club. Everything was crude and unfinished. The door at the bottom was thick and heavy and locked with a keypad. Her father punched in a code and the door opened. A blast of cool air rolled out.

Starry followed her father through the door and into a narrow hallway. They turned a corner into a large, unfinished sitting area that Rhys was remodeling into a private party suite. Two floor lamps were the only source of light. The middle of the concrete floor was covered with a thick rug patterned in shades of crimson. A few plush chairs and sofas were pushed up against the walls. A large hook was bolted in one corner of the ceiling. It was meant to hold the hanging pod chair now leaning against a sofa, but Starry suspected it would be put to a different use tonight.

She blinked as her eyes adjusted. A part of her didn't want to see what was in this room. Her heart hammered in her throat as she swept her gaze to four lumps sitting on the floor against the back wall. Emma, Jack, Craig, and Andrews. Their ankles were bound with zip ties. Their arms were pulled behind their backs and bound at the wrists. Craig had a gag in his mouth, tightly tied around his head. He must have been making a lot of noise. Jack and Emma seemed okay, but horribly frightened. Tears glistened in their eyes. Andrews appeared unconscious, his shoulders and head slumped forward.

Jack and Emma looked up at Starry, their eyes widening with surprise and then hope—as if she had come here to save them.

Not quite.

Starry turned away from Emma's gaze and made an effort to ignore the trembling in her fingers. She was beginning to feel numb. Eventually, the trembling would subside. That was exactly what she needed.

"Okay," she said, turning to her father. "How do you want me to do it?"

"Patience, Starry." He waited for his two bodyguards to enter the room, and then stayed near the entrance so he could see around the corner. A flash of anger sparked in his eyes as he informed Starry that Rhys was on his way.

His anger wasn't lost on Starry. She shared the sentiment. "Oh, yes . . . Rhys," she hissed. "I was an idiot to trust him, wasn't I? Tell me how he contacted you, because I know it wasn't through his phone."

Her father's jaw tightened. "Ginger was the only one who contacted me. I figure Rhys didn't because he's either lying to both of us, or you were keeping an eye on him. Am I right?"

She nodded. "I'd like to rule out the lying, but who the hell knows."

Then again, maybe Rhys hadn't meant for all of this to happen.

A moment later, he entered the room, his face flushed as if he'd been running. "Sorry," he gasped. "There was a big commotion with Ginger upstairs. A few customers saw what happened and I had to smooth it over."

Starry couldn't tear her eyes off him. He approached her, his lips twisting into a frown, his eyes intense and filled with guilt. "I'm sorry about up there," he whispered, closing in on her. He stopped right in front of her, but didn't touch her. "Ginger had barely signaled to me that your father was here, and I didn't want to screw things up." He glanced at her father, his expression stony. "I had to keep them here and there wasn't time to explain."

"Screw what up?" she asked, and pointed at her father. "*His* plans? I was right. He will always come before me, won't he?"

But that's how it had to be. She'd chosen the same thing. The syndicate first. Her father second. Everything else was lesser.

"That's right," her father said flatly, boring his eyes into Rhys'. "And you will both prove to me that you understand and agree. Rhys, Andrews is yours. I want you to teach him a lesson before you kill him. Show me you have what it takes. Be creative." He pointed to a corner of the room.

Starry whipped around. She had missed it before as her eyes were adjusting, but now she could see it plain as day: a small table set with an array of torture tools, each of them glinting wickedly in the dim light. The bone saw was the largest. The pliers were the shiniest.

Those types of tools had bothered Starry when she was a child, but never since then. Now, however, the sight of them disgusted her. Her father was going to make her use them on Emma. This wasn't about simply killing her.

It was so much more than that.

A mixture of awe and contempt filled her to the brim as she turned to face her father. She admired him because she longed for and deeply respected his power, but at the same time, could she still love him after this? She had been so sure up in Rhys' office that she loved him, but now as she looked into his icy gray eyes, she didn't know if it was love or . . . fear.

It might have always been fear. Her entire life.

The worst thing was she wasn't sure if she would ever know the difference.

TWENTY-EIGHT

Emma shifted on the concrete floor, her skin burning around the zip ties biting into her already aching wrists. She and Jack had been so close to escaping after her meeting with Starry. They had run out of the club using a back exit, but Glenn had been waiting for them in the alleyway with two other men. All with guns. But why? Starry had said she was going to let them go. Had she lied?

Emma wasn't so sure. Right now Starry looked more furious than triumphant as she glared at a table Glenn was pointing to. Emma couldn't see what was on it, but she doubted it was anything good—not after what Glenn had just told the man called Rhys to do.

Rhys.

Who was he? Andrews had said he was one of Glenn's underlings, but he seemed more than that. Emma furrowed her brow as she watched him march over to the table in the corner. He seemed important to

Starry. A boyfriend, maybe? But the tension between him and Starry felt thick as a brick wall. Nothing was breaking that anytime soon.

Emma opened her mouth to speak to Starry, to plead with her to have some mercy on her own sister, but a warning look from Jack made her swallow her words. Glenn's men had already punched Craig in the face for speaking. Then they had gagged him with a scarf and kicked him in the stomach. Andrews hadn't fared any better. In fact, Emma wasn't sure what they had done to him before they had dragged him down here a few minutes after her and Jack and Craig. He seemed barely conscious, his head lolling to one side. The gash on the side of his face had opened again, fresh blood oozing from the wound.

Keeping her eyes on Jack, Emma tried to control the fear coursing through her. Jack didn't seem nearly as frightened as she felt. He looked calm, every muscle in his face relaxed. Maybe he was keeping himself calm for her sake, but she knew him better than that. He could be cool under pressure. She had seen it first-hand when he'd found Alex's dead body. She had seen it in the stairwell when he'd fought Glenn's men. Maybe he got it from his father because Craig looked just as composed. He had relaxed against the wall, his eyes open but not panicked. Had he accepted this was the end? Emma refused to resign herself to such a fate. Her father had spent eighteen years trying to defeat Glenn.

The last thing she wanted to do was give in to him without a fight.

Although she had no idea how to fight when she was bound hand and foot with no hope of rescue.

"Jack," she whispered between her teeth. "What do you think they're going to do to us?"

His eyes filled with sadness as he studied her face. He was close enough for her to feel his warmth. Even if she was about to die, she felt significantly better than she had strung up in Glenn's torture room, alone and in pain. Here, Jack was right next to her.

Jack flicked his eyes to Rhys, who was picking up something from the table in the corner. "Nothing good," he whispered. "I think he's going to torture Andrews. And then us, maybe."

Terror slammed into Emma. "Why us?" she mouthed. There was nothing Glenn could possibly get from Jack. There was nothing new she could tell him, either. If anything, she had thought Glenn wanted to adopt her into the syndicate.

But that had been before she'd tried to talk Starry into betraying him, of course.

She'd screwed up everything. Again. She had only wanted to do the right thing by trying to finish what her father had started. Now she was going to die because of it.

Jack shook his head, fear creeping into his calm expression. "You heard Glenn," he whispered. "He wants to use us to prove a point. I don't think Starry has any loyalty to you, Emma. It's over." He shifted on the concrete and winced as he fought back a cough.

Emma inched closer to him. "Your ribs. Are you okay?"

Jack squeezed his eyes shut and mouthed, *I'll be fine.*

No he wouldn't. Emma looked up as Rhys turned around from the table with a bundle of nylon rope in his hands.

That was it? Rope?

Emma wasn't sure what Rhys was planning as he marched over to Andrews. He shoved the man's knee and Andrews groaned and rolled his head up to look at Rhys. He stayed silent as Rhys grabbed his elbow and yanked him up to his feet. His arms were secured behind his back by a pair of handcuffs instead of zip ties.

"Hang him by his wrists," he growled to Glenn's two bodyguards, and tossed them the rope. He shoved Andrews forward. The man almost fell on his face since his feet were bound together, but Glenn's men rushed forward and caught him. They started dragging him over to a corner of the room.

Andrews looked over his shoulder at Rhys, who was following along. "You can't do this," he hissed. "It's too sick."

Rhys just smiled.

Glenn laughed from the middle of the room. "Good call, Rhys. You've chosen something personal. I like that. I like it a lot."

Andrews continued glaring at Rhys as the bodyguards dragged him along. "You're going to regret this," he growled.

"Am I, now? How do you figure that?"

"You'll regret working for Glenn, just like I do," Andrews answered. "He's too powerful for his own good. He'll use you up just like he does everyone."

Emma thought about what Andrews had told her in the parking lot. She didn't admire him as a person in the slightest, but she did admire his courage. She doubted anyone broke free of Glenn without that kind of grit.

"Oh, I see," Glenn sighed from the middle of the room. The bodyguards hauling Andrews stopped and turned him so he could look at Glenn. "This is about you losing power. The syndicate keeps getting bigger, yet your slice of the pie stays the same. So you thought you'd get me out of the way so you could take more power."

Andrews pursed his lips and looked away.

Glenn took a step forward. "I always promised you'd grow with the syndicate, Andrews. Once I'd laid the groundwork, the entire West Coast ecstasy operation was going to be yours. I'm disappointed you decided to trust someone like Sam and this Craig bastard instead of the man who took you in when you were a homeless teenager on the streets."

"No," Andrews retorted, snapping his eyes to Glenn. "You're wrong. It wasn't about more power. I took Sam's offer because I've wanted out from under you for years now. So did Chavez." He looked up at Starry, who was watching him with a horrified expression on her face. "Things will go too far," he said to her, his voice trembling. "They already have. He's killed friends of mine, people he promised he would never harm. Innocent families. He's too greedy. He's got too much power, Starry, and you can change it. Right now. I know you can."

The fear in Starry's eyes vanished, replaced by fury. Emma saw Glenn in that look and it scared her.

"My dad has done more for you than you'll ever know," Starry snapped at Andrews. "He sacrifices everything for the syndicate and everyone in it. The least you could do is acknowledge the fact that you're too much of a coward to sacrifice as much as he does. You're a liar and a traitor."

Andrews looked away and triumph replaced the fury on Starry's face. Emma winced in disappointment. Starry seemed to like her position of power far too much. That was probably the most frightening thing of all, Emma realized. Where was the warm, attentive person she had glimpsed at the bar only a little while ago? She knew it was buried in there somewhere, but

Starry seemed so intent on her own powerful position that nothing could drag that person back out right now.

Glenn's bodyguards turned Andrews back around and hauled him to a corner of the room Emma had a hard time seeing unless she craned her neck up to look past Jack and Craig. But she didn't want to see it anyway. A few minutes later Andrews was crying out in pain.

"What are they doing to him?" Emma whispered to Jack, who had been leaning forward to watch.

He sat back against the wall. "They've hung him up by his wrists," he answered flatly. "Think about it. He's a big guy and his arms are behind his back. His shoulders are probably going to dislocate with all that weight on them."

"How is that personal?"

"No idea."

Emma squeezed her eyes shut, her heart pounding in her chest as she remembered Glenn's whip slicing across her flesh all over again. She forced her attention up to Glenn to see a smug grin lifting his lips as he watched the torture.

Sick. He was sick with power. He had controlled her father and stolen Starry away from him for some reason Emma couldn't even fathom. Why hadn't he taken her too? She supposed none of it mattered now. All that mattered was the fear growing stronger and stronger in her gut. Her skin felt cold and clammy. Jack grew blurry in her vision. He had promised to do everything in his power to help her, and he had kept that promise as much as possible. She wanted to get closer to him and soak up some of his strength and courage. His breathing was irregular, but that was from his cracked ribs, not fear. She was trembling from head to foot as Andrews' screams filled the room. All she could think about was what Rhys might decide to do to her or Jack or Craig. Were they next?

"Are they going to string us up too?" she whispered shakily to Jack under her breath.

He jerked his head in Starry's direction. "Whatever it is they plan on doing, I'm wondering if she might be the one who'll do it."

Emma blinked away her tears and looked up to see Starry watching her with pure hatred swirling in her eyes. At least she wasn't stopping her and Jack from whispering to each other. Emma met her gaze, desperately trying to communicate pleas for help. It wasn't going to work. Starry seemed distracted, almost as if she didn't see Emma at all.

A hot tear rolled down Emma's cheek. Her body was sore, her wrists burning, her stomach turning upside down with dread. Andrews' shrieks were dying into whimpers now.

"You did this to *her*," he cried. "Why . . . *why* did you do this to her?" He took in a sharp gasp. "She didn't deserve it. She betrayed the syndicate, but she didn't deserve this much pain. I told you I didn't love her, but I did. Too much." His cries filled the whole room. He sounded more hurt by the experience of living through the mirrored pain of someone he loved than the actual pain itself.

"We all knew you loved her," Glenn sighed loudly. "That's the whole point here."

Emma stared down at her knees and thought about the pain her father had experienced. She'd already tasted a small portion of it, and she was sure she was about to taste some more. Why had she delivered those Chinese eggs? If only she'd left the package on the couch, she wouldn't be here. None of this would be happening. Her father would still be alive.

No.

All of this had been set in motion long before she had delivered the package. *She* might not be in danger now, but her father would have followed through with his plans. And even if he'd been able to step into running the syndicate with Starry, where would that have left Emma?

She realized that was why her father had so desperately wanted her to pick a college somewhere far away. She would have been out of the way, leaving him free to carry out his plans with the syndicate without putting her in any danger. Maybe. She wondered if he had planned to reunite her and Starry at some point if Starry agreed to bring down the syndicate with him.

But none of that would happen now, and nothing guaranteed the results would have been any better if things had gone exactly to plan.

Emma thought about her father's words again: *Promise me you'll always stick to what you know is right.*

His heart had been in the right place. She didn't know if his actions had been right, but maybe being tied to someone like Glenn meant no actions could ever be truly "right," no matter how good the intentions.

Lifting her eyes to Glenn, Emma was surprised yet again at how much he looked like her father. The difference was his cocky attitude. That wasn't like her father at all.

Then it struck her. Maybe the only thing that mattered at this point was *her* attitude. Her father had raised her with courage. He'd never once allowed his relationship with Glenn to influence his love for her. He'd taught her to be a good person despite all of his secrets. She wanted that kind of courage—courage in the face of impossible odds. If she could find it, she knew nobody could take it away from her.

Not even someone as powerful as Glenn.

TWENTY-NINE

Starry tried to block out Andrews' cries and whimpers and moved her attention to Jack and Emma. Jack looked in control of his emotions, but he was also in pain. His breathing was labored and irregular. His cracked ribs were probably the culprit. Her father's men had not been gentle with their captives.

He met her eyes and she held his wounded gaze, realizing he was about the same age Andrews had been when her father had rescued him off the streets. Jack and Emma were both too young to die, but it couldn't be helped. It occurred to her then how much her father relied on saving people he thought were worth saving—how much he used that to his advantage to control them. He'd wanted to do the same with Emma, and Starry had to admit she felt a similar desire. Emma was broken and lost and lonely. When Starry looked at her, she saw a part of herself she desperately wanted to fix.

It was a vulnerable part. A weak part. Innocent. *Normal.*

And normal was inadequate.

Normal disappeared and was forgotten.

Normal had to be eliminated, especially within herself.

Starry watched two tears slide down Emma's cheeks and wondered how her sister could cry so silently. She was probably afraid that drawing attention to herself would get her killed or hurt faster.

She was right. It would.

Starry felt a surge of desperation well up inside of her. She wanted to tell Emma she was sorry that this was how things had to play out, that some things were more important than family ties. Some things transcended an individual and their selfish desires. The syndicate was one of them. It involved and affected millions of people. Her and Emma's desires were nothing in the big picture. Starry could fill her father's shoes if he died, but so could a dozen other people. He just wanted it to be her. *She* wanted it to be her. It was what she had been raised for.

Andrews had started shrieking again. He was pleading between the screams—something Starry thought she would never hear from him.

"Please, Rhys," he gasped. "It's getting worse. Please."

"Worse?" Rhys laughed. "Good time to add even more, then." He marched over to the table and picked up the wicked looking bone saw. It was the size of a small chef's knife.

Starry shook her head, annoyed. Andrews was in enough pain already. Rhys had chosen something emotionally painful as well as physically painful. It was a good choice, but adding more to it would muddle it up in the man's head. Too much pain and he would shut down too fast. Clean, slow torture was better torture. It was a fine balance Rhys obviously hadn't learned.

She grabbed his arm as he passed by her with the bone saw. "The saw is too much," she whispered. She reached for the saw, but Rhys yanked it away and turned to face her. His expression was filled with fearful determination.

"It's fine," he said, and then glanced over at her father still silently watching them. "I have to prove myself, Starry. We have to fix this."

There was that word "we" again, as if Rhys still thought everything was going to work out between them. "I know you do," she said, "but you've got a lot to learn. You're doing it all wrong. Keep his mind on his current pain. Talk to him about his dead girlfriend. Were you the one who tortured her or something? How did you know about that?"

Rhys lowered the bone saw in his hand. "I was there when Glenn tortured and killed her."

"Good, then you know details. Work with that, then if it looks like he's handling it too well, add some weight to his body to increase the pain in his shoulders."

Rhys looked over at Andrews. "You're right," he sighed, and returned the bone saw to the table.

He walked over to Andrews and started talking to him in a low, even voice. It was quiet enough that she couldn't even make out what he was saying. Meant only for Andrews. Perfect. The man started weeping, his emotional pain overpowering his physical pain.

He wasn't the only one weeping. Emma had erupted into tears as well. Starry could tell she was trying her hardest to keep her sobbing to a minimum. Jack was simply staring straight ahead at nothing, his face as white as a sheet. Craig, whom Starry had managed to ignore until that moment, looked irritatingly calm. She wanted to kick him in the face, but suppressed the urge as he lifted his eyes and moved his lips around the gag in his mouth. He was trying to speak.

Starry glared at him. It angered her how everything was going. It felt slow and drawn out, like her father was simply observing and waiting for someone to take charge. It could be Rhys. He was definitely taking charge of what her father had handed him.

But she didn't want it to be him.

She kept quiet and looked at her father as he folded his arms and took a small step back. His bodyguards, who had joined him again, followed. That was when Starry realized he really was waiting for her to step forward and command the room, even past telling Rhys what to do. This was between her and Rhys—the two people he cared about most. Who was stronger? Who had it in them to make the real decisions? Who could handle his precious syndicate when he needed them to?

Well, it wasn't Rhys.

It was her.

Marching over to Craig, she crouched down and pulled the gag from his mouth. It was time to get to the bottom of his connection to Sam and why the hell he was after her father.

"Tell me what you were planning before the shit hit the fan," she demanded. "And don't tell me it was to get Emma to talk me into betraying the syndicate. There has to be more to it than that. What were you and Sam really planning?"

Craig looked her in the eyes. "It was simple: kill Glenn and reunite you and Emma. He hoped you would do the right thing and help him dismantle the syndicate once you learned about all the lies you've been fed, but killing Glenn was his first priority."

Starry slammed her fist into his jaw. Red blossomed across his skin as he calmly maintained eye contact. "Tell me why *you* would go along with all of that," she ordered. If she was going to have to kill her sister, she wanted all of the facts first. "Were you planning to take Sam's place? Were you planning to kill him once he was in?"

Craig blinked and then let out a long, slow breath. Starry nearly hit him again for taking too long to answer.

"I'm doing all of this because I owe Sam," he said, and then glanced over at Emma. "I owe Sam because I'm the one who killed his wife."

Starry's mouth fell open. "*What?*" she hissed, and looked at Emma, whose expression conveyed everything Starry was feeling. Shock. Disbelief. Fury.

What the hell was this? Their mother had died during childbirth.

"It was a car accident," Craig said. "The road was icy and I couldn't stop . . ."

"Son of a bitch," Glenn hissed between his teeth, and Starry turned around to see him marching toward her and Craig. He peered at Craig's face in the dim light. "You're *him*. I thought you were dead. The state wouldn't charge you with manslaughter. They wouldn't even arrest you since it was clearly an accident, so Sam took matters into his own hands."

Starry stood up straight and turned to face her father. "Why lie to me about how my mother died? And how the hell could you not recognize her killer?"

Her father gestured at her to be quiet, his eyes still focused completely on Craig. "It was so long ago," he said. "You had a different name back then. Kentaro Kurosawa. I'll never forget that name."

Craig steeled his eyes, refusing to respond. At least Starry knew why she hadn't been able to find more information on Craig. He had changed his name, and from the look of the pure and utter shock on Jack's face, he hadn't been aware of it either.

"I never bothered digging," Glenn said. "You were out of the picture. Sam sent me a photo of your body to prove what he'd done, and I trusted him." His face hardened as he took a few steps forward. "That was one of the reasons I kept out of his business all these years. I figured if he was vindictive and clever enough to murder his wife's killer and get away with it, he was more like me than I thought and deserved my respect." He raised his gun and aimed it at Craig's head. Starry stepped back, clearing a path for the bullet she knew was coming. "Guess I was right, but in a completely different way than I expected. You were the perfect man to take over if he died. Why would I look for a dead man? I guess it all worked out, though. You're gonna die, anyway. For real this time."

Starry gently put her hand on his arm before he could pull the trigger. "Wait," she said, glancing at Jack and Emma who still looked completely shell-shocked. "I want to hear it from you, Dad. How did Mom really die? It wasn't because of childbirth at all?"

Her father lowered his gun half an inch as he moved his attention to her. "No. I had to lie about that or you would have found the news articles about the accident. That would have led you to her real obituary, which would have led you to Sam." He jerked his gun at Craig and scowled. "That bastard hit your mother with his car. He hit a patch of ice and didn't stop in time. Lucy died in the hospital a few hours later. It was an accident, but he should still pay for it." He gritted his teeth and aimed his gun at Craig's head once more. *"I thought he had."*

Starry's jaw grew slack as she turned to look at Craig. Her mother's killer. The reason for all of this. The reason she had been separated from her sister and birth father. She didn't know how to feel about it. On one hand, she wanted to kill Craig, but on the other, it had been an accident. An *accident*.

But her father didn't accept accidents. Everyone had to pay for what they took.

And Craig was going to pay.

"Please, one second," Craig begged Glenn, his panic so palpable Starry could practically smell it. He turned to Jack, tears spilling from his eyes. "I'm so sorry," he whispered. "Please forgive me. I promised Sam I would finish what he started. It just wasn't a promise I could break. I didn't—"

"Shut up!" Glenn pulled the trigger and Craig slumped onto his side, blood spattering the wall behind him.

Jack gasped, but Starry couldn't tear her attention away from Craig's blood dripping down the concrete wall. Her emotions roiled into a hot, ugly mess. Anger. Frustration. Irritation. And then a strange sort of relief took over, wiping everything else away. So it was true. All Sam had wanted was revenge on his brother and to reunite her and Emma. He had used Craig's guilt to help him, and that made her pause. Maybe Sam had been more like her father than she'd originally thought. Maybe nothing would have been different if she had been raised by him instead of her uncle.

Then again, there was Emma.

Emma was not like her.

Emma was currently burying her face between her knees. "I don't understand," she whimpered. "I don't understand. I don't understand. This can't be happening."

Starry looked away from her sister. She couldn't think about what Emma might be feeling, how this one piece of information about their mother tied them together even more, how fresh grief bonded them in a new way.

What was this? What was *any* of this? It seemed there was no turning back. Everything had to end. Now. She had to cement her place in the syndicate forever just so she could sever the pain filling up her heart, just as her father did every time he killed someone. And there was only one way to do it.

Facing her father, she lifted a hand. "Let me finish this. Give me a gun."

He jerked his head at the bodyguard on his right, who handed over his pistol.

She took it, feeling the heft of the weapon in her hand. Plenty of bullets in the clip.

Rhys stepped away from Andrews, who looked like he was close to passing out from his unceasing pain. "Starry, are you sure?" Rhys asked her softly. There was a pleading look in his eyes.

"Sure about what?" she snapped.

He shook his head. "Nothing."

"That's my girl," her father chuckled as she turned to face Emma. "Show me what you're made of, Starry. No need to torture her. Just kill her and I'll know I can trust you to do your job from here on out."

She already knew he trusted her. He wouldn't have allowed her to have a weapon if he didn't. She spun around to face Emma, who still had her face buried in her knees. Her entire body trembled as sobs kept leaking from her throat.

"I don't wanna die," she whimpered. "Dad, why did you leave me here like this? We always had each other and now you're gone."

Jack turned to her and quieted his own sobbing. "Emma, look at me," he said firmly. "You're not alone, okay? No matter what happens, I'm right here." His knee brushed against hers and she looked up, her face red and wet. Her eyes were filled with something Starry couldn't put her finger on.

Or maybe she could.

She and Jack cared about each other. Deeply.

Starry took a tiny step back, her grip on the gun faltering. Had Rhys ever looked at her like that? Had her father? Had *anyone*? She wanted to think that her father cared about her that deeply, but she wasn't sure. And Rhys . . . she had no idea what the hell he felt now. Either way, it seemed unfair that Jack and Emma could share such a sentiment in a situation like this, right after they'd watched Craig die. It made Starry furious. She marched forward and kicked Jack's knee away from Emma's.

Emma looked up, her eyes widening as Starry aimed the gun between her eyes. "Starry," she said. "Why are you doing this?"

Starry paused, her anger spiraling into something she couldn't control. "Does it matter?" She steadied her aim. It was unfaltering. She could do this.

She *would*.

She was in charge of herself more than anyone.

Emma's tears stopped falling. "It's okay," she said as a sudden calm seemed to settle over her. "I understand why you have to kill us. You can't help it. He raised you this way. If he had taken me instead of you, I'd be doing the same thing."

Starry's aim lowered half a centimeter. "No you wouldn't. You're too good, Emma. You could never, *ever* be like me."

Emma straightened and took a deep breath. She seemed more in control. Starry wondered how she could be so calm when she knew she was going to die.

"I still love you as my sister," Emma said. "I love you no matter what you do."

Starry's hatred exploded into fury. "*Shut up!*" she screamed, her heart pounding so hard she was sure it was going to shatter her ribcage into a million pieces. This was it. She was the one in control. Not Rhys. Not her father. This was her choice. Her power. And she was going to nail it down for good. She was going to put a stop to the pain, the guilt, the loathing she felt for what she was about to do. "You don't love me. You can never love me."

Emma fastened her gaze squarely on Starry's, every speck of fear flitting away from her eyes.

Furious, Starry prepared to pull the trigger, but seeing Emma's sudden, unshrinking courage made her hesitate. Emma was innocent and unarmed. She had to be scared out of her mind, but she was facing that fear with her eyes wide open.

Starry wondered if she could do the same. Was she that brave?

"I do love you," Emma said. "You're my sister."

Starry stiffened. "And that's why you're going to die." She looked down the sights of her gun, right between Emma's eyes.

"I knew you had it in you," Glenn laughed from behind Starry. He was at least ten feet away from her, but Starry felt as if he was right up close to her ear, breathing, waiting, smiling. He sounded so proud of her in that moment—the moment he was absolutely certain she was going to kill her own sister.

And with that image slamming her in the gut, she realized the gruesome truth: she was a coward. She was so terrified of her father that she had honestly thought she loved him and would do anything to stay in his favor. She had believed she needed him. But as she tried to pull the trigger to shoot Emma, she could see now that what she felt for her father wasn't love or loyalty. It was nothing but fear, just as she had suspected earlier.

And the mere fact that she could see it clearly now gave her a trickle of hope and courage to do something she never thought she could do.

The only problem was *how* could she do it? How could she turn on her father and survive? Even with one of his men unarmed, it was impossible.

Her throat closed up, and without moving an inch, she slid her eyes to Rhys. He was standing off to the side, watching her. He glanced worriedly at Emma and then back to Starry, his eyebrows knotting together in an expression so distraught Starry wondered if he didn't want her to shoot Emma.

But why wouldn't he? He knew as well as she did that her only other choice was to try to kill her father, and that was possible suicide. Why would he want her to risk so much just to save a girl he didn't even know?

Either way, she'd made up her mind. With Rhys' help or not, it was time to take a stand.

THIRTY

The moment Starry spun around, Rhys charged at the man closest to him: the unarmed bodyguard on her father's right side. They went down in a sprawl of limbs, and Starry aimed at her father's chest, their eyes meeting as he trained his own gun on her. His eyes widened with a mixture of shock and disappointment. It was the disappointment that struck Starry. She realized it was the same sort of heartache welling up in her own eyes.

There was no saying goodbye.

One shot and it would be over.

And she shot first.

Then something slammed into her. It was the armed bodyguard. She didn't know why he hadn't shot at her, but perhaps he'd had orders not to. A loud *oof!* left her throat and she flew through the air. Her head whipped back, smacking the concrete, and her gun went spinning across the floor. She sat up immediately, everything blurry, just as a gunshot sounded. Rhys stumbled backward, his hand to his chest.

"Rhys!" Starry scrambled to her feet, but fell back down as the room spun in circles. She looked up in time to see the bodyguard who had pushed her out of the way aiming his gun at Rhys for a second shot.

No.

No.

Starry flew to her feet again. She would not let that bastard hurt Rhys, no matter how much the room was spinning. She lifted her leg for a high kick to the man's head, completely missing her target and hitting his shoulder instead. It was enough. His shot went wide and he staggered off balance. Rhys lunged at him, snapping the man's neck with a sickening crunch as they both crashed to the floor.

Starry looked around the room, her breath stopping in her throat as her eyes landed on her father. He was lying on the floor a few feet away, face up.

She had shot him straight through the heart.

White specks floated across her vision and she fell to her knees. He was dead. She had killed him. Why wasn't she crying? She felt numb inside. Everything was blurry.

Rhys didn't get up. Starry remembered him clutching a hand to his chest a moment ago. "Rhys?" she gasped, panic rising in her voice. The idea of losing him now made her entire world shatter, but at the same time a surge of hope filled her heart. He had risked himself for her.

He was on her side.

The white specks in her vision turned black. She blinked quickly, but everything looked so dark. "Rhys," she cried. "Rhys?" She crawled to his side.

"I'm right here." The sound of his voice filled her with relief as he reached up to cup her face in his hands. "It's okay, Starry. You're safe. It's okay."

Her vision finally cleared and Rhys' eyes came into focus. "A–are you hurt?" She looked down at his chest.

He was bleeding.

Everywhere.

It came from his left side, near his heart. There was so much blood soaking through his pinstriped shirt, Starry couldn't tell if a bullet had lodged in him or not. Her elbows turned to jelly and she nearly collapsed. "Rhys. You . . ."

He shrugged and looked down at his wound as if it was nothing more than a paper cut. "I'll live," he laughed weakly. "All the bullet did was graze me. I'm fine."

Starry almost smacked him. "But you're losing a lot of blood. We have to get help." She shook her head and looked over at Jack and Emma still bound near the wall. Relief filled her as she saw that they were completely unharmed. They looked even more shell-shocked, if that was possible, with their faces wet with tears, their eyes red and wide. At least they were okay. Andrews had passed out during the fight and hung silent in the corner.

Rhys let out a little groan and Starry snapped her attention back to him. She had to get it together. Things were done with no way of undoing them and she had to move forward. She had to prioritize. She *had* to.

And right now the priority was Rhys.

"We've got to stop the bleeding," she said. She jumped up and grabbed a clean towel from the table. Her father had probably put it there for cleaning up. He hated the feel of blood on his hands. That suddenly struck her as ludicrous and she had to force down a hysterical giggle.

She unbuttoned Rhys' bloodied shirt and pulled it away from his side to get a better look at the wound, her thoughts going back to the time she'd tended her father's wounded shoulder. No. No. She wouldn't think about that. She wouldn't think about him. She wouldn't.

Blinking back her tears, she studied Rhys' wound. The bullet had done more than just graze him. It had gouged a furrow in his flesh deep enough that she worried bone chips from his ribcage could be floating around in there. "We should get you to Pearce," she said, and pressed the towel against the wound, realizing Pearce was now under her. Not her father. *Her.*

The syndicate was hers.

She guided Rhys' hand onto the towel to hold it in place and then sat back on the floor, her breaths shallow. Did she know enough to run the syndicate? There was so much that her father hadn't taught her yet. His Top Eight—Top Six now, she realized—knew enough. They would help.

If she could control them. If they accepted her. They would have to accept her. Or she would kill them.

But all of that meant her father was truly gone.

A deep, aching grief welled up in her throat as she glanced over at his dead body. She wasn't sure she could bring herself to get any closer to him than she was at the moment. Looking away, she tried to swallow her grief before it burst out of her. She could not lose her grip.

A sudden shuffling noise caught her attention and she whipped around to see Jack and Emma struggling to get to their feet. They looked ridiculous, propped up against each other back to back. They both froze when they saw her.

"What the hell are you doing?" she asked, and waved a hand at her father's body. "He's dead! The danger's over. You don't have to escape. I'll cut you free in a minute, okay?"

Emma slumped back to the floor, her eyes filled with hope as she looked at Starry. "Did you kill him to save us?"

Starry narrowed her eyes and looked at Jack, who looked fearfully back at her. She couldn't blame him. He probably thought she was going to kill them both. There was no way they would ever agree to join the syndicate.

Starry opened her mouth, but closed it when Rhys spoke. "We need to call Wilson and Perez to get rid of the bodies," he said, gingerly struggling to a sitting position. "We can trust them now that we know Craig was behind all of this."

"Yeah, you're right. But text them. Don't call. And use my phone. Yours is still hacked." She pulled her phone out of her bra and handed it to him.

Rhys nodded. "Let's get a story together and convince Wilson and Perez that Andrews and Craig killed your father and the others. If they don't buy it and have a problem with what really happened, we'll have to get rid of them too and figure out something else."

Wincing, Starry tried not to think about the industrial incinerator her father owned—the one he used to burn the bodies he never wanted found. It ran so hot it burned teeth to ash. *She* owned that incinerator now. She owned everything, even all of her father's money.

So much money.

She turned to Rhys, studying him closely. "Were you on my side the whole time?" she asked.

Rhys looked away. "No. I've gone back and forth so many times I lost count, but I finally realized how much it was going to hurt you to kill your sister. I couldn't let your father do that to you. I couldn't let him control you anymore."

Starry raised an eyebrow. "But why? Your loyalty to him outweighed everything before."

"I still love him, and I'm sorry that he's dead, but there are more important things than loyalty, Starry."

"Like what?"

Sighing, Rhys rolled his eyes and then focused directly on her. "Don't you get it? I'm in love with you. How else do you want me to show it?"

Oh.

Her heart pounded even harder now than it had in the past hour. "You're in love with me?" she whispered.

He winced as he pressed the towel against his wound. "I've been in a lot of relationships, Star. Nobody compares to you."

Starry stared at him for an eternity before she finally leaned forward to kiss him. There was nothing else left to do because she had already decided she was in love with him too—or, at least, she cared about him so deeply that the thought of losing him sent her into a full-blown panic.

"I don't know what to say," she mumbled against his lips. "You're a bastard. You've lied to me, you just helped me kill my father, and now you want me to forget all of that and run the syndicate with you because you love me. How am I supposed to react to that?"

He shrugged. "However you want. I'll never control you like he did."

Starry let Rhys' words sink in. She was surprised at how significant they felt. He really wasn't going to control her. She knew that clear down to her bones. Then again, nobody would ever control her again. She would make sure of it.

"It's nice to know I can trust you," she said and brushed a finger over his lips. "That means everything to me."

Rhys smiled and looked over at Glenn's body. "It means everything to me too. I didn't think I would be so relieved that he's gone. I think he had more power over me than I realized, and not in a good way."

Starry got up and walked over to her father. He was on his back, his glassy eyes staring up at the ceiling. He had been her world for so long. He deserved a goodbye, and she needed one too.

Dropping to her knees, she took his hand and held it gently between her palms. He was still warm, and that put her over the edge. Tears blurred her vision as she leaned close to his face. "I'm sorry, Dad, but you pushed us here. You pushed so hard, we didn't have a choice. Even though I hate you, I love you too . . . and . . . *ugh*, I hate you for that. But I'll never forget the good things.

You always wanted the best for me, in your own screwed up way. We just didn't agree in the end about what the best thing was. I'll miss you, and you'll always be my father."

Gritting her teeth, she let go of his hand and let it fall to the carpet. She looked over at Emma, who was still watching her with hope in her eyes. Right. There was still Emma and Jack to deal with.

Starry got to her feet and walked over to her sister. "What *am* I going to do with you two?" she sighed.

Jack glanced at his father. A pool of dark red blood had formed beneath his head. "I thought you were going to let us go."

Starry crouched down to look Emma in the eyes, and then Jack. "I didn't risk so much just to kill you, so I suppose I have to let you go now. I doubt you'll agree to join the syndicate, no matter what I offer you, am I right?"

Emma looked away and nodded.

"But I have to be able to trust you," Starry said, glancing at Jack. She didn't trust him as much as she trusted Emma, but she supposed there were ways to keep him in line.

Emma looked at her again, curiosity sweeping across her face. "We won't ever do anything against your syndicate," she said. "I promise."

Starry nodded. "That's the kind of promise I need from you both. You're going to have to accept that this is what I do. If you don't like it, we can push a replay button on everything that just happened, but I don't think any of us want to repeat our fathers' mistakes."

Emma's eyes turned wet again, but she swallowed her tears and nodded. "I understand this is how things are. Just don't hate me if I keep hoping you'll change one day."

Starry laughed at the ridiculousness of such a thought, but nodded. "Emma, I don't think I could ever hate you. I could kill you if you drove me to it, but I could never hate you."

"Starry," Rhys said from behind her. He still had the towel pressed to his wound, her cell phone in his other hand. "We've got to hurry. Wilson and Perez will be here any minute. I think if you're going to let Emma and Jack go, it should be now. Keeping them here will complicate everything. And you should probably kill Andrews while you're at it. He's out cold anyway."

Starry nodded. "You're right." She stood up and walked to the table of tools to grab a knife and returned to Emma and Jack. "I hope you know," she said to Emma as she bent down to cut through the zip tie around her ankles, "that even though I'm letting you go, I will always know where you are and what you're doing."

Emma's eyes widened. "So this is it? We can just walk out of here?"

Starry smiled sadly at Emma's faith in her. She could probably promise the girl the moon and she'd believe it. Then again, Starry knew there was no way she could lie to Emma now, simply because she *was* trusting and innocent and, most of all, her sister.

"Not quite yet," she answered. "There's going to be a lot of stuff to take care of first, but yes, you will eventually be able to walk free. Right now we'll get you up to Rhys' apartment until all of this shit is sorted out." She waved a hand at Andrews and the dead bodies and then looked Emma in the eyes, pausing before she slipped her knife through the zip tie. "Thank you, Emma."

Emma looked down at the knife poised against the zip tie around her ankles. She looked confused. "For what?"

Starry took a deep breath, knowing Emma would never truly understand what she was about to say. "For giving me a reason to stand up to my father." It was, after all, Emma's show of courage that had finally opened her eyes.

And with that, she cut Emma free.

THIRTY-ONE

The café reminded Emma of the one in Brooklyn next to the laundromat. Instead of Brooklyn, it was in San Francisco, and in addition to croissant sandwiches, the café served gourmet donuts. Jack was excited about the donuts. He was currently buying one at the counter and said he would find somewhere else to sit and eat until Emma and Starry were finished talking.

"This is it," Starry said as she took a sip of her coffee and leaned back in her chair. "You and Jack have surprised me."

Emma lifted an eyebrow as she flicked a donut sprinkle off the table. This café was owned by Starry's syndicate, and it was all Emma could do to keep herself from laughing at the thought of some hardcore drug dealer covering her donut in rainbow sprinkles. It was probably staffed by innocent college kids with no idea who they really worked for, but that thought wasn't nearly so funny. "What do you mean?" she asked.

Starry rolled her eyes. "You've kept your word, just like you said you would. My source in the NYPD says you've never breathed a word about me or Rhys during the whole investigation, and my people here tell me you're the most boring surveillance subjects I've ever assigned them."

Emma's shoulders drooped. She was disappointed in how long it was taking for Starry to believe anything she said. "The case is closed now. As far as law enforcement is concerned, Jack and I are just innocent kids who got caught up in a syndicate turf war. If I tell them what really happened I would lose the only family I have left. I can't face that. You know I can't. I'll never give you a reason to distrust me."

Starry scowled at Jack now sitting near the window. "I think I worry more about him than you."

"Jack's fine," Emma said. "He hates what happened to his dad, but he'll be okay, and he's grateful to you for sparing us. Plus, you gave him his father's ashes and we held a proper funeral and everything, so he's made his peace, just as I have." She recalled when Starry had handed her Sam's ashes and told her it was up to her what to do with them. She had taken a week to say goodbye to her father and then let Starry arrange for the ashes to be secretly buried in Lucy's plot in New York.

Starry turned to a black leather bag she had set on the chair beside her and pulled out an electronic tablet. "Here's the last thing for you to approve and then we're completely done. You'll never have to see me again unless there's a problem."

Emma frowned. As much as she disapproved of and hated the syndicate and everything Starry did within it, she still felt a connection to her sister that was going to be difficult to let go.

Taking the tablet, she looked down at a bunch of numbers. After a moment, she realized she was looking at her own bank account information.

Starry was giving her money. A *lot* of money.

Emma looked up from the tablet, shocked.

"As soon as you enter in a new passcode there at the bottom, that money will move over to a new account I can't touch," Starry explained. "I know you probably don't believe me when I say I won't access your accounts, but I promise it's the truth."

Emma set down the tablet. "No," she said firmly. There was no way she was going to take any of the syndicate's dirty money. She and Jack had been living fine on their own until now. Starry had funneled the funds from Sam's bank account to a new one under Emma's name months ago. It had only been the money her father had made from his work as a CPA— retirement funds and such—but it had been enough to help the both of them get by until they found work. It was honest money.

"What do you mean *no?*" Starry asked. She folded her arms and glared.

"I don't want your drug money."

Starry cleared her throat. "Oh, come on, Emma. I thought you'd be grateful. You *should* be grateful. Sam risked everything for that money, and it was a pain in the ass freeing it up from Andrews' and Craig's accounts. It's rightfully yours now. I don't have any business touching it."

So it was her father's money. Emma wasn't sure that made any difference, though. It was still drug money. Her eyebrows pulled together. "I will never understand where your logic comes from."

"Come on, think about it. You and Jack can pay off your student loans right now and get your own place together. A *nice* place. No more debt, no more disgusting dorms, no more waitressing in that shitty restaurant . . ." When Emma's expression didn't change, Starry unfolded her arms and sat back in her chair. "Still don't get it? All right, then. Let's just say I think you'll have more reason to trust me, and me to trust you, if I allow you and Jack as much freedom and independence as possible. This is a step in that direction."

It made sense, and Emma appreciated Starry's reasons, but she wasn't sure if she agreed with how it was being handled. She focused on the tablet again.

How could she feel right owning that kind of money? Maybe she just wouldn't spend it.

"Put your new passcode in," Starry ordered.

Emma glanced up at her sister, knowing it wasn't going to do any good to argue. "Fine." She punched in a number she knew she wouldn't forget. She watched the screen as the banking program went through a set of automatic commands, and in less than two minutes her new account was set up. She pulled out her phone and made sure the account worked on her end and then handed over the tablet.

"Well, that's it," Starry said, taking the tablet. She slipped it into her bag and stood up, her expression forlorn as she looked down at Emma. "I guess this is goodbye."

A pang of sorrow hit Emma in the gut. She didn't know why. It wasn't like she *wanted* to be involved in Starry's life, but letting go of a sister she had discovered only six months ago wasn't an easy thing to swallow. She stood up and faced Starry with as much courage as she could. "Bye."

Starry smiled softly, gave her a curt nod, and turned around. As soon as she stepped onto the sidewalk, a man in an expensive suit jumped out of a black Hummer parked along the curb and opened the door for her.

Emma watched until Starry was inside the vehicle and then turned to Jack and smiled. He got up from the table and joined her, donut crumbs still clinging to his lips. "So, it's over, right? We don't have to see her again?"

She picked up her purse. "It's over for now, but I doubt she'll ever fully trust us."

"That's to be expected." Jack put an arm around her and they walked out of the café.

Emma looked over at Starry's Hummer as it pulled away from the curb. The windows were tinted, so Emma couldn't see inside, but she smiled at Starry's window anyway and gave a little wave goodbye. Something inside of her blossomed as she watched the Hummer drive away.

"What's going on?" Jack asked. "You're usually depressed after meeting with her."

Turning to him, she smiled even wider. "I don't know. I feel like I'm doing the opposite of what Glenn and my dad did. They resented each other and wanted to make each other pay for their mistakes, but Starry and I aren't like that. Maybe it'll make a difference in the long run, you know?"

Jack's eyes softened as he stopped on the sidewalk and pulled her into his arms. "This is why I love you," he said. "You always want to do the right thing, no matter how crazy the situation. And if it's any comfort, I do think you'll make a positive difference in your sister's life, even if she doesn't choose what you want."

"I hope so." Emma felt her smile droop as Jack let her go and they kept walking. She told herself for the thousandth time that she was in the only place she could possibly be and that none of it was her fault. Her father had unwittingly put her here, but it was okay. It had to be. Her choices and attitude from here on out were what truly mattered. She and Jack were attending college now. The people Starry hired to keep an eye on them weren't intrusive at all. Emma had never even seen them, so half the time she forgot they existed. She and Jack had a shot at a decent, happy life if they played by Starry's rules.

The only problem was the money. Maybe this was an area where she could learn from Starry. Maybe things didn't have to be so black and white. She could keep her promise and use her father's money to do something that felt right in her heart.

She closed her eyes, the sun warm on her skin as she decided her dad would be proud of her. And really, that was what she had always wanted most from him.

THIRTY-TWO

Starry slipped off her suit jacket and pulled her handgun out of her shoulder holster. Setting both on the empty seat beside her, she leaned her head back and stared at the Hummer's ceiling. Once again, Emma had surprised her. She hadn't complained about being watched. She hadn't lied about anything. Neither she nor Jack had acted upset about what they imagined Starry did day in and day out. They had accepted everything, and it seemed as if they would continue to do so, despite Starry's doubts.

Turning her attention to the city outside her window, Starry felt a surge of frustration at Emma's innocence. She was so easy to manipulate, which was exactly what Starry *didn't* want to do to her only sister. She had tried her hardest not to manipulate Emma and Jack. She had given them everything they'd needed so far, and yet it didn't feel as if they were taking advantage of her.

She wondered how long it would last.

"The Chinese consul has changed the location for your meeting this afternoon," Starry's assistant said from the front passenger seat as he typed on a tablet in his hand.

"I expected that," Starry said, still looking out the window. She was poised to push the syndicate beyond its current borders far more quickly and efficiently than her father had ever planned. "Tell him we'll meet him there fifteen minutes before the scheduled time."

"Yes, ma'am." The man smiled at her in the rearview mirror, and she returned the smile even while chiding herself for being so congenial. Her father had never smiled so kindly to a man below him.

Her phone dinged and she pulled it out of her bag.

RHYS: *Hey, love, how did the meeting go?*

Her smile widened. Rhys always made her feel good. He was one of her Top Eight now, but he was closer to her than any of the other men, of course. She didn't keep anything from him, and vice versa.

STARRY: *Went well. No fight.*

RHYS: *That's good! How do you feel?*

Her smile faded as she stared down at her phone. She and Rhys had talked a lot about Emma and whether or not they should worry about her and Jack doing something stupid against the syndicate. So far nothing was amiss, and Starry felt confident with the way things were going.

STARRY: *I feel better knowing she has what she needs. It's weird forcing myself to trust someone like this, that's all. I'm not sure I'll ever be comfortable with it.*

RHYS: *Trusting someone doesn't mean you're weak. Maybe it means the opposite.*

Starry kept her fingers poised over the keypad on her phone. Rhys was right. Everything she was doing was a step to the left of what her father had always done. Where he had been ruthless, she showed mercy. Where he was wary and suspicious, she was willing to trust and confide. She wasn't sure if any of that would make the syndicate stronger or weaker in the long run, but so far it was the former.

RHYS: *So I'll see you tomorrow?*

STARRY: *Yes. I miss you already.*

RHYS: *Miss you too.*

When Starry looked up, traffic was stopped at an intersection where she could see the Golden Gate Bridge out her window, its perfectly symmetrical shape magnificent against a backdrop of wispy clouds and blue sky. It was powerfully majestic and imposing—traits Starry strived for. She was surprised she had never really looked at it before. Something about it made her feel weak and insignificant, like a piece of glass about to shatter into a beautiful mess.

But for the first time in her life, she savored such a vulnerable feeling. It felt safe, as if acknowledging her triviality next to something so huge protected her from the same fate as her father. She wouldn't make his mistakes, and both she and the syndicate would grow stronger because of it.

She held on to that thought as the light turned green.

Thank you for reading STREETS OF GLASS. Please consider leaving an honest review on Amazon.com, Goodreads, your blog, or another form of social media. Reviews can dramatically boost visibility for a published book, effectively increasing sales and allowing an author to continue their craft—and you to continue reading!

To keep updated on Michelle's newest work and sales, subscribe to her newsletter found on her website, www.michelledargyle.com

ACKNOWLEDGMENTS

Trust is a fragile thing. I had no idea that was what this book was about until I finished it and set it aside. Since trust has become a hard thing for me as of late, both with learning to trust myself and others, it's no surprise now that I've written a character like Starry who's greatest challenge is to learn to trust *anyone*.

But like Starry, I've had to put my fears aside and trust those close to me. Amy Carlin, Natalie Whipple, Jenn Johansson, Katy Glemser, Megan Hall, and Lisa Clegg. I would not be where I am without you. I'm not sure I would have even survived. Thank you for being there when I needed you most.

Special thanks to my parents, Robert and Shelly, for your endless wisdom and understanding. You've helped me learn that sometimes the strongest ties are borne from the greatest anguish.

Thank you to my editor, Diane Dalton. You're not only an amazing friend literally on the other side of the world, but the most talented editor I know. My writing wouldn't be what it is without you, and my life wouldn't be as rich without your friendship.

A deep thank you to those who helped specifically on this book. You have no idea what it means to know you have my back. Special thanks to my writing group: Janci Patterson, J.R. Johansson, Megan Walker, Christopher Husberg, James Goldberg, Heidi Summers, Heather Clark, Bree Despain, Cavan Helps, and Lee Ann Setzer. I cried after critiques sometimes, but it was worth it to get to this point. Thank you for your honesty and for caring as much as you do.

And thank you to all those I have forgotten to mention here. If you know me at all, you know I would never intentionally leave you off.

ABOUT THE AUTHOR

Michelle lives and writes in Utah, surrounded by the Rocky Mountains. She's a foodie and also adores anything Star Wars-related. She loves to read and write books in the time she grabs between her sword-wielding husband and energetic daughter. She believes a simple life is the best life.

Michelle mainly writes contemporary upper YA fiction, but occasionally branches into other genres.

Follow Michelle on Facebook, Twitter, and Instagram. You can also be the first to hear about new releases and announcements by subscribing to her newsletter at www.michelledargyle.com